Books by Ursula K. Le Guin

Novels

Tehanu
Always Coming Home
The Eye of the Heron°
The Beginning Place°
Malafrena
Very Far Away from Anywhere Else
The Word for World Is Forest
The Dispossessed°
The Lathe of Heaven
The Farthest Shore
The Tombs of Atuan
A Wizard of Earthsea
The Left Hand of Darkness°
City of Illusions
Planet of Exile
Rocannon's World

Short Stories

Four Ways to Forgiveness°
A Fisherman of the Inland Sea°
Searoad°
Buffalo Gals°
The Compass Rose°
Orsinian Tales°
The Wind's Twelve Quarters°

For Children

Catwings Return • Catwings
A Ride on the Red Mare's Back
Fire and Stone
A Visit from Dr. Katz
Leese Webster

Poetry and Criticism

Going Out With Peacocks
Hard Words
Dancing at the Edge of the World
Wild Oats and Fireweed
The Language of the Night
Wild Angels

°available from HarperPrism

URSULA K. LE GUIN

Four Ways to

Forgiveness

HarperPrism
An Imprint of HarperPaperbacks

"Betrayals," copyright © 1994 by Ursula K. Le Guin; first appeared in *Blue Motel*.
"Forgiveness Day," copyright © 1994 by Ursula K. Le Guin; first appeared in *Asimov's*.
"A Man of the People," copyright © 1995 by Ursula K. Le Guin; first appeared in *Asimov's*.
"A Woman's Liberation," copyright © 1995 by Ursula K. Le Guin; first appeared in *Asimov's*.

HarperPaperbacks   *A Division of* HarperCollins*Publishers*
10 East 53rd Street, New York, N.Y. 10022

Cover illustration by Danilo Ducak

A hardcover edition of this book was published in 1995 by HarperPrism.

First mass market printing: August 1996

Printed in the United States of America

HarperPrism is an imprint of HarperPaperbacks. HarperPaperbacks, HarperPrism, and colophon are trademarks of HarperCollins*Publishers*.

10 9 8 7 6 5 4 3 2 1

Contents

Four Ways to Forgiveness

Betrayals

"On the planet O there has not been a war for five thousand years," she read, "and on Gethen there has never been a war." She stopped reading, to rest her eyes and because she was trying to train herself to read slowly, not gobble words down in chunks the way Tikuli gulped his food. "There has never been a war": in her mind the words stood clear and bright, surrounded by and sinking into an infinite, dark, soft incredulity. What would that world be, a world without war? It would be the real world. Peace was the true life, the life of working and learning and bringing up children to work and learn. War, which devoured work, learning, and children, was the denial of reality. But my people, she thought, know only how to deny. Born in the dark shadow of power misused, we set peace outside our world, a guiding and unattainable light. All we know to do is fight. Any peace one of us can make in our life is only a denial that the war is going on, a shadow of the shadow, a doubled unbelief.

So as the cloud-shadows swept over the marshes and the page of the book open on her lap, she sighed and closed her eyes, thinking, "I am a liar." Then she opened her eyes and read more about the other worlds, the far realities.

Tikuli, sleeping curled up around his tail in the weak sunshine, sighed as if imitating her, and scratched a dreamflea. Gubu was out in the reeds, hunting; she could not see him, but now and then the plume of a reed quivered, and once a marsh hen flew up cackling in indignation.

Absorbed in a description of the peculiar social customs of the Ithsh, she did not see Wada till he was at the gate letting himself in. "Oh, you're here already," she said, taken by surprise and feeling unready, incompetent, old, as she always felt with other people. Alone, she only felt old when she was overtired or ill. Maybe living alone was the right thing for her after all. "Come on in," she said, getting up and dropping her book and picking it up and feeling her back hair where the knot was coming loose. "I'll just get my bag and be off, then."

"No hurry," the young man said in his soft voice. "Eyid won't be here for a while yet."

Very kind of you to tell me I don't have to hurry to leave my own house, Yoss thought, but said nothing, obedient to the insufferable, adorable selfishness of the young. She went in and got her shopping bag, reknotted her hair, tied a scarf over it, and came out onto the little open porch. Wada had sat down in her chair; he jumped up when she came out. He was a shy boy, the gentler, she thought, of the two lovers. "Have fun," she said with a smile, knowing she embarrassed him. "I'll be back in a couple of hours — before sunset." She went down to her gate, let herself out, and set off the way Wada had come, along the path up to the winding wooden causeway across the marshes to the village.

She would not meet Eyid on the way. The girl would be coming from the north on one of the bog-paths, having left the village at a different time and in a different direction than Wada, so that nobody would notice that for a few hours every week or so the two young people were gone at the same time. They were madly in love, had been in love for three years, and would have lived in partnership long since if Wada's father and Eyid's father's brother hadn't quarreled over a piece of reallocated Corporation land and set up a feud between the families that had so far stopped short of bloodshed, but put a love match out of the question. The land was valuable; the families, though poor, each aspired to be leaders of the village. Nothing would heal the grudge. The whole village took sides in it. Eyid and Wada had nowhere to go, no skills to keep them alive in the cities, no tribal relations in another village who might take them in. Their passion was trapped in the hatred of the old. Yoss had come on them, a year ago now, in each other's arms on the cold ground of an island in the marshes — blundering onto them as once she had blundered onto a pair of fendeer fawns holding utterly still in the nest of grass where the doe had left them. This pair had been as frightened, as beautiful and vulnerable as the fawns, and they had begged her "not to tell" so humbly, what could she do? They were shivering with cold, Eyid's bare legs were muddy, they clung to each other like children. "Come to my house," she said sternly. "For mercy sake!" She stalked off. Timidly, they followed her. "I will be back in an hour or so," she said when she had got them indoors, into her one room with the bed alcove right beside the chimney. "Don't get things muddy!"

That time she had roamed the paths keeping watch, in case anybody was out looking for them. Nowadays she mostly went into the village while "the fawns" were in her house having their sweet hour.

They were too ignorant to think of any way to thank her. Wada, a peat-cutter, might have supplied her fire without anyone being suspicious, but they never left so much as a flower, though they always made up the bed very neat and tight. Perhaps indeed they were not very grateful. Why should they be? She gave them only what was their due: a bed, an hour of pleasure, a moment of peace. It wasn't their fault, or her virtue, that nobody else would give it to them.

Her errand today took her in to Eyid's uncle's shop. He was the village sweets-seller. All the holy abstinence she had intended when she came here two years ago, the single bowl of unflavored grain, the draft of pure water, she'd given that up in no time. She got diarrhea from a cereal diet, and the water of the marshes was undrinkable. She ate every fresh vegetable she could buy or grow, drank wine or bottled water or fruit juice from the city, and kept a large supply of sweets — dried fruits, raisins, sugar-brittle, even the cakes Eyid's mother and aunts made, fat disks with a nutmeat squashed onto the top, dry, greasy, tasteless, but curiously satisfying. She bought a bagful of them and a brown wheel of sugar-brittle, and gossiped with the aunts, dark, darting-eyed little women who had been at old Uad's wake last night and wanted to talk about it. "Those people" — Wada's family, indicated by a glance, a shrug, a sneer — had misbehaved as usual, got drunk, picked fights, boasted, got sick, and vomited all over the place, greedy upstart louts that they were. When she stopped by the newsstand to pick up a paper (another vow long since broken; she had been going to read only the *Arkamye* and learn it by heart), Wada's mother was there, and she heard how "those people" — Eyid's family — had boasted and picked fights and vomited all over the place at the wake last night. She did not merely hear; she asked for details, she drew the gossip out; she loved it.

What a fool, she thought, starting slowly home on the causeway path, what a fool I was to think I could ever drink water and be silent! I'll never, never be able to let anything go, anything at all. I'll never be free, never be worthy of freedom. Even old age can't make me let go. Even losing Safnan can't make me let go.

Before the Five Armies they stood. Holding up his sword, Enar said to Kamye: My hands hold your death, my Lord! Kamye answered: Brother, it is your death they hold.

She knew those lines, anyway. Everybody knew those lines. And so then Enar dropped his sword, because he was a hero and a holy man, the Lord's younger brother. But I can't drop my death. I'll hold it to the end, I'll cherish it, hate it, eat it, drink it, listen to it, give it my bed, mourn it, everything but let it go.

She looked up out of her thoughts into the afternoon on the marshes: the sky a cloudless misty blue, reflected in one distant curving channel of water, and the sunlight golden over the dun levels of the reedbeds and among the stems of the reeds. The rare, soft west wind blew. A perfect day. The beauty of the world, the beauty of the world! A sword in my hand, turned against me. Why do you make beauty to kill us, my Lord?

She trudged on, pulling her headscarf tighter with a little dissatisfied jerk. At this rate she would soon be wandering around the marshes shouting aloud, like Abberkam.

And there he was, the thought had summoned him: lurching along in the blind way he had as if he never saw anything but his thoughts, striking at the roadway with his big stick as if he was killing a snake. Long grey hair blowing around his face. He wasn't shouting, he only shouted at night, and not for a long time now, but he was talking, she saw his lips move; then he saw her, and shut his mouth, and drew himself into himself, wary as a wild animal. They approached each other on the narrow causeway path, not another human being in all the wilderness of reeds and mud and water and wind.

"Good evening, Chief Abberkam," Yoss said when there were only a few paces between them. What a big man he was; she never could believe how tall and broad and heavy he was till she saw him again, his dark skin still smooth as a young man's, but his head stooped and his hair grey and wild. A huge hook nose and the mistrustful, unseeing eyes. He muttered some kind of greeting, hardly slowing his gait.

The mischief was in Yoss today; she was sick of her own thoughts and sorrows and shortcomings. She stopped, so that he had to stop or else run right into her, and said, "Were you at the wake last night?"

He stared down at her; she felt he was getting her into focus, or part of her; he finally said, "Wake?"

"They buried old Uad last night. All the men got drunk, and it's a mercy the feud didn't finally break out."

"Feud?" he repeated in his deep voice.

Maybe he wasn't capable of focusing any more, but she was driven to talk to him, to get through to him. "The Dewis and Kamanners. They're quarreling over that arable island just north of the village. And the two poor children, they want to be partners, and their fathers threaten to kill them if they look at each other. What idiocy! Why don't they divide the island and let the children pair and let their children share it? It'll come to blood one of these days, I think."

"To blood," the Chief said, repeating again like a half-wit, and then slowly, in that great, deep voice, the voice she had heard crying out in agony in the night across the marshes, "Those men. Those shopkeepers. They have the souls of owners. They won't kill. But they won't share. If it's property, they won't let go. Never."

She saw again the lifted sword.

"Ah," she said with a shudder. "So then the children must wait . . . till the old people die . . . "

"Too late," he said. His eyes met hers for one instant, keen and strange; then he pushed back his hair impatiently, growled something by way of good-bye, and started on so abruptly that she almost crouched aside to make way for him. That's how a chief walks, she thought wryly, as she went on. Big, wide, taking up space, stamping the earth down. And this, this is how an old woman walks, narrowly, narrowly.

There was a strange noise behind her — gunshots, she thought, for city usages stay in the nerves — and she turned sharp round. Abberkam had stopped and was coughing explosively, tremendously, his big frame hunched around the spasms that nearly wracked him off his feet. Yoss knew that kind of coughing. The Ekumen was supposed to have medicine for it, but she'd left the city before any of it came. She went to Abberkam and when the paroxysm was over and he stood gasping, grey-faced, she said, "That's berlot: are you getting over it or are you getting it?"

He shook his head.

She waited.

While she waited she thought, what do I care if he's sick or not? Does he care? He came here to die. I heard him howling out on the marshes in the dark, last winter. Howling in agony. Eaten out with shame, like a man with cancer who's been all eaten out by the cancer but can't die.

"It's all right," he said, hoarse, angry, wanting her only to get away from him; and she nodded and went on her way. Let him die. How could he want to live knowing what he'd lost, his power, his honor, and what he'd done? Lied, betrayed his supporters, embezzled. The perfect politician. Big Chief Abberkam, hero of the Liberation, leader of the World Party, who had destroyed the World Party by his greed and folly.

She glanced back once. He was moving very slowly or perhaps had stopped, she was not sure. She went on, taking the right-hand way where the causeway forked, going down onto the bog-path that led to her little house.

Three hundred years ago these marshlands had been a vast, rich agricultural valley, one of the first to be irrigated and cultivated by the Agricultural Plantation Corporation when they brought their slaves from Werel to the Yeowe Colony. Too well irrigated, too well cultivated; fertilizing chemicals and salts of the soil had accumulated till nothing would grow, and the Owners went elsewhere for their profit. The banks of the irrigation canals slumped here and there and the waters of the river wandered free again, pooling and meandering, slowly washing the lands clean. The reeds grew, miles and miles of reeds bowing a little under the wind, under the cloud-shadows and the wings of long-legged birds. Here and there on an island of rockier soil a few fields and a slave-village remained, a few sharecroppers left behind, useless people on useless land. The freedom of desolation. And all through the marshes there were lonely houses.

Growing old, the people of Werel and Yeowe might turn to silence, as their religion recommended them to do: when their children were grown, when they had done their work as householder and citizen, when as their body weakened their soul might make itself strong, they left their life behind and came empty-handed to lonely places. Even on the Plantations, the Bosses had let old slaves go out into the wilderness, go free. Here in the North, freedmen from the cities had come out to the marshlands and lived as recluses in the lonely houses. Now, since the Liberation, even women came.

Some of the houses were derelict, and any soul-maker might claim them; most, like Yoss's thatched cabin, were owned by villagers who maintained them and gave them to a recluse rent-free as a religious duty, a means of enriching the soul. Yoss liked knowing that she was a source of spiritual profit to her landlord, a grasping man whose account with Providence was probably otherwise all on the debit side. She liked to feel useful. She took it for another sign of her incapacity to let the world go, as the Lord Kamye bade her do. *You are no longer useful,* he had told her in a hundred ways, over and over, since she was sixty; but she would not listen. She left the noisy world and came out to the marshes, but she let the world go on chattering and gossiping and singing and crying in her ears. She would not hear the low voice of the Lord.

Eyid and Wada were gone when she got home; the bed was made up very tight, and the foxdog Tikuli was sleeping on it, curled up around his tail. Gubu the spotted cat was prancing around asking about dinner. She picked him up and petted his silken, speckled back while he nuzzled under her ear, making his steady roo-roo-roo of pleasure and affection; then she fed him. Tikuli took no notice, which was odd. Tikuli was sleeping too much. She sat on the bed and scratched the roots of his stiff, red-furred ears. He woke and yawned and looked at her with soft amber eyes, his red plume of tail stirring. "Aren't you hungry?" she asked him. I will eat to please you,

Tikuli answered, getting down off the bed rather stiffly. "Oh, Tikuli, you're getting old," Yoss said, and the sword stirred in her heart. Her daughter Safnan had given her Tikuli, a tiny red cub, a scurry of paws and plume-tail — how long ago? Eight years. A long time. A lifetime for a foxdog.

More than a lifetime for Safnan. More than a lifetime for her children, Yoss's grandchildren, Enkamma and Uye.

If I am alive, they are dead, Yoss thought, as she always thought; if they are alive, I am dead. They went on the ship that goes like light; they are translated into the light. When they return into life, when they step off the ship on the world called Hain, it will be eighty years from the day they left, and I will be dead, long dead; I am dead. They left me and I am dead. Let them be alive, Lord, sweet Lord, let them be alive, I will be dead. I came here to be dead. For them. I cannot, I cannot let them be dead for me.

Tikuli's cold nose touched her hand. She looked intently at him. The amber of his eyes was dimmed, bluish. She stroked his head, scratched the roots of his ears, silent.

He ate a few bites to please her, and climbed back up onto the bed. She made her own dinner, soup and rewarmed soda cakes, and ate it, not tasting it. She washed the three dishes she had used, made up the fire, and sat by it trying to read her book slowly, while Tikuli slept on the bed and Gubu lay on the hearth gazing into the fire with round golden eyes, going roo-roo-roo very softly. Once he sat up and made his battlecall, "Hoooo!" at some noise he heard out in the marshes, and stalked about a bit; then he settled down again to staring and roo-ing. Later, when the fire was out and the house utterly dark in the starless darkness, he joined Yoss and Tikuli in the warm bed, where earlier the young lovers had had their brief, sharp joy.

She found she was thinking about Abberkam, the next couple of days, as she worked in her little vegetable garden, cleaning it up for the winter. When the Chief first came, the villagers had been all abuzz with excitement about his living in a house that belonged to the headman of their village. Disgraced, dishonored, he was still a very famous man. An elected Chief of the Heyend, one of the principal Tribes of Yeowe, he had come to prominence during the last years of the War of Liberation, leading a great movement for what he called Racial Freedom. Even some of the villagers had embraced the main principle of the World Party: No one was to live on Yeowe but its own people. No Werelians, the hated ancestral colonizers, the Bosses and Owners. The War had ended slavery; and in the last few years the diplomats of the Ekumen had negotiated an end to Werel's economic power over its former colony-planet. The Bosses and Owners, even those whose families had lived on Yeowe for centuries, had all withdrawn to Werel, the Old World, next outward from the sun. They had run, and their soldiers had been driven after them. They must never return, said the World Party. Not as traders, not as visitors, they would never again pollute the soil and soul of Yeowe. Nor would any other foreigner, any other Power. The Aliens of the Ekumen had helped Yeowe free itself; now they too must go. There was no place for them here. "This is our world. This is the free world. Here we will make our souls in the image of Kamye the Swordsman," Abberkam had said over and over, and that image, the curved sword, was the symbol of the World Party.

And blood had been shed. From the Uprising at Nadami on, thirty years of fighting, rebellions, retaliations, half her lifetime, and even after Liberation, after all the Werelians were gone, the fighting went on. Always, always, the young men were ready to rush out and kill whoever the old men told them to kill, each other, women, old people, children; always there was a war to be fought in the name of Peace, Freedom, Justice, the Lord. Newly freed tribes fought over land, the city chiefs fought for power. All Yoss had worked for all her life as an educator in the capital had come to pieces not only during the War of Liberation but after it, as the city disintegrated in one ward-war after another.

In all fairness, she thought, despite his waving Kamye's sword, Abberkam, in leading the World Party, had tried to avoid war and had partly succeeded. His preference was for the winning of power by policy and persuasion, and he was a master of it. He had come very near success. The curved sword was everywhere, the rallies cheering his speeches were immense. ABBERKAM AND RACIAL FREEDOM! said huge posters stretched across the city avenues. He was certain to win the first free election ever held on Yeowe, to be Chief of the World Council. And then, nothing much at first, the rumors. The defections. His son's suicide. His son's mother's accusations of debauchery and gross luxury.

The proof that he had embezzled great sums of money given his party for relief of districts left in poverty by the withdrawal of Werelian capital. The revelation of the secret plan to assassinate the Envoy of the Ekumen and put the blame on Abberkam's old friend and supporter Demeye. . . . That was what brought him down. A chief could indulge himself sexually, misuse power, grow rich off his people and be admired for it, but a chief who betrayed a companion was not forgiven. It was, Yoss thought, the code of the slave.

Mobs of his own supporters turned against him, attacking the old APCY Manager's Residency, which he had taken over. Supporters of the Ekumen joined with forces still loyal to him to defend him and restore order to the capital city. After days of street warfare, hundreds of men killed fighting and thousands more in riots around the continent, Abberkam surrendered. The Ekumen supported a provisional government in declaring amnesty. Their people walked him through the bloodstained, bombed-out streets in absolute silence. People watched, people who had trusted him, people who had revered him, people who had hated him, watched him walk past in silence, guarded by the foreigners, the Aliens he had tried to drive from their world.

She had read about it in the paper. She had been living in the marshes for over a year then. "Serve him right," she had thought, and not much more. Whether the Ekumen was a true ally or a new set of Owners in disguise, she didn't know, but she liked to see any chief go down. Werelian Bosses, strutting tribal headmen, or ranting demagogues, let them taste dirt. She'd eaten enough of their dirt in her life.

When a few months later they told her in the village that Abberkam was coming to the marshlands as a recluse, a soulmaker, she had been surprised and for a moment ashamed at having assumed his talk had all been empty rhetoric. Was he a religious man, then? — Through all the luxury, the orgies, the thefts, the powermongering, the murders? No! Since he'd lost his money and power, he'd stayed in view by making a spectacle of his poverty and piety. He was utterly shameless. She was surprised at the bitterness of her indignation. The first time she saw him she felt like spitting at the big, thick-toed, sandaled feet, which were all she saw of him; she refused to look at his face.

But then in the winter she had heard the howling out on the marshes, at night, in the freezing wind. Tikuli and Gubu had pricked an ear but been unfrightened by the awful noise. That led her after a minute to recognize it as a human voice — a man shouting aloud, drunk? mad? — howling, beseeching, so that she had got up to go to him, despite her terror; but he was not calling out for human aid. "Lord, my Lord, Kamye!" he shouted, and looking out her door she saw him up on the causeway, a shadow against the pale night clouds, striding and tearing at his hair and crying like an animal, like a soul in pain.

After that night she did not judge him. They were equals. When she next met him she looked him in the face and spoke, forcing him to speak to her.

That was not often; he lived in true seclusion. No one came across the marshes to see him. People in the village often enriched their souls by giving her food, harvest surplus, leftovers, sometimes at the holy days a dish cooked for her; but she saw no one take anything out to Abberkam's house. Maybe they had offered and he was too proud to take. Maybe they were afraid to offer.

She dug up her root bed with the miserable short-handled spade Em Dewi had given her, and thought about Abberkam howling, and about the way he had coughed. Safnan had nearly died of the berlot when she was four. Yoss had heard that terrible cough for weeks. Had Abberkam been going to the village to get medicine, the other day? Had he got there, or turned back?

She put on her shawl, for the wind had turned cold again, the autumn was getting on. She went up to the causeway and took the right-hand turn.

Abberkam's house was of wood, riding a raft of tree trunks sunk in the peaty water of the marsh. Such houses were very old, going back two hundred years or more to when there had been trees growing in the valley. It had been a farmhouse and was much larger than her hut, a rambling, dark place, the roof in ill repair, some windows boarded over, planks on the porch loose as she stepped up on it. She said his name, then said it again louder. The wind whined in the reeds. She knocked, waited, pushed the heavy door open. It was dark indoors. She was in a kind of vestibule. She heard him talking in the next room. "Never down to the adit, in the intent, take it out, take it out," the deep, hoarse voice said, and then he coughed. She opened the door; she had to let her eyes adjust to the darkness for a minute before she could see where she was. It was the old front room of the house. The windows were shuttered, the fire dead. There was a sideboard, a table, a couch, but a bed stood near the fireplace. The tangled covers had slid to the floor, and Abberkam was naked on the bed, writhing and raving in fever. "Oh, Lord!" Yoss said. That huge, black, sweat-oiled breast and belly whorled with grey hair, those powerful arms and groping hands, how was she going to get near him?

She managed it, growing less timid and cautious as she found him weak in his fever, and, when he was lucid, obedient to her requests. She got him covered up, piled up all the blankets he had and a rug from the floor of an unused room on top; she built up the fire as hot as she could make it; and after a couple of hours he began to sweat, sweat pouring out of him till the sheets and mattress were soaked. "You are immoderate," she railed at him in the depths of the night, shoving and hauling at him, making him stagger over to the decrepit couch and lie there wrapped in the rug so she could get his bedding dry at the fire. He shivered and coughed, and she brewed up the herbals she had brought, and drank the scalding tea along with him. He fell suddenly asleep and slept like death, not wakened even by the cough that wracked him. She fell as suddenly asleep and woke to find herself lying on bare hearthstones, the fire dying, the day white in the windows.

Abberkam lay like a mountain range under the rug, which she saw now to be filthy; his breath wheezed but was deep and regular. She got up piece by piece, all ache and pain, made up the fire and got warm, made tea, investigated the pantry. It was stocked with essentials; evidently the Chief ordered in supplies from Veo, the nearest town of any size.

She made herself a good breakfast, and when Abberkam roused, got some more herbal tea into him. The fever had broken. The danger now was water in the lungs, she thought; they had warned her about that with Safnan, and this was a man of sixty. If he stopped coughing, that would be a danger sign. She made him lie propped up. "Cough," she told him.

"Hurts," he growled.

"You have to," she said, and he coughed, hak-hak.

"More!" she ordered, and he coughed till his body was shaken with the spasms.

"Good," she said. "Now sleep." He slept.

Tikuli, Gubu would be starving! She fled home, fed her pets, petted them, changed her under-clothes, sat down in her own chair by her own fireside for half an hour with Gubu going roo-roo under her ear. Then she went back across the marshes to the Chief's house.

She got his bed dried out by nightfall and moved him back into it. She stayed that night, but left him in the morning, saying, "I'll be back in the evening." He was silent, still very sick, indifferent to his own plight or hers.

The next day he was clearly better: the cough was phlegmy and rough, a good cough; she well remembered when Safnan had finally begun cough-ing a good cough. He was fully awake from time to time, and when she brought him the bottle she had made serve as a bedpan he took it from her and turned away from her to piss in it. Modesty, a good sign in a Chief, she thought. She felt pleased with him and with herself. She had been useful. "I'm going to leave you tonight; don't let the covers slip off. I'll be back in the morning," she told him, pleased with herself, her decisiveness, her unanswerability.

But when she got home in the clear, cold evening, Tikuli was curled up in a corner of the room where he had never slept before. He would not eat, and crept back to his corner when she tried to move him, pet him, make him sleep on the bed. Let me be, he said, looking away from her, turning his eyes away, tucking his dry, black, sharp nose into the curve of his foreleg. Let me be, he said patiently, let me die, that is what I am doing now.

She slept, because she was very tired. Gubu stayed out in the marshes all night. In the morning Tikuli was just the same, curled up on the floor in the place where he had never slept, waiting.

"I have to go," she told him, "I'll be back soon — very soon. Wait for me, Tikuli."

He said nothing, gazing away from her with dim amber eyes. It was not her he waited for.

She strode across the marshes, dry-eyed, angry, useless. Abberkam was much the same as he had been; she fed him some grain pap, looked to his needs, and said, "I can't stay. My kit is sick, I have to go back."

"Kit," the big man said in his rumble of voice.

"A foxdog. My daughter gave him to me." Why was she explaining, excusing herself? She left; when she got home Tikuli was where she had left him. She did some mending, cooked up some food she thought Abberkam might eat, tried to read the book about the worlds of the Ekumen, about the world that had no war, where it was always winter, where people were both men and women. In the middle of the afternoon she thought she must go back to Abberkam, and was just getting up when Tikuli too stood up. He walked very slowly over to her. She sat down again in her chair and stooped to pick him up, but he put his sharp muzzle into her hand, sighed, and lay down with his head on his paws. He sighed again.

She sat and wept aloud for a while, not long; then she got up and got the gardening spade and went outdoors. She made the grave at the corner of the stone chimney, in a sunny nook. When she went in and picked Tikuli up she thought with a thrill like terror, "He is not dead!" He was dead, only he was not cold yet; the thick red fur kept the body's warmth in. She wrapped him in her blue scarf and took him in her arms, carried him to his grave, feeling that faint warmth still through the cloth, and the light rigidity of the body, like a wooden statue. She filled the grave and set a stone that had fallen from the chimney on it. She could not say anything, but she had an image in her mind like a prayer, of Tikuli running in the sunlight somewhere.

She put out food on the porch for Gubu, who had kept out of the house all day, and set off up the causeway. It was a silent, overcast evening. The reeds stood grey and the pools had a leaden gleam.

Abberkam was sitting up in bed, certainly better, perhaps with a touch of fever but nothing serious; he was hungry, a good sign. When she brought him his tray he said, "The kit, it's all right?"

"No," she said and turned away, able only after a minute to say, "Dead."

"In the Lord's hands," said the hoarse, deep

voice, and she saw Tikuli in the sunlight again, in some presence, some kind presence like the sunlight.

"Yes," she said. "Thank you." Her lips quivered and her throat closed up. She kept seeing the design on her blue scarf, leaves printed in a darker blue. She made herself busy. Presently she came back to see to the fire and sit down beside it. She felt very tired.

"Before the Lord Kamye took up the sword, he was a herdsman," Abberkam said. "And they called him Lord of the Beasts, and Deer-Herd, because when he went into the forest he came among the deer, and lions also walked with him among the deer, offering no harm. None were afraid."

He spoke so quietly that it was a while before she realised he was saying lines from the *Arkamye*.

She put another block of peat on the fire and sat down again.

"Tell me where you come from, Chief Abberkam," she said.

"Gebba Plantation."

"In the east?"

He nodded.

"What was it like?"

The fire smouldered, making its pungent smoke. The night was intensely silent. When she first came out here from the city the silence had wakened her, night after night.

"What was it like?" he said almost in a whisper. Like most people of their race, the dark iris filled his eyes, but she saw the white flash as he glanced over at her. "Sixty years ago," he said. "We lived in the Plantation compound. The canebrakes; some of us worked there, cut cane, worked in the mill. Most of the women, the little children. Most men and the boys over nine or ten went down the mines. Some of the girls, too, they wanted them small, to work the shafts a man couldn't get into. I was big. They sent me down the mines when I was eight years old."

"What was it like?"

"Dark," he said. Again she saw the flash of his eyes. "I look back and think how did we live? how did we stay living in that place? The air down the mine was so thick with the dust that it was black. Black air. Your lantern light didn't go five feet into that air. There was water in most of the workings, up to a man's knees. There was one shaft where a soft-coal face had caught fire and was burning so the whole system was full of smoke. They went on working it, because the lodes ran behind that coke. We wore masks, filters. They didn't do much good. We breathed the smoke. I always wheeze some like I do now. It's not just the berlot. It's the old smoke. The men died of the black lung. All the men. Forty, forty-five years old, they died. The Bosses gave your tribe money when a man died. A death bonus. Some men thought that made it worth while dying."

"How did you get out?"

"My mother," he said. "She was a chief's daughter from the village. She taught me. She taught me religion and freedom."

He has said that before, Yoss thought. It has become his stock answer, his standard myth.

"How? What did she say?"

A pause. "She taught me the Holy Word," Abberkam said. "And she said to me, 'You and your brother, you are the true people, you are the Lord's people, his servants, his warriors, his lions: only you. Lord Kamye came with us from the Old World and he is ours now, he lives among us.' She named us Abberkam, Tongue of the Lord, and Domerkam, Arm of the Lord. To speak the truth and fight to be free."

"What became of your brother?" Yoss asked after a time.

"Killed at Nadami," Abberkam said, and again both were silent for a while.

Nadami had been the first great outbreak of the Uprising which finally brought the Liberation to Yeowe. At Nadami plantation slaves and city freed-people had first fought side by side against the own-ers. If the slaves had been able to hold together against the owners, the Corporations, they might have won their freedom years sooner. But the liber-ation movement had constantly splintered into trib-al rivalries, chiefs vying for power in the newly freed territories, bargaining with the Bosses to consolidate their gains. Thirty years of war and destruction before the vastly outnumbered Werelians were defeated, driven offworld, leaving the Yeowans free to turn upon one another.

"Your brother was lucky," said Yoss.

Then she looked across at the Chief, wondering how he would take this challenge. His big, dark face had a softened look in the firelight. His grey, coarse hair had escaped from the loose braid she had made of it to keep it from his eyes, and straggled around his face. He said slowly and softly, "He was my younger brother. He was Enar on the Field of the Five Armies."

Oh, so then you're the Lord Kamye himself?

Yoss retorted in her mind, moved, indignant, cynical. What an ego! — But, to be sure, there was another implication. Enar had taken up his sword to kill his Elder Brother on that battlefield, to keep him from becoming Lord of the World. And Kamye had told him that the sword he held was his own death; that there is no lordship and no freedom in life, only in the letting go of life, of longing, of desire. Enar had laid down his sword and gone into the wilderness, into the silence, saying only, "Brother, I am thou." And Kamye had taken up that sword to fight the Armies of Desolation, knowing there is no victory.

So who was he, this man? this big fellow? this sick old man, this little boy down in the mines in the dark, this bully, thief, and liar who thought he could speak for the Lord?

"We're talking too much," Yoss said, though neither of them had said a word for five minutes. She poured a cup of tea for him and set the kettle off the fire, where she had kept it simmering to keep the air moist. She took up her shawl. He watched her with that same soft look in his face, an expression almost of confusion.

"It was freedom I wanted," he said. "Our freedom."

His conscience was none of her concern. "Keep warm," she said.

"You're going out now?"

"I can't get lost on the causeway."

It was a strange walk, though, for she had no lantern, and the night was very black. She thought, feeling her way along the causeway, of that black air he had told her of down in the mines, swallowing light. She thought of Abberkam's black, heavy body. She thought how seldom she had walked alone at night. When she was a child on Banni Plantation, the slaves were locked in the compound at night. Women stayed on the women's side and never went alone. Before the War, when she came to the city as a freedwoman, studying at the training school, she'd had a taste of freedom; but in the bad years of the War and even since the Liberation a woman couldn't go safely in the streets at night. There were no police in the working quarters, no streetlights; district warlords sent their gangs out raiding; even in daylight you had to look out, try to stay in the crowd, always be sure there was a street you could escape by.

She grew anxious that she would miss her turning, but her eyes had grown used to the dark by the time she came to it, and she could even make out the blot of her house down in the formlessness of the reedbeds. The Aliens had poor night vision, she had heard. They had little eyes, little dots with white all round them, like a scared calf. She didn't like their eyes, though she liked the colors of their skin, mostly dark brown or ruddy brown, warmer than her greyish-brown slave skin or the blue-black hide Abberkam had got from the owner who had raped his mother. Cyanid skins, the Aliens said politely, an ocular adaptation to the radiation spectrum of the Werelian System sun.

Gubu danced about her on the pathway down, silent, tickling her legs with his tail. "Look out," she scolded him, "I'm going to walk on you." She was grateful to him, picked him up as soon as they were indoors. No dignified and joyous greeting from

Tikuli, not this night, not ever. Roo-roo-roo, Gubu went under her ear, listen to me, I'm here, life goes on, where's dinner?

The Chief got a touch of pneumonia after all, and she went into the village to call the clinic in Veo. They sent out a practitioner, who said he was doing fine, just keep him sitting up and coughing, the herbal teas were fine, just keep an eye on him, that's right, and went away, thanks very much. So she spent her afternoons with him. The house without Tikuli seemed very drab, the late autumn days seemed very cold, and anyhow what else did she have to do? She liked the big, dark raft-house. She wasn't going to clean house for the Chief or any man who didn't do it for himself, but she poked about in it, in rooms Abberkam evidently hadn't used or even looked at. She found one upstairs, with long low windows all along the west wall, that she liked. She swept it out and cleaned the windows with their small, greenish panes. When he was asleep she would go up to that room and sit on a ragged wool rug, its only furnishing. The fireplace had been sealed up with loose bricks, but heat came up it from the peat fire burning below, and with her back against the warm bricks and the sunlight slanting in, she was warm. She felt a peacefulness there that seemed to belong to the room, the shape of its air, the greenish, wavery glass of the windows. There she would sit in silence, unoccupied, content, as she had never sat in her own house.

The Chief was slow to get his strength back. Often he was sullen, dour, the uncouth man she had first thought him, sunk in a stupor of self-centered shame and rage. Other days he was ready to talk; even to listen, sometimes.

"I've been reading a book about the worlds of the Ekumen," Yoss said, waiting for their bean-cakes to be ready to turn and fry on the other side. For the last several days she had made and eaten dinner with him in the late afternoon, washed up, and gone home before dark. "It's very interesting. There isn't any question that we're descended from the people of Hain, all of us. Us and the Aliens too. Even our animals have the same ancestors."

"So they say," he grunted.

"It isn't a matter of who says it," she said. "Anybody who will look at the evidence sees it; it's a genetic fact. That you don't like it doesn't alter it."

"What is a 'fact' a million years old?" he said. "What has it to do with you, with me, with us? This is our world. We are ourselves. We have nothing to do with them."

"We do now," she said rather fliply, flipping the bean-cakes.

"Not if I had had my way," he said.

She laughed. "You don't give up, do you?"

"No," he said.

After they were eating, he in bed with his tray, she at a stool on the hearth, she went on, with a sense of teasing a bull, daring the avalanche to fall; for all he was still sick and weak, there was that menace in him, his size, not of body only. "Is that what it was all about, really?" she asked. "The World Party. Having the planet for ourselves, no Aliens? Just that?"

"Yes," he said, the dark rumble.

"Why? The Ekumen has so much to share with us. They broke the Corporations' hold over us. They're on our side."

"We were brought to this world as slaves," he said, "but it is our world to find our own way in. Kamye came with us, the Herdsman, the Bondsman, Kamye of the Sword. This is his world. Our earth. No one can give it to us. We don't need to share other people's knowledge or follow their gods. This is where we live, this earth. This is where we die to rejoin the Lord."

After a while she said, "I have a daughter, and a grandson and granddaughter. They left this world four years ago. They're on a ship that is going to Hain. All these years I live till I die are like a few minutes, an hour to them. They'll be there in eighty years — seventy-six years, now. On that other earth. They'll live and die there. Not here."

"Were you willing for them to go?"

"It was their choice."

"Not yours."

"I don't live their lives."

"But you grieve," he said.

The silence between them was heavy.

"It is wrong, wrong, wrong!" he said, his voice strong and loud. "We had our own destiny, our own way to the Lord, and they've taken it from us — we're slaves again! The wise Aliens, the scientists with all their great knowledge and inventions, our ancestors, they say they are — 'Do this!' they say, and we do it. 'Do that!' and we do it. 'Take your children on the wonderful ship and fly to our wonderful worlds!' And the children are taken, and they'll never come home. Never know their home. Never know who they are. Never know whose hands might have held them."

He was orating; for all she knew it was a speech he had made once or a hundred times, ranting and magnificent; there were tears in his eyes. There were tears in her eyes also. She would not let him use her, play on her, have power over her.

"If I agreed with you," she said, "still, still, why did you cheat, Abberkam? You lied to your own people, you stole!"

"Never," he said. "Everything I did, always, every breath I took, was for the World Party. Yes, I spent money, all the money I could get, what was it for except the cause? Yes, I threatened the Envoy, I wanted to drive him and all the rest of them off this world! Yes, I lied to them, because they want to control us, to own us, and I will do anything to save my people from slavery — anything!"

He beat his great fists on the mound of his knees, and gasped for breath, sobbing.

"And there is nothing I can do, O Kamye!" he cried, and hid his face in his arms.

She sat silent, sick at heart.

After a long time he wiped his hands over his face, like a child, wiping the coarse, straggling hair back, rubbing his eyes and nose. He picked up the tray and set it on his knees, picked up the fork, cut a piece of bean-cake, put it in his mouth, chewed, swallowed. If he can, I can, Yoss thought, and did the same. They finished their dinner. She got up and came to take his tray. "I'm sorry," she said.

"It was gone then," he said very quietly. He looked up at her directly, seeing her, as she felt he seldom did.

She stood, not understanding, waiting.

"It was gone then. Years before. What I believed at Nadami. That all we needed was to drive them out and we would be free. We lost our way as the war went on and on. I knew it was a lie. What did it matter if I lied more?"

She understood only that he was deeply upset and probably somewhat mad, and that she had been wrong to goad him. They were both old, both defeated, they had both lost their child. Why did she want to hurt him? She put her hand on his hand for a moment, in silence, before she picked up his tray.

As she washed up the dishes in the scullery, he called her, "Come here, please!" He had never done so before, and she hurried into the room.

"Who were you?" he asked.

She stood staring.

"Before you came here," he said impatiently.

"I went from the plantation to education school," she said. "I lived in the city. I taught physics. I administered the teaching of science in the schools. I brought up my daughter."

"What is your name?"

"Yoss. Seddewi Tribe, from Banni."

He nodded, and after a moment more she went back to the scullery. He didn't even know my name, she thought.

Every day she made him get up, walk a little, sit in a chair; he was obedient, but it tired him. The next afternoon she made him walk about a good while, and when he got back to bed he closed his eyes at once. She slipped up the rickety stairs to the west-window room and sat there a long time in perfect peace.

She had him sit up in the chair while she made their dinner. She talked to cheer him up, for he never complained at her demands, but he looked gloomy and bleak, and she blamed herself for upsetting him yesterday. Were they not both here to leave all that behind them, all their mistakes and failures as well as their loves and victories? She told him about Wada and Eyid, spinning out the story of the star-crossed lovers, who were, in fact, in bed in her house that afternoon. "I didn't used to have anywhere to go when they came," she said. "It could be rather inconvenient, cold days like today. I'd have to hang around the shops in the village. This is better, I must say. I like this house."

He only grunted, but she felt he was listening intently, almost that he was trying to understand, like a foreigner who did not know the language.

"You don't care about the house, do you?" she said, and laughed, serving up their soup. "You're honest, at least. Here I am pretending to be holy, to be making my soul, and I get fond of things, attached to them, I love things." She sat down by the fire to eat her soup. "There's a beautiful room upstairs," she said, "the front corner room, looking west. Something good happened in that room, lovers lived there once, maybe. I like to look out at the marshes from there."

When she made ready to go he asked, "Will they be gone?"

"The fawns? Oh yes. Long since. Back to their hateful families. I suppose if they could live together, they'd soon be just as hateful. They're very ignorant. How can they help it? The village is narrow-minded, they're so poor. But they cling to their love for each other, as if they knew it . . . it was their truth . . . "

"'Hold fast to the noble thing,'" Abberkam said. She knew the quotation.

"Would you like me to read to you?" she asked. "I have the *Arkamye,* I could bring it."

He shook his head, with a sudden, broad smile. "No need," he said. "I know it."

"All of it?"

He nodded.

"I meant to learn it — part of it anyway — when I came here," she said, awed. "But I never did. There never seems to be time. Did you learn it here?"

"Long ago. In the jail, in Gebba City," he said. "Plenty of time there. . . . These days, I lie here and say it to myself." His smile lingered as he looked up at her. "It gives me company in your absence."

She stood wordless.

"Your presence is sweet to me," he said.

She wrapped herself in her shawl and hurried out with scarcely a word of good-bye.

She walked home in a crowd of confused, conflicted feelings. What a monster the man was! He had been flirting with her: there was no doubt about it. Coming on to her, was more like it. Lying in bed like a great felled ox, with his wheezing and his grey hair! That soft, deep voice, that smile, he knew the uses of that smile, he knew how to keep it rare. He knew how to get round a woman, he'd got round a thousand if the stories were true, round them and into them and out again, here's a little semen to remember your Chief by, and bye-bye, baby. Lord!

So, why had she taken it into her head to tell him about Eyid and Wada being in her bed? Stupid woman, she told herself, striding into the mean east wind that scoured the greying reeds. Stupid, stupid, old, old woman.

Gubu came to meet her, dancing and batting with soft paws at her legs and hands, waving his short, end-knotted, black-spotted tail. She had left the door unlatched for him, and he could push it open. It was ajar. Feathers of some kind of small bird were strewn all over the room and there was a little blood and a bit of entrail on the hearthrug. "Monster," she told him. "Murder outside!" He danced his battle dance and cried Hoo! Hoo! He slept all night curled up in the small of her back, obligingly getting up, stepping over her, and curling up on the other side each time she turned over.

She turned over frequently, imagining or dreaming the weight and heat of a massive body, the weight of hands on her breasts, the tug of lips at her nipples, sucking life.

She shortened her visits to Abberkam. He was able to get up, see to his needs, get his own breakfast; she kept his peatbox by the chimney filled and his larder supplied, and she now brought him dinner but did not stay to eat it with him. He was mostly grave and silent, and she watched her tongue. They were wary with each other. She missed her hours upstairs in the western room; but that was done with, a kind of dream, a sweetness gone.

Eyid came to Yoss's house alone one afternoon, sullen-faced. "I guess I won't come back out here," she said.

"What's wrong?"

The girl shrugged.

"Are they watching you?"

"No. I don't know. I might, you know. I might get stuffed." She used the old slave word for pregnant.

"You used the contraceptives, didn't you?" She had bought them for the pair in Veo, a good supply.

Eyid nodded vaguely. "I guess it's wrong," she said, pursing her mouth.

"Making love? Using contraceptives?"

"I guess it's wrong," the girl repeated, with a quick, vengeful glance.

"All right," Yoss said.

Eyid turned away.

"Good-bye, Eyid."

Without speaking, Eyid went off by the bog-path.

Hold fast to the noble thing, Yoss thought, bitterly.

She went round the house to Tikuli's grave, but it was too cold to stand outside for long, a still, aching, midwinter cold. She went in and shut the door. The room seemed small and dark and low. The dull peat fire smoked and smouldered. It made no noise burning. There was no noise outside the house. The wind was down, the ice-bound reeds were still.

I want some wood, I want a wood fire, Yoss thought. A flame leaping and crackling, a story-telling fire, like we used to have in the grandmothers' house on the plantation.

The next day she went off one of the bog-paths to a ruined house half a mile away and pulled some loose boards off the fallen-in porch. She had a roaring blaze in her fireplace that night. She took to going to the ruined house once or more daily, and built up a sizeable woodpile next to the stacked peat in the nook on the other side of the chimney from her bed nook. She was no longer going to Abberkam's house; he was recovered, and she wanted a goal to walk to. She had no way to cut the longer boards, and so shoved them into the fireplace a bit at a time; that way one would last all the evening. She sat by the bright fire and tried to learn the First Book of the *Arkamye*. Gubu lay on the hearthstone sometimes watching the flames and whispering roo, roo, sometimes asleep. He hated so to go out into the icy reeds that she made him a little dirt-box in the scullery, and he used it very neatly.

The deep cold continued, the worst winter she had known on the marshes. Fierce drafts led her to cracks in the wood walls she had not known about; she had no rags to stuff them with and used mud and wadded reeds. If she let the fire go out, the little house grew icy within an hour. The peat fire, banked, got her through the nights. In the daytime often she put on a piece of wood for the flare, the brightness, the company of it.

She had to go into the village. She had put off going for days, hoping that the cold might relent, and had run out of practically everything. It was colder than ever. The peat blocks now on the fire were earthy and burned poorly, smouldering, so she put a piece of wood in with them to keep the fire lively and the house warm. She wrapped every jacket and shawl she had around her and set off with her sack. Gubu blinked at her from the hearth. "Lazy lout," she told him. "Wise beast."

The cold was frightening. If I slipped on the ice and broke a leg, no one might come by for days, she thought. I'd lie here and be frozen dead in a few hours. Well, well, well, I'm in the Lord's hands, and dead in a few years one way or the other. Only, dear Lord, let me get to the village and get warm!

She got there, and spent a good while at the sweet-shop stove catching up on gossip, and at the news vendor's woodstove, reading old newspapers about a new war in the eastern province. Eyid's aunts and Wada's father, mother, and aunts all asked her how the Chief was. They also all told her to go by her landlord's house, Kebi had something for her. He had a packet of cheap nasty tea for her. Perfectly willing to let him enrich his soul, she thanked him for the tea. He asked her about Abberkam. The Chief had been ill? He was better now? He pried; she replied indifferently. It's easy to live in silence, she thought; what I could not do is live with these voices.

She was loath to leave the warm room, but her bag was heavier than she liked to carry, and the icy spots on the road would be hard to see as the light failed. She took her leave and set off across the village again and up onto the causeway. It was later than she had thought. The sun was quite low, hiding behind one bar of cloud in an otherwise stark sky, as if grudging even a half hour's warmth and brightness. She wanted to get home to her fire, and stepped right along.

Keeping her eyes on the way ahead for fear of

ice, at first she only heard the voice. She knew it, and she thought, Abberkam has gone mad again! For he was running towards her, shouting. She stopped, afraid of him, but it was her name he was shouting. "Yoss! Yoss! It's all right!" he shouted, coming up right on her, a huge wild man, all dirty, muddy, ice and mud in his grey hair, his hands black, his clothes black, and she could see the whites all round his eyes.

"Get back!" she said, "get away, get away from me!"

"It's all right," he said, "but the house, but the house — "

"What house?"

"Your house, it burned. I saw it, I was coming to the village, I saw the smoke down in the marsh — "

He went on, but Yoss stood paralysed, unhearing. She had shut the door, let the latch fall. She never locked it, but she had let the latch fall, and Gubu would not be able to get out. He was in the house. Locked in: the bright, desperate eyes: the little voice crying —

She started forward. Abberkam blocked her way.

"Let me get by," she said. "I have to get by." She set down her bag and began to run.

Her arm was caught, she was stopped as if by a sea wave, swung right round. The huge body and voice were all around her. "It's all right, the kit is all right, it's in my house," he was saying. "Listen, listen to me, Yoss! The house burned. The kit is all right."

"What happened?" she said, shouting, furious. "Let me go! I don't understand! What happened?"

"Please, please be quiet," he begged her, releasing her. "We'll go by there. You'll see it. There isn't much to see."

Very shakily, she walked along with him while he told her what had happened. "But how did it start?" she said, "how could it?"

"A spark; you left the fire burning? Of course, of course you did, it's cold. But there were stones out of the chimney, I could see that. Sparks, if there was any wood on the fire — maybe a floorboard caught — the thatch, maybe. Then it would all go, in this dry weather, everything dried out, no rain. Oh my Lord, my sweet Lord, I thought you were in there. I thought you were in the house. I saw the fire, I was up on the causeway — then I was down at the door of the house, I don't know how, did I fly, I don't know — I pushed, it was latched, I pushed it in, and I saw the whole back wall and ceiling burning, blazing. There was so much smoke, I couldn't tell if you were there, I went in, the little animal was hiding in a corner — I thought how you cried when the other one died, I tried to catch it, and it went out the door like a flash, and I saw no one was there, and made for the door, and the roof fell in." He laughed, wild, triumphant. "Hit me on the head, see?" He stooped, but she still was not tall enough to see the top of his head. "I saw your bucket and tried to throw water on the front wall, to save something, then I saw that was crazy, it was all on fire, nothing left. And I went up the path, and the little animal, your pet, was waiting there, all shaking. It let me pick it up, and I didn't know what to do with it, so I ran back to my house, and left it there. I shut the door. It's safe there. Then I thought you must be in the village, so I came back to find you."

They had come to the turnoff. She went to the side of the causeway and looked down. A smear of smoke, a huddle of black. Black sticks. Ice. She shook all over and felt so sick she had to crouch down, swallowing cold saliva. The sky and the reeds went from left to right, spinning, in her eyes; she could not stop them spinning.

"Come, come on now, it's all right. Come on with me." She was aware of the voice, the hands and arms, a large warmth supporting her. She walked along with her eyes shut. After a while she could open them and look down at the road, carefully.

"Oh, my bag — I left it — It's all I have," she said suddenly with a kind of laugh, turning around and nearly falling over because the turn started the spinning again.

"I have it here. Come on, it's just a short way now." He carried the bag oddly, in the crook of his arm. The other arm was around her, helping her stand up and walk. They came to his house, the dark raft-house. It faced a tremendous orange-and-yellow sky, with pink streaks going up the sky from where the sun had set; the sun's hair, they used to call that, when she was a child. They turned from the glory, entering the dark house.

"Gubu?" she said.

It took a while to find him. He was cowering under the couch. She had to haul him out, he would not come to her. His fur was full of dust and came out in her hands as she stroked it. There was a little foam on his mouth, and he shivered and was silent in her arms. She stroked and stroked the silvery, speckled back, the spotted sides, the silken white belly fur. He closed his eyes finally; but the instant she moved a little, he leapt, and ran back under the couch.

She sat and said, "I'm sorry, I'm sorry, Gubu, I'm sorry."

Hearing her speak, the Chief came back into the room. He had been in the scullery. He held his wet hands in front of him and she wondered why he didn't dry them. "Is he all right?" he asked.

"It'll take a while," she said. "The fire. And a strange house. They're . . . cats are territorial. Don't like strange places."

She could not arrange her thoughts or words, they came in pieces, unattached.

"That is a cat, then?"

"A spotted cat, yes."

"Those pet animals, they belonged to the Bosses, they were in the Bosses' houses," he said. "We never had any around."

She thought it was an accusation. "They came from Werel with the Bosses," she said, "yes. So did we." After the sharp words were out she thought that maybe what he had said was an apology for ignorance.

He still stood there holding out his hands stiffly. "I'm sorry," he said. "I need some kind of bandage, I think."

She focused slowly on his hands.

"You burned them," she said.

"Not much. I don't know when."

"Let me see." He came nearer and turned the big hands palm up: a fierce red blistered bar across the bluish inner skin of the fingers of one, and a raw bloody wound in the base of the thumb of the other.

"I didn't notice till I was washing," he said. "It didn't hurt."

"Let me see your head," she said, remembering; and he knelt and presented her with a matted shaggy sooty object with a red-and-black burn right across the top of it. "Oh, Lord," she said.

His big nose and eyes appeared under the grey tangle, close to her, looking up at her, anxious. "I know the roof fell onto me," he said, and she began to laugh.

"It would take more than a roof falling onto you!" she said. "Have you got anything — any clean cloths — I know I left some clean dish towels in the scullery closet — Any disinfectant?"

She talked as she cleaned the head wound. "I don't know anything about burns except try to keep them clean and leave them open and dry. We should call the clinic in Veo. I can go into the village, tomorrow."

"I thought you were a doctor or a nurse," he said.

"I'm a school administrator!"

"You looked after me."

"I knew what you had. I don't know anything about burns. I'll go into the village and call. Not tonight, though."

"Not tonight," he agreed. He flexed his hands, wincing. "I was going to make us dinner," he said. "I didn't know there was anything wrong with my hands. I don't know when it happened."

"When you rescued Gubu," Yoss said in a matter-of-fact voice, and then began crying. "Show me what you were going to eat, I'll put it on," she said through tears.

"I'm sorry about your things," he said.

"Nothing mattered. I'm wearing almost all my clothes," she said, weeping. "There wasn't anything. Hardly any food there even. Only the *Arkamye*. And my book about the worlds." She thought of the pages blackening and curling as the fire read them. "A friend sent me that from the city, she never approved of me coming here, pretending to drink water and be silent. She was right, too, I should go back, I should never have come. What a liar I am, what a fool! Stealing wood! Stealing wood so I could have a nice fire! So I could be warm and cheerful! So I set the house on fire, so everything's gone, ruined, Kebi's house, my poor little cat, your hands, it's my fault. I forgot about sparks from wood fires, the chimney was built for peat fires, I forgot. I forget everything, my mind betrays me, my memory lies, I lie. I dishonor my Lord, pretending to turn to him when I can't turn to him, when I can't let go the world. So I burn it! So the sword cuts your hands." She took his hands in hers and bent her head over them. "Tears are disinfectant," she said. "Oh I'm sorry, I am sorry!"

His big, burned hands rested in hers. He leaned forward and kissed her hair, caressing it with his lips and cheek. "I will say you the *Arkamye*," he said. "Be still now. We need to eat something. You feel very cold. I think you have some shock, maybe. You sit there. I can put a pot on to heat, anyhow."

She obeyed. He was right, she felt very cold. She huddled closer to the fire. "Gubu?" she whispered. "Gubu, it's all right. Come on, come on, little one." But nothing moved under the couch.

Abberkam stood by her, offering her something: a glass: it was wine, red wine.

"You have wine?" she said, startled.

"Mostly I drink water and am silent," he said. "Sometimes I drink wine and talk. Take it."

She took it humbly. "I wasn't shocked," she said.

"Nothing shocks a city woman," he said gravely. "Now I need you to open up this jar."

"How did you get the wine open?" she asked as she unscrewed the lid of a jar of fish stew.

"It was already open," he said, deep-voiced, imperturbable.

They sat across the hearth from each other to eat, helping themselves from the pot hung on the firehook. She held bits of fish down low so they could be seen from under the couch and whispered to Gubu, but he would not come out.

"When he's very hungry, he will," she said. She was tired of the teary quaver in her voice, the knot in her throat, the sense of shame. "Thank you for the food," she said. "I feel better."

She got up and washed the pot and the spoons; she had told him not to get his hands wet, and he did not offer to help her, but sat on by the fire, motionless, like a great dark lump of stone.

"I'll go upstairs," she said when she was done. "Maybe I can get hold of Gubu and take him with me. Let me have a blanket or two."

He nodded. "They're up there. I lighted the fire," he said. She did not know what he meant; she had knelt to peer under the couch. She knew as she did so that she was grotesque, an old woman bundled up in shawls with her rear end in the air, whispering, "Gubu, Gubu!" to a piece of furniture. But there was a little scrabbling, and then Gubu came straight into her hands. He clung to her shoulder with his nose hidden under her ear. She sat up on her heels and looked at Abberkam, radiant. "Here he is!" she said. She got to her feet with some difficulty, and said, "Good night."

"Good night, Yoss," he said. She dared not try to carry the oil lamp, and made her way up the stairs in the dark, holding Gubu close with both hands till she was in the west room and had shut the door. Then she stood staring. Abberkam had unsealed the fireplace, and some time this evening he had lighted the peat laid ready in it; the ruddy glow flickered in the long, low windows black with night, and the scent of it was sweet. A bedstead that had been in another unused room now stood in this one, made up, with mattress and blankets and a new white wool rug thrown over it. A jug and basin stood on the shelf by the chimney. The old rug she had used to sit on had been beaten and scrubbed, and lay clean and threadbare on the hearth.

Gubu pushed at her arms; she set him down, and he ran straight under the bed. He would be all right there. She poured a little water from the jug into the basin and set it on the hearth in case he was thirsty. He could use the ashes for his box. Everything we need is here, she thought, still looking with a sense of bewilderment at the shadowy room, the soft light that struck the windows from within.

She went out, closing the door behind her, and went downstairs. Abberkam sat still by the fire. His eyes flashed at her. She did not know what to say.

"You liked that room," he said.

She nodded.

"You said maybe it was a lovers' room once. I thought maybe it was a lovers' room to be."

After a while she said, "Maybe."

"Not tonight," he said, with a low rumble: a laugh, she realised. She had seen him smile once, now she had heard him laugh.

"No. Not tonight," she said stiffly.

"I need my hands," he said, "I need everything, for that, for you."

She said nothing, watching him.

"Sit down, Yoss, please," he said. She sat down in the hearth-seat facing him.

"When I was ill I thought about these things," he said, always a touch of the orator in his voice. "I betrayed my cause, I lied and stole in its name, because I could not admit I had lost faith in it. I feared the Aliens because I feared their gods. So many gods! I feared that they would diminish my Lord. Diminish him!" He was silent for a minute, and drew breath; she could hear the deep rasp in his chest. "I betrayed my son's mother many times, many times. Her, other women, myself. I did not hold to the one noble thing." He opened up his hands, wincing a little, looking at the burns across them. "I think you did," he said.

After a while she said, "I only stayed with Safnan's father a few years. I had some other men. What does it matter, now?"

"That's not what I mean," he said. "I mean that you did not betray your men, your child, yourself. All right, all that's past. You say, what does it matter now, nothing matters. But you give me this chance even now, this beautiful chance, to me, to hold you, hold you fast."

She said nothing.

"I came here in shame," he said, "and you honored me."

"Why not? Who am I to judge you?"

"'Brother, I am thou.'"

She looked at him in terror, one glance, then looked into the fire. The peat burned low and warm, sending up one faint curl of smoke. She thought of the warmth, the darkness of his body.

"Would there be any peace between us?" she said at last.

"Do you need peace?"

After a while she smiled a little.

"I will do my best," he said. "Stay in this house a while."

She nodded.

Forgiveness Day

~~~

Solly had been a space brat, a Mobile's child, living on this ship and that, this world and that; she'd traveled five hundred light-years by the time she was ten. At twenty-five she had been through a revolution on Alterra, learned *aiji* on Terra and farthinking from an old hilfer on Rokanan, breezed through the Schools on Hain, and survived an assignment as Observer in murderous, dying Kheakh, skipping another half millennium at near-lightspeed in the process. She was young, but she'd been around.

She got bored with the Embassy people in Voe Deo telling her to watch out for this, remember that; she was a Mobile herself now, after all. Werel had its quirks — what world didn't? She'd done her homework, she knew when to curtsy and when not to belch, and vice versa. It was a relief to get on her own at last, in this gorgeous little city, on this gorgeous little continent, the first and only

Envoy of the Ekumen to the Divine Kingdom of Gatay.

She was high for days on the altitude, the tiny, brilliant sun pouring vertical light into the noisy streets, the peaks soaring up incredibly behind every building, the dark blue sky where great near stars burned all day, the dazzling nights under six or seven lolloping bits of moon, the tall black people with their black eyes, narrow heads, long, narrow hands and feet, gorgeous people, her people! She loved them all. Even if she saw a little too much of them.

The last time she had had completely to herself was a few hours in the passenger cabin of the airskimmer sent by Gatay to bring her across the ocean from Voe Deo. On the airstrip she was met by a delegation of priests and officials from the King and the Council, magnificent in scarlet and brown and turquoise, and swept off to the Palace, where there was a lot of curtsying and no belching, of course, for hours — an introduction to his little shrunken old majesty, introductions to High Muckamucks and Lord Hooziwhats, speeches, a banquet — all completely predictable, no problems at all, not even the impenetrable giant fried flower on her plate at the banquet. But with her, from that first moment on the airstrip and at every moment thereafter, discreetly behind or beside or very near her, were two men: her Guide and her Guard.

The Guide, whose name was San Ubattat, was provided by her hosts in Gatay; of course he was reporting on her to the government, but he was a most obliging spy, endlessly smoothing the way for her, showing her with a bare hint what was expected or what would be a gaffe, and an excellent linguist, ready with a translation when she needed one. San was all right. But the Guard was something else.

He had been attached to her by the Ekumen's hosts on this world, the dominant power on Werel, the big nation of Voe Deo. She had promptly protested to the Embassy back in Voe Deo that she didn't need or want a bodyguard. Nobody in Gatay was out to get her and even if they were, she preferred to look after herself. The Embassy sighed. Sorry, they said. You're stuck with him. Voe Deo has a military presence in Gatay, which after all is a client state, economically dependent. It's in Voe Deo's interest to protect the legitimate government of Gatay against the native terrorist factions, and you get protected as one of their interests. We can't argue with that.

She knew better than to argue with the Embassy, but she could not resign herself to the Major. His military title, rega, she translated by the archaic word "Major," from a skit she'd seen on Terra. That Major had been a stuffed uniform, covered with medals and insignia. It puffed and strutted and commanded, and finally blew up into bits of stuffing. If only this Major would blow up! Not that he strutted, exactly, or even commanded, directly. He was stonily polite, woodenly silent, stiff and cold as rigor mortis. She soon gave up any effort to talk to him; whatever she said, he replied Yessum or Nomum with the prompt stupidity of a man who does not and will not actually listen, an officer officially incapable of humanity. And he was with her in every public situation, day and night, on the street, shopping, meeting with businessmen and officials, sight-seeing, at court, in the balloon ascent above the mountains — with her everywhere, everywhere but bed.

Even in bed she wasn't quite as alone as she would often have liked; for the Guide and the Guard went home at night, but in the anteroom of her bedroom slept the Maid — a gift from His Majesty, her own private asset.

She remembered her incredulity when she first learned that word, years ago, in a text about slavery. "On Werel, members of the dominant caste are called *owners;* members of the serving class are called *assets.* Only owners are referred to as men or women; assets are called bondsmen, bondswomen."

So here she was, the owner of an asset. You don't turn down a king's gift. Her asset's name was Rewe. Rewe was probably a spy too, but it was hard to believe. She was a dignified, handsome woman some years older than Solly and about the same intensity of skin color, though Solly was pinkish brown and Rewe was bluish brown. The palms of her hands were a delicate azure. Rewe's manners were exquisite and she had tact, astuteness, an infallible sense of when she was wanted and when not. Solly of course treated her as an equal, stating right out at the beginning that she believed no human being had a right to dominate, much less own, another, that she would give Rewe no orders, and that she hoped they might become friends. Rewe accepted this, unfortunately, as a new set of orders. She smiled and said yes. She was infinitely yielding. Whatever Solly said or did sank into that acceptance and was lost, leaving Rewe unchanged: an attentive, obliging, gentle physical presence, just out of reach. She smiled, and said yes, and was untouchable.

And Solly began to think, after the first fizz of the first days in Gatay, that she needed Rewe, really needed her as a woman to talk with. There was no way to meet owner women, who lived hidden away in their bezas, women's quarters, "at home," they called it. All bondswomen but Rewe were somebody else's property, not hers to talk to. All she ever met was men. And eunuchs.

That had been another thing hard to believe, that a man would voluntarily trade his virility for a little social standing; but she met such men all the time in King Hotat's court. Born assets, they earned partial independence by becoming eunuchs, and as such often rose to positions of considerable power and trust among their owners. The eunuch Tayandan, majordomo of the palace, ruled the King, who didn't rule, but figureheaded for the Council. The Council was made up of various kinds of lord but only one kind of priest, Tualites. Only assets worshiped Kamye, and the original religion of Gatay had been suppressed when the monarchy became Tualite a century or so ago. If there was one thing she really disliked about Werel, aside from slavery and gender-dominance, it was the religions. The songs about Lady Tual were beautiful, and the statues of her and the great temples in Voe Deo were wonderful, and the *Arkamye* seemed to be a good story though long-winded; but the deadly self-righteousness, the intolerance, the stupidity of the priests, the hideous doctrines that justified every cruelty in the name of the faith! As a matter of fact, Solly said to herself, was there anything she *did* like about Werel?

And answered herself instantly: I love it, I love it. I love this weird little bright sun and all the broken bits of moons and the mountains going up like ice walls and the people — the people with their black eyes without whites like animals' eyes, eyes like dark glass, like dark water, mysterious — I want to love them, I want to know them, I want to reach them!

But she had to admit that the pissants at the Embassy had been right about one thing: being a woman was tough on Werel. She fit nowhere. She went about alone, she had a public position, and so was a contradiction in terms: proper women stayed at home, invisible. Only bondswomen went out in the streets, or met strangers, or worked at any public job. She behaved like an asset, not like an owner. Yet she was something very grand, an envoy of the Ekumen, and Gatay very much wanted to join the Ekumen and not to offend its envoys. So the officials and courtiers and businessmen she talked to on the business of the Ekumen did the best they could: they treated her as if she were a man.

The pretense was never complete and often broke right down. The poor old King groped her industriously, under the vague impression that she was one of his bedwarmers. When she contradicted Lord Gatuyo in a discussion, he stared with the blank disbelief of a man who has been talked back to by his shoe. He had been thinking of her as a woman. But in general the disgenderment worked, allowing her to work with them; and she began to fit herself into the game, enlisting Rewe's help in making clothes that resembled what male owners wore in Gatay, avoiding anything that to them would be specifically feminine. Rewe was a quick, intelligent seamstress. The bright, heavy, close-fitted trousers were practical and becoming, the embroidered jackets were splendidly warm. She liked wearing them. But she felt unsexed by these men who could not accept her for what she was. She needed to talk to a woman.

She tried to meet some of the hidden owner women through the owner men, and met a wall of politeness without a door, without a peephole. What a wonderful idea; we will certainly arrange a visit when the weather is better! I should be overwhelmed with the honor if the Envoy were to entertain Lady Mayoyo and my daughters, but my foolish, provincial girls are so unforgivably timid — I'm sure you understand. Oh, surely, surely, a tour of the inner gardens — but not at present, when the vines are not in flower! We must wait until the vines are in flower!

There was nobody to talk to, nobody, until she met Batikam the Makil.

It was an event: a touring troupe from Voe Deo. There wasn't much going on in Gatay's little mountain capital by way of entertainment, except for temple dancers — all men, of course — and the soppy fluff that passed as drama on the Werelian network. Solly had doggedly entered some of these wet pastels, hoping for a glimpse into the life "at home," but she couldn't stomach the swooning maidens who died of love while the stiff-necked jackass heroes, who all looked like the Major, died nobly in battle, and Tual the Merciful leaned out of the clouds smiling upon their deaths with her eyes slightly crossed and the whites showing, a sign of divinity. Solly had noticed that Werelian men never entered the network for drama. Now she knew why. But the receptions at the palace and the parties in her honor given by various lords and businessmen were pretty dull stuff: all men, always, because they wouldn't have the slave girls in while the Envoy was there; and she couldn't flirt even with the nicest men, couldn't remind them that they were men, since that would remind them that she was a woman not behaving like a lady. The fizz had definitely gone flat by the time the makil troupe came.

She asked San, a reliable etiquette advisor, if it would be all right for her to attend the performance. He hemmed and hawed and finally, with more than usual oily delicacy, gave her to understand that it would be all right so long as she went dressed as a man. "Women, you know, don't go in public. But sometimes, they want so much to see the entertainers, you know? Lady Amatay used to go with Lord Amatay, dressed in his clothes, every year; everybody knew, nobody said anything — you know. For you, such a great person, it would be all right. Nobody will say anything. Quite, quite all right. Of course, I come with you, the rega comes with you. Like friends, ha? You know, three good men friends going to the entertainment, ha? Ha?"

Ha, ha, she said obediently. What fun! — But it was worth it, she thought, to see the makils.

They were never on the network. Young girls at home were not to be exposed to their performances, some of which, San gravely informed her, were unseemly. They played only in theaters. Clowns, dancers, prostitutes, actors, musicians, the makils formed a kind of subclass, the only assets not personally owned. A talented slave boy bought by the Entertainment Corporation from his owner was thenceforth the property of the Corporation, which trained and looked after him the rest of his life.

They walked to the theater, six or seven streets away. She had forgotten that the makils were all transvestites, indeed she did not remember it when she first saw them, a troop of tall slender dancers sweeping out onto the stage with the precision and power and grace of great birds wheeling, flocking, soaring. She watched unthinking, enthralled by their beauty, until suddenly the music changed and the clowns came in, black as night, black as owners, wearing fantastic trailing skirts, with fantastic jutting jeweled breasts, singing in tiny, swoony voices, "Oh do not rape me please kind Sir, no no, not now!" They're men, they're men! Solly realized then, already laughing helplessly. By the time Batikam finished his star turn, a marvelous dramatic monologue, she was a fan. "I want to meet him," she said to San at a pause between acts. "The actor — Batikam."

San got the bland expression that signified he was thinking how it could be arranged and how to make a little money out of it. But the Major was on guard, as ever. Stiff as a stick, he barely turned his head to glance at San. And San's expression began to alter.

If her proposal was out of line, San would have signaled or said so. The Stuffed Major was simply controlling her, trying to keep her as tied down as one of "his" women. It was time to challenge him. She turned to him and stared straight at him. "Rega

Teyeo," she said, "I quite comprehend that you're under orders to keep me in order. But if you give orders to San or to me, they must be spoken aloud, and they must be justified. I will not be managed by your winks or your whims."

There was a considerable pause, a truly delicious and rewarding pause. It was difficult to see if the Major's expression changed; the dim theater light showed no detail in his blue-black face. But there was something frozen about his stillness that told her she'd stopped him. At last he said, "I'm charged to protect you, Envoy."

"Am I endangered by the makils? Is there impropriety in an envoy of the Ekumen congratulating a great artist of Werel?"

Again the frozen silence. "No," he said.

"Then I request you to accompany me when I go backstage after the performance to speak to Batikam."

One stiff nod. One stiff, stuffy, defeated nod. Score one! Solly thought, and sat back cheerfully to watch the lightpainters, the erotic dances, and the curiously touching little drama with which the evening ended. It was in archaic poetry, hard to understand, but the actors were so beautiful, their voices so tender that she found tears in her eyes and hardly knew why.

"A pity the makils always draw on the *Arkamye*," said San, with smug, pious disapproval. He was not a very high-class owner, in fact he owned no assets; but he was an owner, and a bigoted Tualite, and liked to remind himself of it. "Scenes from the *Incarnations of Tual* would be more befitting such an audience."

"I'm sure you agree, Rega," she said, enjoying her own irony.

"Not at all," he said, with such toneless politeness that at first she did not realise what he had said; and then forgot the minor puzzle in the bustle of finding their way and gaining admittance to the backstage and to the performers' dressing room.

When they realised who she was, the managers tried to clear all the other performers out, leaving her alone with Batikam (and San and the Major, of course); but she said no, no, no, these wonderful artists must not be disturbed, just let me talk a moment with Batikam. She stood there in the bustle of doffed costumes, half-naked people, smeared makeup, laughter, dissolving tension after the show, any backstage on any world, talking with the clever, intense man in elaborate archaic woman's costume. They hit it off at once. "Can you come to my house?" she asked. "With pleasure," Batikam said, and his eyes did not flick to San's or the Major's face: the first bondsman she had yet met who did not glance to her Guard or her Guide for permission to say or do anything, anything at all. She glanced at them only to see if they were shocked. San looked collusive, the Major looked rigid. "I'll come in a little while," Batikam said. "I must change."

They exchanged smiles, and she left. The fizz was back in the air. The huge close stars hung clustered like grapes of fire. A moon tumbled over the icy peaks, another jigged like a lopsided lantern above the curlicue pinnacles of the palace. She strode along the dark street, enjoying the freedom of the male robe she wore and its warmth, making San trot to keep up; the Major, long-legged, kept pace with her. A high, trilling voice called, "Envoy!" and she turned with a smile, then swung round, seeing the Major grappling momentarily with someone in the shadow of a portico. He broke free, caught up to her without a word, seized her arm in an iron grip, and dragged her into a run. "Let go!" she said, struggling; she did not want to use an aiji break on him, but nothing less was going to get her free.

He pulled her nearly off-balance with a sudden dodge into an alley; she ran with him, letting him keep hold on her arm. They came unexpectedly out into her street and to her gate, through it, into the house, which he unlocked with a word — how did he do that? — "What is all this?" she demanded, breaking away easily, holding her arm where his grip had bruised it.

She saw, outraged, the last flicker of an exhilarated smile on his face. Breathing hard, he asked, "Are you hurt?"

"Hurt? Where you yanked me, yes — what do you think you were doing?"

"Keeping the fellow away."

"What fellow?"

He said nothing.

"The one who called out? Maybe he wanted to talk to me!"

After a moment the Major said, "Possibly. He was in the shadow. I thought he might be armed. I must go out and look for San Ubattat. Please keep the door locked until I come back." He was out the door as he gave the order; it never occurred to him that she would not obey, and she did obey, raging. Did he think she couldn't look after herself? That she needed him interfering in her life, kicking slaves around, "protecting" her? Maybe it was time he saw what an aiji fall looked like. He was strong and quick, but had no real training. This kind of amateur interference was intolerable, really intolerable; she must protest to the Embassy again.

As soon she let him back in with a nervous, shamefaced San in tow, she said, "You opened my door with a password. I was not informed that you had right of entrance day and night."

He was back to his military blankness. "Nomum," he said.

"You are not to do so again. You are not to seize hold of me ever again. I must tell you that if you do, I will injure you. If something alarms you, tell me what it is and I will respond as I see fit. Now will you please go."

"With pleasure, mum," he said, wheeled, and marched out.

"Oh, Lady — Oh, Envoy," San said, "that was a dangerous person, extremely dangerous people, I am so sorry, disgraceful," and he babbled on. She finally got him to say who he thought it was, a religious dissident, one of the Old Believers who held to the original religion of Gatay and wanted to cast out or kill all foreigners and unbelievers. "A bondsman?" she asked with interest, and he was shocked — "Oh, no, no, a real person, a man — but most misguided, a fanatic, a heathen fanatic! Knifemen, they call themselves. But a man, Lady — Envoy, certainly a man!"

The thought that she might think that an asset might touch her upset him as much as the attempted assault. If such it had been.

As she considered it, she began to wonder if, since she had put the Major in his place at the theater, he had found an excuse to put her in her place by "protecting" her. Well, if he tried it again, he'd find himself upside down against the opposite wall.

"Rewe!" she called, and the bondswoman appeared instantly as always. "One of the actors is coming. Would you like to make us a little tea, something like that?" Rewe smiled, said, "Yes," and vanished. There was a knock at the door. The Major opened it — he must be standing guard outside — and Batikam came in.

It had not occurred to her that the makil would still be in women's clothing, but it was how he dressed offstage too, not so magnificently, but with elegance, in the delicate, flowing materials and dark, subtle hues that the swoony ladies in the dramas wore. It gave considerable piquancy, she felt, to her own male costume. Batikam was not as handsome as the Major, who was a stunning-looking man till he opened his mouth; but the makil was magnetic, you had to look at him. He was a dark greyish brown, not the blue-black that the owners were so vain of (though there were plenty of black assets too, Solly had noticed: of course, when every bondswoman was her owner's sexual servant). Intense, vivid intelligence and sympathy shone in his face through the makil's stardust black makeup, as he looked around with a slow, lovely laugh at her, at San, and at the Major standing at the door. He laughed like a woman, a warm ripple, not the ha, ha of a man. He held out his hands to Solly, and she came forward and took them. "Thank you for coming, Batikam!" she said, and he said, "Thank you for asking me, Alien Envoy!"

"San," she said, "I think this is your cue?"

Only indecision about what he ought to do could have slowed San down till she had to speak. He still hesitated a moment, then smiled with unction and said, "Yes, so sorry, a very good night to you, Envoy! Noon hour at the Office of Mines, tomorrow, I believe?" Backing away, he backed right into the Major, who stood like a post in the doorway. She looked at the Major, ready to order him out without ceremony, how dare he shove back in! — and saw the expression on his face. For once his blank mask had cracked, and what was revealed was contempt. Incredulous, sickened contempt. As if he was obliged to watch someone eat a turd.

"Get out," she said. She turned her back on both of them. "Come on, Batikam; the only privacy I have is in here," she said, and led the makil to her bedroom.

He was born where his fathers before him were born, in the old, cold house in the foothills above Noeha. His mother did not cry out as she bore him, since she was a soldier's wife, and a soldier's mother, now. He was named for his great-uncle, killed on duty in the Sosa. He grew up in the stark discipline of a poor household of pure veot lineage. His father, when he was on leave, taught him the arts a soldier must know; when his father was on duty the old Asset-Sergeant Habbakam took over the lessons, which began at five in the morning, summer or winter, with worship, shortsword practice, and a cross-country run. His mother and grandmother taught him the other arts a man must know, beginning with good manners before he was two, and after his second birthday going on to history, poetry, and sitting still without talking.

The child's day was filled with lessons and fenced with disciplines; but a child's day is long. There was room and time for freedom, the freedom of the farmyard and the open hills. There was the companionship of pets, foxdogs, running dogs, spotted cats, hunting cats, and the farm cattle and the greathorses; not much companionship otherwise. The family's assets, other than Habbakam and the two housewomen, were sharecroppers, working the stony foothill land that they and their owners had lived on forever. Their children were light-skinned, shy, already stooped to their lifelong work, ignorant of anything beyond their fields and hills. Sometimes they swam with Teyeo, summers, in the pools of the river. Sometimes he rounded up a couple of them to play soldiers with him. They stood awkward, uncouth, smirking when he shouted "Charge!" and rushed at the invisible enemy. "Follow me!" he cried shrilly, and they lumbered after him, firing their tree-branch guns at random, pow, pow. Mostly he went alone, riding his good mare Tasi or afoot with a hunting cat pacing by his side.

A few times a year visitors came to the estate, relatives or fellow officers of Teyeo's father, bringing their children and their housepeople. Teyeo silently and politely showed the child guests about, introduced them to the animals, took them on rides. Silently and politely, he and his cousin Gemat came to hate each other; at age fourteen they fought for an hour in a glade behind the house, punctiliously following the rules of wrestling, relentlessly hurting each other, getting bloodier and wearier and more desperate, until by unspoken consent they called it off and returned in silence to the house, where everyone was gathering for dinner. Everyone looked at them and said nothing. They washed up hurriedly, hurried to table. Gemat's nose leaked blood all through the meal; Teyeo's jaw was so sore he could not open it to eat. No one commented.

Silently and politely, when they were both fifteen, Teyeo and Rega Toebawe's daughter fell in love. On the last day of her visit they escaped by unspoken collusion and rode out side by side, rode for hours, too shy to talk. He had given her Tasi to ride. They dismounted to water and rest the horses in a wild valley of the hills. They sat near each other, not very near, by the side of the little quiet-running stream. "I love you," Teyeo said. "I love you," Emdu said, bending her shining black face down. They did not touch or look at each other. They rode back over the hills, joyous, silent.

When he was sixteen Teyeo was sent to the Officers' Academy in the capital of his province. There he continued to learn and practice the arts of war and the arts of peace. His province was the most rural in Voe Deo; its ways were conservative, and his training was in some ways anachronistic. He was of course taught the technologies of modern warfare, becoming a first-rate pod pilot and an expert in telereconnaissance; but he was not taught the modern ways of thinking that accompanied the technologies in other schools. He learned the poetry and history of Voe Deo, not the history and politics of the Ekumen. The Alien presence on Werel remained remote, theoretical to him. His reality was the old reality of the veot class, whose men held themselves apart from all men not soldiers and in brotherhood with all soldiers, whether owners, assets, or enemies. As for women, Teyeo considered his rights over them absolute, binding him absolutely to responsible chivalry to women of his own class and protective, merciful treatment of bondswomen. He believed all foreigners to be basically hostile, untrustworthy heathens. He honored the Lady Tual, but worshiped the Lord Kamye. He expected no justice, looked for no reward, and valued above all competence, courage, and self-respect. In some respects he was utterly unsuited to the world he was to enter, in others well prepared for it, since he was to spend seven years on Yeowe fighting a war in which there was no justice, no reward, and never even an illusion of ultimate victory.

Rank among veot officers was hereditary. Teyeo entered active service as a rega, the highest of the three veot ranks. No degree of ineptitude or distinction could lower or raise his status or his pay. Material ambition was no use to a veot. But honor and responsibility were to be earned, and he earned them quickly. He loved service, loved the life, knew he was good at it, intelligently obedient, effective in command; he had come out of the Academy with the highest recommendations, and being posted to the capital, drew notice as a promising officer as well as a likable young man. At twenty-four he was absolutely fit, his body would do anything he asked of it. His austere upbringing had given him little taste for indulgence but an intense appreciation of pleasure, so the luxuries and entertainments of the capital were a discovery of delight to him. He was reserved and rather shy, but companionable and cheerful. A handsome young man, in with a set of other young men very like him, for a year he knew what it is to live a completely privileged life with complete enjoyment of it. The brilliant intensity of that enjoyment stood against the dark background of the war in Yeowe, the slave revolution on the colony planet, which had gone on all his lifetime, and was now intensifying. Without that background, he could not have been so happy. A whole life of games and diversions had no interest for him; and when his orders came, posted as a pilot and division commander to Yeowe, his happiness was pretty nearly complete.

He went home for his thirty-day leave. Having received his parents' approbation, he rode over the hills to Rega Toebawe's estate and asked for his daughter's hand in marriage. The rega and his wife told their daughter that they approved his offer and asked her, for they were not strict parents, if she would like to marry Teyeo. "Yes," she said. As a grown, unmarried woman, she lived in seclusion in the women's side of the house, but she and Teyeo were allowed to meet and even to walk together, the chaperone remaining at some distance. Teyeo told her it was a three-year posting; would she marry in haste now, or wait three years and have a proper wedding? "Now," she said, bending down her narrow, shining face. Teyeo gave a laugh of delight, and she laughed at him. They were married nine days later — it couldn't be sooner, there had to be some fuss and ceremony, even if it was a soldier's wedding — and for seventeen days Teyeo and Emdu made love, walked together, made love, rode together, made love, came to know each other, came to love each other, quarreled, made up, made love, slept in each other's arms. Then he left for the war on another world, and she moved to the women's side of her husband's house.

His three-year posting was extended year by year, as his value as an officer was recognised and as the war on Yeowe changed from scattered containing actions to an increasingly desperate retreat. In his seventh year of service an order for compassionate leave was sent out to Yeowe Headquarters for Rega Teyeo, whose wife was dying of complications of berlot fever. At that point, there was no headquarters on Yeowe; the Army was retreating from three directions towards the old colonial capital; Teyeo's division was fighting a rear-guard defense in the sea marshes; communications had collapsed.

Command on Werel continued to find it inconceivable that a mass of ignorant slaves with the crudest kind of weapons could be defeating the Army of Voe Deo, a disciplined, trained body of soldiers with an infallible communications network, skimmers, pods, every armament and device permitted by the Ekumenical Convention Agreement. A strong faction in Voe Deo blamed the setbacks on this submissive adherence to Alien rules. The hell with Ekumenical Conventions. Bomb the damned dusties back to the mud they were made of. Use the biobomb, what was it for, anyway? Get our men off the foul planet and wipe it clean. Start fresh. If we don't win the war on Yeowe, the next revolution's going to be right here on Werel, in our own cities, in our own homes! The jittery government held on against this pressure. Werel was on probation, and Voe Deo wanted to lead the planet to Ekumenical status. Defeats were minimised, losses were not made up, skimmers, pods, weapons, men were not replaced. By the end of Teyeo's seventh year, the Army on Yeowe had been essentially written off by its government. Early in the eighth year, when the Ekumen was at last permitted to send its Envoys to Yeowe, Voe Deo and the other countries that had supplied auxiliary troops finally began to bring their soldiers home.

It was not until he got back to Werel that Teyeo learned his wife was dead.

He went home to Noeha. He and his father greeted each other with a silent embrace, but his mother wept as she embraced him. He knelt to her in apology for having brought her more grief than she could bear.

He lay that night in the cold room in the silent house, listening to his heart beat like a slow drum. He was not unhappy, the relief of being at peace and the sweetness of being home were too great for that; but it was a desolate calm, and somewhere in it was anger. Not used to anger, he was not sure what he felt. It was as if a faint, sullen red flare colored every image in his mind, as he lay trying to think through the seven years on Yeowe, first as a pilot, then the ground war, then the long retreat, the killing and the being killed. Why had they been left there to be hunted down and slaughtered? Why had the government not sent them reinforcements? The questions had not been worth asking then, they were not worth asking now. They had only one answer: We do what they ask us to do, and we don't complain. I fought every step of the way, he thought without pride. The new knowledge sliced keen as a knife through all other knowledge — And while I was fighting, she was dying. All a waste, there on Yeowe. All a waste, here on Werel. He sat up in the dark, the cold, silent, sweet dark of night in the hills. "Lord Kamye," he said aloud, "help me. My mind betrays me."

During the long leave home he sat often with his mother. She wanted to talk about Emdu, and at first he had to force himself to listen. It would be easy to forget the girl he had known for seventeen days seven years ago, if only his mother would let him forget. Gradually he learned to take what she wanted to give him, the knowledge of who his wife had been. His mother wanted to share all she could with him of the joy she had had in Emdu, her beloved child and friend. Even his father, retired now, a quenched, silent man, was able to say, "She was the light of the house." They were thanking him for her. They were telling him that it had not all been a waste.

But what lay ahead of them? Old age, the empty house. They did not complain, of course, and seemed content in their severe, placid round of daily work; but for them the continuity of the past with the future was broken.

"I should remarry," Teyeo said to his mother. "Is there anyone you've noticed . . . ?"

It was raining, a grey light through the wet windows, a soft thrumming on the eaves. His mother's face was indistinct as she bent to her mending.

"No," she said. "Not really." She looked up at him, and after a pause asked, "Where do you think you'll be posted?"

"I don't know."

"There's no war now," she said, in her soft, even voice.

"No," Teyeo said. "There's no war."

"Will there be . . . ever? do you think?"

He stood up, walked down the room and back, sat down again on the cushioned platform near her; they both sat straight-backed, still except for the slight motion of her hands as she sewed; his hands lay lightly one in the other, as he had been taught when he was two.

"I don't know," he said. "It's strange. It's as if there hadn't been a war. As if we'd never been on Yeowe — the Colony, the Uprising, all of it. They don't talk about it. It didn't happen. We don't fight wars. This is a new age. They say that often on the net. The age of peace, brotherhood across the stars. So, are we brothers with Yeowe, now? Are we brothers with Gatay and Bambur and the Forty States? Are we brothers with our assets? I can't make sense of it. I don't know what they mean. I don't know where I fit in." His voice too was quiet and even.

"Not here, I think," she said. "Not yet."

After a while he said, "I thought . . . children . . ."

"Of course. When the time comes." She smiled at him. "You never could sit still for half an hour. . . . Wait. Wait and see."

She was right, of course; and yet what he saw in the net and in town tried his patience and his pride. It seemed that to be a soldier now was a disgrace. Government reports, the news and the analyses, constantly referred to the Army and particularly the veot class as fossils, costly and useless, Voe Deo's principal obstacle to full admission to the Ekumen. His own uselessness was made clear to him when his request for a posting was met by an indefinite extension of his leave on half pay. At thirty-two, they appeared to be telling him, he was superannuated.

Again he suggested to his mother that he should accept the situation, settle down, and look for a wife. "Talk to your father," she said. He did so; his father said, "Of course your help is welcome, but I can run the farm well enough for a while yet. Your mother thinks you should go to the capital, to Command. They can't ignore you if you're there. After all. After seven years' combat — your record — "

Teyeo knew what that was worth, now. But he was certainly not needed here, and probably irritated his father with his ideas of changing this or that way things were done. They were right: he should go to the capital and find out for himself what part he could play in the new world of peace.

His first half-year there was grim. He knew almost no one at Command or in the barracks; his generation was dead, or invalided out, or home on half pay. The younger officers, who had not been on Yeowe, seemed to him a cold, buttoned-up lot, always talking money and politics. Little business-men, he privately thought them. He knew they were afraid of him — of his record, of his reputation. Whether he wanted to or not he reminded them that there had been a war that Werel had fought and lost, a civil war, their own race fighting against itself, class against class. They wanted to dismiss it as a meaningless quarrel on another world, nothing to do with them.

Teyeo walked the streets of the capital, watched the thousands of bondsmen and bondswomen hurrying about their owners' business, and wondered what they were waiting for.

"The Ekumen does not interfere with the social, cultural, or economic arrangements and affairs of any people," the Embassy and the government spokesmen repeated. "Full membership for any nation or people that wishes it is contingent only on absence, or renunciation, of certain specific methods and devices of warfare," and there followed the list of terrible weapons, most of them mere names to Teyeo, but a few of them inventions of his own country: the biobomb, as they called it, and the neuronics.

He personally agreed with the Ekumen's judgment on such devices, and respected their patience in waiting for Voe Deo and the rest of Werel to prove not only compliance with the ban, but acceptance of the principle. But he very deeply resented their condescension. They sat in judgment on everything Werelian, viewing from above. The less they said about the division of classes, the clearer their disapproval was. "Slavery is of very rare occurrence in Ekumenical worlds," said their books, "and disappears completely with full participation in the Ekumenical polity." Was that what the Alien Embassy was really waiting for?

"By our Lady!" said one of the young officers — many of them were Tualites, as well as businessmen — "the Aliens are going to admit the dusties before they admit us!" He was sputtering with indignant rage, like a red-faced old rega faced with an insolent bondsoldier. "Yeowe — a damned planet of savages, tribesmen, regressed into barbarism — preferred over us!"

"They fought well," Teyeo observed, knowing he should not say it as he said it, but not liking to hear the men and women he had fought against called dusties. Assets, rebels, enemies, yes.

The young man stared at him and after a moment said, "I suppose you love 'em, eh? The dusties?"

"I killed as many as I could," Teyeo replied politely, and then changed the conversation. The young man, though nominally Teyeo's superior at Command, was an oga, the lowest rank of veot, and to snub him further would be ill-bred.

They were stuffy, he was touchy; the old days of cheerful good fellowship were a faint, incredible memory. The bureau chiefs at Command listened to his request to be put back on active service and sent him endlessly on to another department. He could not live in barracks, but had to find an apartment, like a civilian. His half pay did not permit him indulgence in the expensive pleasures of the city. While waiting for appointments to see this or that official, he spent his days in the library net of the Officers' Academy. He knew his education had been incomplete and was out of date. If his country was going to join the Ekumen, in order to be useful he must know more about the Alien ways of thinking and the new technologies. Not sure what he needed to know, he floundered about in the network, bewildered by the endless information available, increasingly aware that he was no intellectual and no scholar and would never understand Alien minds, but doggedly driving himself on out of his depth.

A man from the Embassy was offering an introductory course in Ekumenical history in the public net. Teyeo joined it, and sat through eight or ten lecture-and-discussion periods, straight-backed and still, only his hands moving slightly as he took full and methodical notes. The lecturer, a Hainishman who translated his extremely long Hainish name as Old Music, watched Teyeo, tried to draw him out in discussion, and at last asked him to stay in after session. "I should like to meet you, Rega," he said, when the others had dropped out.

They met at a café. They met again. Teyeo did not like the Alien's manners, which he found effusive; he did not trust his quick, clever mind; he felt Old Music was using him, studying him as a specimen of The Veot, The Soldier, probably The Barbarian. The Alien, secure in his superiority, was indifferent to Teyeo's coldness, ignored his distrust, insisted on helping him with information and guidance, and shamelessly repeated questions Teyeo had avoided answering. One of these was, "Why are you sitting around here on half pay?"

"It's not by my own choice, Mr. Old Music," Teyeo finally answered, the third time it was asked. He was very angry at the man's impudence, and so spoke with particular mildness. He kept his eyes away from Old Music's eyes, bluish, with the whites showing like a scared horse. He could not get used to Aliens' eyes.

"They won't put you back on active service?"

Teyeo assented politely. Could the man, however alien, really be oblivious to the fact that his questions were grossly humiliating?

"Would you be willing to serve in the Embassy Guard?"

That question left Teyeo speechless for a moment;

then he committed the extreme rudeness of answering a question with a question. "Why do you ask?"

"I'd like very much to have a man of your capacity in that corps," said Old Music, adding with his appalling candor, "Most of them are spies or blockheads. It would be wonderful to have a man I knew was neither. It's not just sentry duty, you know. I imagine you'd be asked by your government to give information; that's to be expected. And we would use you, once you had experience and if you were willing, as a liaison officer. Here or in other countries. We would not, however, ask you to give information to us. Am I clear, Teyeo? I want no misunderstanding between us as to what I am and am not asking of you."

"You would be able . . . ?" Teyeo asked cautiously.

Old Music laughed and said, "Yes. I have a string to pull in your Command. A favor owed. Will you think it over?"

Teyeo was silent a minute. He had been nearly a year now in the capital and his requests for posting had met only bureaucratic evasion and, recently, hints that they were considered insubordinate. "I'll accept now, if I may," he said, with a cold deference.

The Hainishman looked at him, his smile changing to a thoughtful, steady gaze. "Thank you," he said. "You should hear from Command in a few days."

So Teyeo put his uniform back on, moved back to the City Barracks, and served for another seven years on alien ground. The Ekumenical Embassy was, by diplomatic agreement, a part not of Werel but of the Ekumen — a piece of the planet that no longer belonged to it. The Guardsmen furnished by

Voe Deo were protective and decorative, a highly visible presence on the Embassy grounds in their white-and-gold dress uniform. They were also visibly armed, since protest against the Alien presence still broke out erratically in violence.

Rega Teyeo, at first assigned to command a troop of these guards, soon was transferred to a different duty, that of accompanying members of the Embassy staff about the city and on journeys. He served as a bodyguard, in undress uniform. The Embassy much preferred not to use their own people and weapons, but to request and trust Voe Deo to protect them. Often he was also called upon to be a guide and interpreter, and sometimes a companion. He did not like it when visitors from somewhere in space wanted to be chummy and confiding, asked him about himself, invited him to come drinking with them. With perfectly concealed distaste, with perfect civility, he refused such offers. He did his job and kept his distance. He knew that that was precisely what the Embassy valued him for. Their confidence in him gave him a cold satisfaction.

His own government had never approached him to give information, though he certainly learned things that would have interested them. Voe Dean intelligence did not recruit their agents among veots. He knew who the agents in the Embassy Guard were; some of them tried to get information from him, but he had no intention of spying for spies.

Old Music, whom he now surmised to be the head of the Embassy's intelligence system, called him in on his return from a winter leave at home.

The Hainishman had learned not to make emotional demands on Teyeo, but could not hide a note of affection in his voice greeting him. "Hullo, Rega! I hope your family's well? Good. I've got a particularly tricky job for you. Kingdom of Gatay. You were there with Kemehan two years ago, weren't you? Well, now they want us to send an Envoy. They say they want to join. Of course the old King's a puppet of your government; but there's a lot else going on there. A strong religious separatist movement. A Patriotic Cause, kick out all the foreigners, Voe Deans and Aliens alike. But the King and Council requested an Envoy, and all we've got to send them is a new arrival. She may give you some problems till she learns the ropes. I judge her a bit headstrong. Excellent material, but young, very young. And she's only been here a few weeks. I requested you, because she needs your experience. Be patient with her, Rega. I think you'll find her likable."

He did not. In seven years he had got accustomed to the Aliens' eyes and their various smells and colors and manners. Protected by his flawless courtesy and his stoical code, he endured or ignored their strange or shocking or troubling behavior, their ignorance and their different knowledge. Serving and protecting the foreigners entrusted to him, he kept himself aloof from them, neither touched nor touching. His charges learned to count on him and not to presume on him. Women were often quicker to see and respond to his Keep Out signs than men; he had an easy, almost friendly relationship with an old Terran Observer whom he had accompanied on several long investigatory tours. "You are as peaceful to be with as a cat, Rega," she told him once, and he valued the compliment. But the Envoy to Gatay was another matter.

She was physically splendid, with clear red-brown skin like that of a baby, glossy swinging hair, a free walk — too free: she flaunted her ripe, slender body at men who had no access to it, thrusting it at him, at everyone, insistent, shameless. She expressed her opinion on everything with coarse self-confidence. She could not hear a hint and refused to take an order. She was an aggressive, spoiled child with the sexuality of an adult, given the responsibility of a diplomat in a dangerously unstable country. Teyeo knew as soon as he met her that this was an impossible assignment. He could not trust her or himself. Her sexual immodesty aroused him as it disgusted him; she was a whore whom he must treat as a princess. Forced to endure and unable to ignore her, he hated her.

He was more familiar with anger than he had used to be, but not used to hating. It troubled him extremely. He had never in his life asked for a reposting, but on the morning after she had taken the makil into her room, he sent a stiff little appeal to the Embassy. Old Music responded to him with a sealed voice-message through the diplomatic link: "Love of god and country is like fire, a wonderful friend, a terrible enemy; only children play with fire. I don't like the situation. There's nobody here I can replace either of you with. Will you hang on a while longer?"

He did not know how to refuse. A veot did not refuse duty. He was ashamed at having even thought of doing so, and hated her again for causing him that shame.

The first sentence of the message was enigmatic, not in Old Music's usual style but flowery, indirect, like a coded warning. Teyeo of course knew none of the intelligence codes either of his country or of the Ekumen. Old Music would have to use hints and indirection with him. "Love of god and country" could well mean the Old Believers and the Patriots, the two subversive groups in Gatay, both of them fanatically opposed to foreign influence; the Envoy could be the child playing with fire. Was she being approached by one group or the other? He had seen no evidence of it, unless the man in the shadows that night had been not a knifeman but a messenger. She was under his eyes all day, her house watched all night by soldiers under his command. Surely the makil, Batikam, was not acting for either of those groups. He might well be a member of the Hame, the asset liberation underground of Voe Deo, but as such would not endanger the Envoy, since the Hame saw the Ekumen as their ticket to Yeowe and to freedom.

Teyeo puzzled over the words, replaying them over and over, knowing his own stupidity faced with this kind of subtlety, the ins and outs of the political labyrinth. At last he erased the message and yawned, for it was late; bathed, lay down, turned off the light, said under his breath, "Lord Kamye, let me hold with courage to the one noble thing!" and slept like a stone.

The makil came to her house every night after the theater. Teyeo tried to tell himself there was nothing wrong in it. He himself had spent nights with the makils, back in the palmy days before the war. Expert, artistic sex was part of their business. He knew by hearsay that rich city women often hired them to come supply a husband's deficiencies. But even such women did so secretly, discreetly, not in this vulgar, shameless way, utterly careless of decency, flouting the moral code, as if she had some kind of right to do whatever she wanted wherever and whenever she wanted it. Of course Batikam colluded eagerly with her, playing on her infatuation, mocking the Gatayans, mocking Teyeo — and mocking her, though she didn't know it. What a chance for an asset to make fools of all the owners at once!

Watching Batikam, Teyeo felt sure he was a member of the Hame. His mockery was very subtle; he was not trying to disgrace the Envoy. Indeed his discretion was far greater than hers. He was trying to keep her from disgracing herself. The makil returned Teyeo's cold courtesy in kind, but once or twice their eyes met and some brief, involuntary understanding passed between them, fraternal, ironic.

There was to be a public festival, an observation of the Tualite Feast of Forgiveness, to which the Envoy was pressingly invited by the King and Council. She was put on show at many such events. Teyeo thought nothing about it except how to provide security in an excited holiday crowd, until San told him that the festival day was the highest holy day of the old religion of Gatay, and that the Old Believers fiercely resented the imposition of the foreign rites over their own. The little man seemed genuinely worried. Teyeo worried too when next day

San was suddenly replaced by an elderly man who spoke little but Gatayan and was quite unable to explain what had become of San Ubattat. "Other duties, other duties call," he said in very bad Voe Dean, smiling and bobbing, "very great relishes time, aha? Relishes duties call."

During the days that preceded the festival tension rose in the city; graffiti appeared, symbols of the old religion smeared across walls; a Tualite temple was desecrated, after which the Royal Guard was much in evidence in the streets. Teyeo went to the palace and requested, on his own authority, that the Envoy not be asked to appear in public during a ceremony that was "likely to be troubled by inappropriate demonstrations." He was called in and treated by a Court official with a mixture of dismissive insolence and conniving nods and winks, which left him really uneasy. He left four men on duty at the Envoy's house that night. Returning to his quarters, a little barracks down the street which had been handed over to the Embassy Guard, he found the window of his room open and a scrap of writing, in his own language, on his table: *Fest F is set up for assasnation.*

He was at the Envoy's house promptly the next morning and asked her asset to tell her he must speak to her. She came out of her bedroom pulling a white wrap around her naked body. Batikam followed her, half-dressed, sleepy, and amused. Teyeo gave him the eye-signal *go*, which he received with a serene, patronising smile, murmuring to the woman, "I'll go have some breakfast. Rewe? have you got something to feed me?" He followed the bondswoman out of the room. Teyeo faced the Envoy and held out the scrap of paper.

"I received this last night, ma'am," he said. "I must ask you not to attend the festival tomorrow."

She considered the paper, read the writing, and yawned. "Who's it from?"

"I don't know, ma'am."

"What's it mean? *Assassination?* They can't spell, can they?"

After a moment, he said, "There are a number of other indications — enough that I must ask you — "

"Not to attend the festival of Forgiveness, yes. I heard you." She went to a window seat and sat down, her robe falling wide to reveal her legs; her bare, brown feet were short and supple, the soles pink, the toes small and orderly. Teyeo looked fixedly at the air beside her head. She twiddled the bit of paper. "If you think it's dangerous, Rega, bring a guardsman or two with you," she said, with the faintest tone of scorn. "I really have to be there. The King requested it, you know. And I'm to light the big fire, or something. One of the few things women are allowed to do in public here. . . . I can't back out of it." She held out the paper, and after a moment he came close enough to take it. She looked up at him smiling; when she defeated him she always smiled at him. "Who do you think would want to blow me away, anyhow? The Patriots?"

"Or the Old Believers, ma'am. Tomorrow is one of their holidays."

"And your Tualites have taken it away from them? Well, they can't exactly blame the Ekumen, can they?"

"I think it possible that the government might permit violence in order to excuse retaliation, ma'am."

She started to answer carelessly, realised what he had said, and frowned. "You think the Council's setting me up? What evidence have you?"

After a pause he said, "Very little, ma'am. San Ubattat —"

"San's been ill. The old fellow they sent isn't much use, but he's scarcely dangerous! Is that all?" He said nothing, and she went on, "Until you have real evidence, Rega, don't interfere with my obligations. Your militaristic paranoia isn't acceptable when it spreads to the people I'm dealing with here. Control it, please! I'll expect an extra guardsman or two tomorrow; and that's enough."

"Yes, ma'am," he said, and went out. His head sang with anger. It occurred to him now that her new guide had told him San Ubattat had been kept away by religious duties, not by illness. He did not turn back. What was the use? "Stay on for an hour or so, will you, Seyem?" he said to the guard at her gate, and strode off down the street, trying to walk away from her, from her soft brown thighs and the pink soles of her feet and her stupid, insolent, whorish voice giving him orders. He tried to let the bright icy sunlit air, the stepped streets snapping with banners for the festival, the glitter of the great mountains and the clamor of the markets fill him, dazzle and distract him; but he walked seeing his own shadow fall in front of him like a knife across the stones, knowing the futility of his life.

"The veot looked worried," Batikam said in his velvet voice, and she laughed, spearing a preserved fruit from the dish and popping it, dripping, into his mouth.

"I'm ready for breakfast now, Rewe," she called, and sat down across from Batikam. "I'm starving! He was having one of his phallocratic fits. He hasn't saved me from anything lately. It's his only function, after all. So he has to invent occasions. I wish, I wish he was out of my hair. It's so nice not to have poor little old San crawling around like some kind of pubic infestation. If only I could get rid of the Major now!"

"He's a man of honor," the makil said; his tone did not seem ironical.

"How can an owner of slaves be an honorable man?"

Batikam watched her from his long, dark eyes. She could not read Werelian eyes, beautiful as they were, filling their lids with darkness.

"Male hierarchy members always yatter about their precious honor," she said. "And 'their' women's honor, of course."

"Honor is a great privilege," Batikam said. "I envy it. I envy him."

"Oh, the hell with all that phony dignity, it's just pissing to mark your territory. All you need envy him, Batikam, is his freedom."

He smiled. "You're the only person I've ever known who was neither owned nor owner. That is freedom. *That* is freedom. I wonder if you know it?"

"Of course I do," she said. He smiled, and went on eating his breakfast, but there had been something in his voice she had not heard before. Moved and a little troubled, she said after a while, "You're going away soon."

"Mind reader. Yes. In ten days, the troupe goes on to tour the Forty States."

"Oh, Batikam, I'll miss you! You're the only man, the only person here I can talk to — let alone the sex —"

"Did we ever?"

"Not often," she said, laughing, but her voice shook a little. He held out his hand; she came to him and sat on his lap, the robe dropping open. "Little pretty Envoy breasts," he said, lipping and stroking, "little soft Envoy belly . . ." Rewe came in with a tray and softly set it down. "Eat your breakfast, little Envoy," Batikam said, and she disengaged herself and returned to her chair, grinning.

"Because you're free you can be honest," he said, fastidiously peeling a pini fruit. "Don't be too hard on those of us who aren't and can't." He cut a slice and fed it to her across the table. "It has been a taste of freedom to know you," he said. "A hint, a shadow . . ."

"In a few years at most, Batikam, you *will* be free. This whole idiotic structure of masters and slaves will collapse completely when Werel comes into the Ekumen."

"If it does."

"Of course it will."

He shrugged. "My home is Yeowe," he said.

She stared, confused. "You come from Yeowe?"

"I've never been there," he said. "I'll probably never go there. What use have they got for makils? But it is my home. Those are my people. That is my freedom. When will you see . . ." His fist was clenched; he opened it with a soft gesture of letting something go. He smiled and returned to his breakfast. "I've got to get back to the theater," he said. "We're rehearsing an act for the Day of Forgiveness."

She wasted all day at court. She had made persistent attempts to obtain permission to visit the mines and the huge government-run farms on the far side of the mountains, from which Gatay's wealth flowed. She had been as persistently foiled — by the protocol and bureaucracy of the government, she had thought at first, their unwillingness to let a diplomat do anything but run round to meaningless events; but some businessmen had let something slip about conditions in the mines and on the farms that made her think they might be hiding a more brutal kind of slavery than any visible in the capital. Today she got nowhere, waiting for appointments that had not been made. The old fellow who was standing in for San misunderstood most of what she said in Voe Dean, and when she tried to speak Gatayan he misunderstood it all, through stupidity or intent. The Major was blessedly absent most of the morning, replaced by one of his soldiers, but turned up at court, stiff and silent and set-jawed, and attended her until she gave up and went home for an early bath.

Batikam came late that night. In the middle of one of the elaborate fantasy games and role reversals she had learned from him and found so exciting, his caresses grew slower and slower, soft, dragging across her like feathers, so that she shivered with unappeased desire and, pressing her body against his, realised that he had gone to sleep. "Wake up," she said, laughing and yet chilled, and shook him a little. The dark eyes opened, bewildered, full of fear.

"I'm sorry," she said at once, "go back to sleep, you're tired. No, no, it's all right, it's late." But he went on with what she now, whatever his skill and tenderness, had to see was his job.

In the morning at breakfast she said, "Can you see me as an equal, do you, Batikam?"

He looked tired, older than he usually did. He did not smile. After a while he said, "What do you want me to say?"

"That you do."

"I do," he said quietly.

"You don't trust me," she said, bitter.

After a while he said, "This is Forgiveness Day. The Lady Tual came to the men of Asdok, who had set their hunting cats upon her followers. She came among them riding on a great hunting cat with a fiery tongue, and they fell down in terror, but she blessed them, forgiving them." His voice and hands enacted the story as he told it. "Forgive me," he said.

"You don't need any forgiveness!"

"Oh, we all do. It's why we Kamyites borrow the Lady Tual now and then. When we need her. So, today you'll be the Lady Tual, at the rites?"

"All I have to do is light a fire, they said," she said anxiously, and he laughed. When he left she told him she would come to the theater to see him, tonight, after the festival.

The horse-race course, the only flat area of any size anywhere near the city, was thronged, vendors calling, banners waving; the Royal motorcars drove straight into the crowd, which parted like water and closed behind. Some rickety-looking bleachers had been erected for lords and owners, with a curtained section for ladies. She saw a motorcar drive up to the bleachers; a figure swathed in red cloth was bundled out of it and hurried between the curtains, vanishing. Were there peepholes for them to watch the ceremony through? There were women in the crowds, but bondswomen only, assets. She realised that she, too, would be kept hidden until her moment of the ceremony arrived: a red tent awaited her, alongside the bleachers, not far from the roped enclosure where priests were chanting. She was rushed out of the car and into the tent by obsequious and determined courtiers.

Bondswomen in the tent offered her tea, sweets, mirrors, makeup, and hair oil, and helped her put on the complex swathing of fine red-and-yellow cloth, her costume for her brief enactment of Lady Tual. Nobody had told her very clearly what she was to do, and to her questions the women said, "The priests will show you, Lady, you just go with them. You just light the fire. They have it all ready." She had the impression that they knew no more than she did; they were pretty girls, court assets, excited at being part of the show, indifferent to the religion. She knew the symbolism of the fire she was to light: into it faults and transgressions could be cast and burnt up, forgotten. It was a nice idea.

The priests were whooping it up out there; she peeked out — there were indeed peepholes in the tent fabric — and saw the crowd had thickened. Nobody except in the bleachers and right against the enclosure ropes could possibly see anything, but everybody was waving red-and-yellow banners, munching fried food, and making a day of it, while the priests kept up their deep chanting. In the far right of the little, blurred field of vision through the peephole was a familiar arm: the Major's, of course. They had not let him get into the motorcar with her.

He must have been furious. He had got here, though, and stationed himself on guard. "Lady, Lady," the court girls were saying, "here come the priests now," and they buzzed around her making sure her headdress was on straight and the damnable, hobbling skirts fell in the right folds. They were still plucking and patting as she stepped out of the tent, dazzled by the daylight, smiling and trying to hold herself very straight and dignified as a Goddess ought to do. She really didn't want to fuck up their ceremony.

Two men in priestly regalia were waiting for her right outside the tent door. They stepped forward immediately, taking her by the elbows and saying, "This way, this way, Lady." Evidently she really wouldn't have to figure out what to do. No doubt they considered women incapable of it, but in the circumstances it was a relief. The priests hurried her along faster than she could comfortably walk in the tight-drawn skirt. They were behind the bleachers now; wasn't the enclosure in the other direction? A car was coming straight at them, scattering the few people who were in its way. Somebody was shouting; the priests suddenly began yanking her, trying to run; one of them yelled and let go her arm, felled by a flying darkness that had hit him with a jolt — she was in the middle of a melee, unable to break the iron hold on her arm, her legs imprisoned in the skirt, and there was a noise, an enormous noise, that hit her head and bent it down, she couldn't see or hear, blinded, struggling, shoved face first into some dark place with her face pressed into a stifling, scratchy darkness and her arms held locked behind her.

A car, moving. A long time. Men, talking low. They talked in Gatayan. It was very hard to breathe. She did not struggle; it was no use. They had taped her arms and legs, bagged her head. After a long time she was hauled out like a corpse and carried quickly, indoors, down stairs, set down on a bed or couch, not roughly though with the same desperate haste. She lay still. The men talked, still almost in whispers. It made no sense to her. Her head was still hearing that enormous noise, had it been real? had she been struck? She felt deaf, as if inside a wall of cotton. The cloth of the bag kept getting stuck on her mouth, sucked against her nostrils as she tried to breathe.

It was plucked off; a man stooping over her turned her so he could untape her arms, then her legs, murmuring as he did so, "Don't to be scared, Lady, we don't to hurt you," in Voe Dean. He backed away from her quickly. There were four or five of them; it was hard to see, there was very little light. "To wait here," another said, "everything all right. Just to keep happy." She was trying to sit up, and it made her dizzy. When her head stopped spinning, they were all gone. As if by magic. Just to keep happy.

A small very high room. Dark brick walls, earthy air. The light was from a little biolume plaque stuck on the ceiling, a weak, shadowless glow. Probably quite sufficient for Werelian eyes. Just to keep happy. I have been kidnapped. How about that. She inventoried: the thick mattress she was on; a blanket; a door; a small pitcher and a cup; a drainhole, was it, over in the corner? She swung her legs off the mattress and her feet struck something lying on the floor at the foot of it — she coiled up, peered at the dark mass, the body lying there. A man. The uniform, the skin so black she could not see the features, but she knew him. Even here, even here, the Major was with her.

She stood up unsteadily and went to investigate the drainhole, which was simply that, a cement-lined hole in the floor, smelling slightly chemical, slightly foul. Her head hurt, and she sat down on the bed again to massage her arms and ankles, easing the tension and pain and getting herself back into herself by touching and confirming herself, rhythmically, methodically. I have been kidnapped. How about that. Just to keep happy. What about him?

Suddenly knowing that he was dead, she shuddered and held still.

After a while she leaned over slowly, trying to see his face, listening. Again she had the sense of being deaf. She heard no breath. She reached out, sick and shaking, and put the back of her hand against his face. It was cool, cold. But warmth breathed across her fingers, once, again. She crouched on the mattress and studied him. He lay absolutely still, but when she put her hand on his chest she felt the slow heartbeat.

"Teyeo," she said in a whisper. Her voice would not go above a whisper.

She put her hand on his chest again. She wanted to feel that slow, steady beat, the faint warmth; it was reassuring. Just to keep happy.

What else had they said? Just to wait. Yes. That seemed to be the program. Maybe she could sleep. Maybe she could sleep and when she woke up the ransom would have come. Or whatever it was they wanted.

Forgiveness Day

* * *

She woke up with the thought that she still had her watch, and after sleepily studying the tiny silver readout for a while decided she had slept three hours; it was still the day of the Festival, too soon for ransom probably, and she wouldn't be able to go to the theater to see the makils tonight. Her eyes had grown accustomed to the low light and when she looked she could see, now, that there was dried blood all over one side of the man's head. Exploring, she found a hot lump like a fist above his temple, and her fingers came away smeared. He had got himself crowned. That must have been him, launching himself at the priest, the fake priest, all she could remember was a flying shadow and a hard thump and an ooof! like an aiji attack, and then there had been the huge noise that confused everything. She clicked her tongue, tapped the wall, to check her hearing. It seemed to be all right; the wall of cotton had disappeared. Maybe she had been crowned herself? She felt her head, but found no lumps. The man must have a concussion, if he was still out after three hours. How bad? When would the men come back?

She got up and nearly fell over, entangled in the damned Goddess skirts. If only she was in her own clothes, not this fancy dress, three pieces of flimsy stuff you had to have servants to put on you! She got out of the skirt piece, and used the scarf piece to make a kind of tied skirt that came to her knees. It wasn't warm in this basement or whatever it was; it was dank and rather cold. She walked up and down, four steps turn, four steps turn, four steps turn, and did some warm-ups. They had dumped the man onto the floor. How cold was it? Was shock part of concussion? People in shock needed to be kept warm. She dithered a long time, puzzled at her own indecision, at not knowing what to do. Should she try to heave him up onto the mattress? Was it better not to move him? Where the hell were the men? Was he going to die?

She stooped over him and said sharply, "Rega! Teyeo!" and after a moment he caught his breath.

"Wake up!" She remembered now, she thought she remembered, that it was important not to let concussed people lapse into a coma. Except he already had.

He caught his breath again, and his face changed, came out of the rigid immobility, softened; his eyes opened and closed, blinked, unfocused. "Oh Kamye," he said very softly.

She couldn't believe how glad she was to see him. Just to keep happy. He evidently had a blinding headache, and admitted that he was seeing double. She helped him haul himself up onto the mattress and covered him with the blanket. He asked no questions, and lay mute, lapsing back to sleep soon. Once he was settled she went back to her exercises, and did an hour of them. She looked at her watch. It was two hours later, the same day, the Festival day. It wasn't evening yet. When were the men going to come?

They came early in the morning, after the endless night that was the same as the afternoon and the morning. The metal door was unlocked and thrown clanging open, and one of them came in with a tray while two of them stood with raised, aimed guns in the doorway. There was nowhere to put the tray but the floor, so he shoved it at Solly, said, "Sorry, Lady!" and backed out; the door clanged shut, the bolts banged home. She stood holding the tray. "Wait!" she said.

The man had waked up and was looking groggily around. After finding him in this place with her she had somehow lost his nickname, did not think of him as the Major, yet shied away from his name. "Here's breakfast, I guess," she said, and sat down on the edge of the mattress. A cloth was thrown over the wicker tray; under it was a pile of Gatayan grainrolls stuffed with meat and greens, several pieces of fruit, and a capped water carafe of thin, fancily beaded metal alloy. "Breakfast, lunch, and dinner, maybe," she said. "Shit. Oh well. It looks good. Can you eat? Can you sit up?"

He worked himself up to sit with his back against the wall, and then shut his eyes.

"You're still seeing double?"

He made a small noise of assent.

"Are you thirsty?"

Small noise of assent.

"Here." She passed him the cup. By holding it in both hands he got it to his mouth, and drank the water slowly, a swallow at a time. She meanwhile devoured three grainrolls one after the other, then forced herself to stop, and ate a pini fruit. "Could you eat some fruit?" she asked him, feeling guilty. He did not answer. She thought of Batikam feeding her the slice of pini at breakfast, when, yesterday, a hundred years ago.

The food in her stomach made her feel sick. She took the cup from the man's relaxed hand — he was asleep again — and poured herself water, and drank it slowly, a swallow at a time.

When she felt better she went to the door and explored its hinges, lock, and surface. She felt and peered around the brick walls, the poured concrete floor, seeking she knew not what, something to escape with, something. . . . She should do exercises. She forced herself to do some, but the queasiness returned, and a lethargy with it. She went back to the mattress and sat down. After a while she found she was crying. After a while she found she had been asleep. She needed to piss. She squatted over the hole and listened to her urine fall into it. There was nothing to clean herself with. She came back to the bed and sat down on it, stretching out her legs, holding her ankles in her hands. It was utterly silent.

She turned to look at the man; he was watching her. It made her start. He looked away at once. He still lay half–propped up against the wall, uncomfortable, but relaxed.

"Are you thirsty?" she asked.

"Thank you," he said. Here where nothing was familiar and time was broken off from the past, his soft, light voice was welcome in its familiarity. She poured him a cup full and gave it to him. He managed it much more steadily, sitting up to drink. "Thank you," he whispered again, giving her back the cup.

"How's your head?"

He put up his hand to the swelling, winced, and sat back.

"One of them had a stick," she said, seeing it in a flash in the jumble of her memories — "a priest's staff. You jumped the other one."

"They took my gun," he said. "Festival." He kept his eyes closed.

"I got tangled in those damn clothes. I couldn't help you at all. Listen. Was there a noise, an explosion?"

"Yes. Diversion, maybe."

"Who do you think these boys are?"

"Revolutionaries. Or . . ."

"You said you thought the Gatayan government was in on it."

"I don't know," he murmured.

"You were right, I was wrong, I'm sorry," she said with a sense of virtue at remembering to make amends.

He moved his hand very slightly in an it-doesn't-matter gesture.

"Are you still seeing double?"

He did not answer; he was phasing out again.

She was standing, trying to remember Selish breathing exercises, when the door crashed and clanged, and the same three men were there, two with guns, all young, black-skinned, short-haired, very nervous. The lead one stooped to set a tray down on the floor, and without the least premeditation Solly stepped on his hand and brought her weight down on it. "You wait!" she said. She was staring straight into the faces and gun muzzles of the other two. "Just wait a moment, listen! He has a head injury, we need a doctor, we need more water, I can't even clean his wound, there's no toilet paper, who the hell are you people anyway?"

The one she had stomped was shouting, "Get off! Lady to get off my hand!" but the others heard her. She lifted her foot and got out of his way as he came up fast, backing into his buddies with the guns. "All right, Lady, we are sorry to have trouble," he said, tears in his eyes, cradling his hand. "We are Patriots. You send messish to this Pretender, like our messish. Nobody is to hurt. All right?" He kept backing up, and one of the gunmen swung the door to. Crash, rattle.

She drew a deep breath and turned. Teyeo was watching her. "That was dangerous," he said, smiling very slightly.

"I know it was," she said, breathing hard. "It was stupid. I can't get hold of myself. I feel like pieces of me. But they shove stuff in and run, damn it! We have to have some water!" She was in tears, the way she always was for a moment after violence or a quarrel. "Let's see, what have they brought this time." She lifted the tray up onto the mattress; like the other, in a ridiculous semblance of service in a hotel or a house with slaves, it was covered with a cloth. "All the comforts," she murmured. Under the cloth was a heap of sweet pastries, a little plastic hand mirror, a comb, a tiny pot of something that smelled like decayed flowers, and a box of what she identified after a while as Gatayan tampons.

"It's things for the lady," she said, "God damn them, the stupid Goddamn pricks! A mirror!" She flung the thing across the room. "Of course I can't last a day without looking in the mirror! God *damn* them!" She flung everything else but the pastries after the mirror, knowing as she did so that she would pick up the tampons and keep them under the mattress and, oh, God forbid, use them if she had to, if they had to stay here, how long would it be? ten days or more — "Oh, God," she said again. She got up and picked everything up, put the mirror and the little pot, the empty water jug and the fruit skins from the last meal, onto one of the trays and set it beside the door. "Garbage," she said in Voe Dean. Her outburst, she realised, had been in another language; Alterran, probably. "Have you any idea," she said, sitting down on the mattress again, "how hard you people make it to be a woman? You could turn a woman against being one!"

"I think they meant well," Teyeo said. She realised that there was not the faintest shade of mockery, even of amusement in his voice. If he was enjoying her shame, he was ashamed to show her that he was. "I think they're amateurs," he said.

After a while she said, "That could be bad."

"It might." He had sat up and was gingerly feeling the knot on his head. His coarse, heavy hair was blood-caked all around it. "Kidnapping," he said. "Ransom demands. Not assassins. They didn't have guns. Couldn't have got in with guns. I had to give up mine."

"You mean these aren't the ones you were warned about?"

"I don't know." His explorations caused him a shiver of pain, and he desisted. "Are we very short of water?"

She brought him another cupful. "Too short for washing. A stupid Goddamn mirror when what we need is water!"

He thanked her and drank and sat back, nursing the last swallows in the cup. "They didn't plan to take me," he said.

She thought about it and nodded. "Afraid you'd identify them?"

"If they had a place for me, they wouldn't put me in with a lady." He spoke without irony. "They had this ready for you. It must be somewhere in the city."

She nodded. "The car ride was half an hour or less. My head was in a bag, though."

"They've sent a message to the Palace. They got no reply, or an unsatisfactory one. They want a message from you."

"To convince the government they really have me? Why do they need convincing?"

They were both silent.

"I'm sorry," he said, "I can't think." He lay back. Feeling tired, low, edgy after her adrenaline rush, she lay down alongside him. She had rolled up the Goddess's skirt to make a pillow; he had none. The blanket lay across their legs.

"Pillow," she said. "More blankets. Soap. What else?"

"Key," he murmured.

They lay side by side in the silence and the faint unvarying light.

Next morning about eight, according to Solly's watch, the Patriots came into the room, four of them. Two stood on guard at the door with their guns ready; the other two stood uncomfortably in what floor space was left, looking down at their captives, both of whom sat cross-legged on the mattress. The new spokesman spoke better Voe Dean than the others. He said they were very sorry to cause the lady discomfort and would do what they could to make it comfortable for her, and she must be patient and write a message by hand to the Pretender King, explaining that she would be set free unharmed as soon as the King commanded the Council to rescind their treaty with Voe Deo.

"He won't," she said. "They won't let him."

"Please do not discuss," the man said with frantic harshness. "This is writing materials. This is the message." He set the papers and a stylo down on the mattress, nervously, as if afraid to get close to her.

She was aware of how Teyeo effaced himself, sitting without a motion, his head lowered, his eyes lowered; the men ignored him.

"If I write this for you, I want water, a lot of water, and soap and blankets and toilet paper and pillows and a doctor, and I want somebody to come when I knock on that door, and I want some decent clothes. Warm clothes. Men's clothes."

"No doctor!" the man said. "Write it! Please! Now!" He was jumpy, twitchy, she dared push him no further. She read their statement, copied it out in her large, childish scrawl — she seldom handwrote anything — and handed both to the spokesman. He glanced over it and without a word hurried the other men out. Clash went the door.

"Should I have refused?"

"I don't think so," Teyeo said. He stood up and stretched, but sat down again looking dizzy. "You bargain well," he said.

"We'll see what we get. Oh, God. What is going *on*?"

"Maybe," he said slowly, "Gatay is unwilling to yield to these demands. But when Voe Deo — and your Ekumen — get word of it, they'll put pressure on Gatay."

"I wish they'd get moving. I suppose Gatay is horribly embarrassed, saving face by trying to conceal the whole thing — is that likely? How long can they keep it up? What about your people? Won't they be hunting for you?"

"No doubt," he said, in his polite way.

It was curious how his stiff manner, his manners, which had always shunted her aside, cut her out, here had quite another effect: his restraint and formality reassured her that she was still part of the world outside this room, from which they came and to which they would return, a world where people lived long lives.

What did long life matter? she asked herself, and didn't know. It was nothing she had ever thought about before. But these young Patriots lived in a world of short lives. Demands, violence, immediacy, and death, for what? for a bigotry, a hatred, a rush of power.

"Whenever they leave," she said in a low voice, "I get really frightened."

Teyeo cleared his throat and said, "So do I."

Exercises.

"Take hold — no, take *hold*, I'm not made of glass! — Now —"

"Ha!" he said, with his flashing grin of excitement, as she showed him the break, and he in turn repeated it, breaking from her.

"All right, now you'd be waiting — here" — thump — "see?"

"Ai!"

"I'm sorry — I'm sorry, Teyeo — I didn't think about your head — Are you all right? I'm really sorry —"

"Oh, Kamye," he said, sitting up and holding his black, narrow head between his hands. He drew several deep breaths. She knelt penitent and anxious.

"That's," he said, and breathed some more, "that's not, not fair play."

"No of course it's not, it's aiji — all's fair in love and war, they say that on Terra — Really, I'm sorry, I'm terribly sorry, that was so stupid of me!"

He laughed, a kind of broken and desperate laugh, shook his head, shook it again. "Show me," he said. "I don't know what you did."

Exercises.

"What do you do with your mind?"

"Nothing."

"You just let it wander?"

"No. Am I and my mind different beings?"

"So . . . you don't focus on something? You just wander with it?"

"No."

"So you *don't* let it wander."

"Who?" he said, rather testily.

A pause.

"Do you think about —"

"No," he said. "Be still."

A very long pause, maybe a quarter hour.

"Teyeo, I can't. I itch. My mind itches. How long have you been doing this?"

A pause, a reluctant answer: "Since I was two."

He broke his utterly relaxed motionless pose, bent his head to stretch his neck and shoulder muscles. She watched him.

"I keep thinking about long life, about living long," she said. "I don't mean just being alive a long time, hell, I've been alive about eleven hundred years, what does that mean, nothing. I mean . . . Something about thinking of life as long makes a difference. Like having kids does. Even thinking about having kids. It's like it changes some balance. It's funny I keep thinking about that now, when my chances for a long life have kind of taken a steep fall. . . ."

He said nothing. He was able to say nothing in a way that allowed her to go on talking. He was one of the least talkative men she had ever known. Most men were so wordy. She was fairly wordy herself. He was quiet. She wished she knew how to be quiet.

"It's just practice, isn't it?" she asked. "Just sitting there."

He nodded.

"Years and years and years of practice. . . . Oh, God. Maybe . . ."

"No, no," he said, taking her thought immediately.

"But why don't they *do* something? What are they *waiting* for? It's been nine *days*!"

From the beginning, by unplanned, unspoken agreement, the room had been divided in two: the line ran down the middle of the mattress and across to the facing wall. The door was on her side, the left;

the shit-hole was on his side, the right. Any invasion of the other's space was requested by some almost invisible cue and permitted the same way. When one of them used the shit-hole the other unobtrusively faced away. When they had enough water to take cat-baths, which was seldom, the same arrangement held. The line down the middle of the mattress was absolute. Their voices crossed it, and the sounds and smells of their bodies. Sometimes she felt his warmth; Werelian body temperature was somewhat higher than hers, and in the dank, still air she felt that faint radiance as he slept. But they never crossed the line, not by a finger, not in the deepest sleep.

Solly thought about this, finding it, in some moments, quite funny. At other moments it seemed stupid and perverse. Couldn't they both use some human comfort? The only time she had touched him was the first day, when she had helped him get onto the mattress, and then when they had enough water she had cleaned his scalp wound and little by little washed the clotted, stinking blood out of his hair, using the comb, which had after all been a good thing to have, and pieces of the Goddess's skirt, an invaluable source of washcloths and bandages. Then once his head healed, they practiced aiji daily; but aiji had an impersonal, ritual purity to its clasps and grips that was a long way from creature comfort. The rest of the time his bodily presence was clearly, invariably uninvasive and untouchable.

He was only maintaining, under incredibly difficult circumstances, the rigid restraint he had always shown. Not just he, but Rewe, too; all of them, all of them but Batikam; and yet was

Batikam's instant yielding to her whim and desire the true contact she had thought it? She thought of the fear in his eyes, that last night. Not restraint, but constraint.

It was the mentality of a slave society: slaves and masters caught in the same trap of radical distrust and self-protection.

"Teyeo," she said, "I don't understand slavery. Let me say what I mean," though he had shown no sign of interruption or protest, merely civil attention. "I mean, I do understand how a social institution comes about and how an individual is simply part of it — I'm not saying why don't you agree with me in seeing it as wicked and unprofitable, I'm not asking you to defend it or renounce it. I'm trying to understand what it feels like to believe that two-thirds of the human beings in your world are actually, rightfully your property. Five-sixths, in fact, including women of your caste."

After a while he said, "My family owns about twenty-five assets."

"Don't quibble."

He accepted the reproof.

"It seems to me that you cut off human contact. You don't touch slaves and slaves don't touch you, in the way human beings ought to touch, in mutuality. You have to keep yourselves separate, always working to maintain that boundary. Because it isn't a natural boundary — it's totally artificial, man-made. I can't tell owners and assets apart physically. Can you?"

"Mostly."

"By cultural, behavioral clues — right?"

After thinking a while, he nodded.

"You are the same species, race, people, exactly the same in every way, with a slight selection towards color. If you brought up an asset child as an owner it would *be* an owner in every respect, and vice versa. So you spend your lives keeping up this tremendous division that doesn't exist. What I don't understand is how you can fail to see how appallingly wasteful it is. I don't mean economically!"

"In the war," he said, and then there was a very long pause; though Solly had a lot more to say, she waited, curious. "I was on Yeowe," he said, "you know, in the civil war."

That's where you got all those scars and dents, she thought; for however scrupulously she averted her eyes, it was impossible not to be familiar with his spare, onyx body by now, and she knew that in aiji he had to favor his left arm, which had a considerable chunk out of it just above the bicep.

"The slaves of the Colonies revolted, you know, some of them at first, then all of them. Nearly all. So we Army men there were all owners. We couldn't send asset soldiers, they might defect. We were all veots and volunteers. Owners fighting assets. I was fighting my equals. I learned that pretty soon. Later on I learned I was fighting my superiors. They defeated us."

"But that — " Solly said, and stopped; she did not know what to say.

"They defeated us from beginning to end," he said. "Partly because my government didn't understand that they could. That they fought better and harder and more intelligently and more bravely than we did."

"Because they were fighting for their freedom!"

"Maybe so," he said in his polite way.

"So . . ."

"I wanted to tell you that I respect the people I fought."

"I know so little about war, about fighting," she said, with a mixture of contrition and irritation. "Nothing, really. I was on Kheakh, but that wasn't war, it was racial suicide, mass slaughter of a biosphere. I guess there's a difference . . . . That was when the Ekumen finally decided on the Arms Convention, you know. Because of Orint and then Kheakh destroying themselves. The Terrans had been pushing for the Convention for ages. Having nearly committed suicide themselves a while back. I'm half-Terran. My ancestors rushed around their planet slaughtering each other. For millennia. They were masters and slaves, too, some of them, a lot of them. . . . But I don't know if the Arms Convention was a good idea. If it's right. Who are we to tell anybody what to do and not to do? The idea of the Ekumen was to offer a way. To open it. Not to bar it to anybody."

He listened intently, but said nothing until after some while. "We learn to . . . close ranks. Always. You're right, I think, it wastes . . . energy, the spirit. You are open."

His words cost him so much, she thought, not like hers that just came dancing out of the air and went back into it. He spoke from his marrow. It made what he said a solemn compliment, which she accepted gratefully, for as the days went on she realized occasionally how much confidence she had lost and kept losing: self-confidence, confidence that they would be ransomed, rescued, that they would get out of this room, that they would get out of it alive.

"Was the war very brutal?"

"Yes," he said. "I can't . . . I've never been able to — to see it — Only something comes like a flash —" He held his hands up as if to shield his eyes. Then he glanced at her, wary. His apparently cast-iron self-respect was, she knew now, vulnerable in many places.

"Things from Kheakh that I didn't even know I saw, they come that way," she said. "At night." And after a while, "How long were you there?"

"A little over seven years."

She winced. "Were you lucky?"

It was a queer question, not coming out the way she meant, but he took it at value. "Yes," he said. "Always. The men I went there with were killed. Most of them in the first few years. We lost three hundred thousand men on Yeowe. They never talk about it. Two-thirds of the veot men in Voe Deo were killed. If it was lucky to live, I was lucky." He looked down at his clasped hands, locked into himself.

After a while she said softly, "I hope you still are."

He said nothing.

"How long has it been?" he asked, and she said, clearing her throat, after an automatic glance at her watch, "Sixty hours."

Their captors had not come yesterday at what had become a regular time, about eight in the morning. Nor had they come this morning.

With nothing left to eat and now no water left, they had grown increasingly silent and inert. It was hours since either had said anything. He had put off asking the time as long as he could prevent himself.

"This is horrible," she said, "this is so horrible. I keep thinking . . ."

"They won't abandon you," he said. "They feel a responsibility."

"Because I'm a woman?"

"Partly."

"Shit."

He remembered that in the other life her coarseness had offended him.

"They've been taken, shot. Nobody bothered to find out where they were keeping us," she said.

Having thought the same thing several hundred times, he had nothing to say.

"It's just such a horrible *place* to die," she said. "It's sordid. I stink. I've stunk for twenty days. Now I have diarrhea because I'm scared. But I can't shit anything. I'm thirsty and I can't drink."

"Solly," he said sharply. It was the first time he had spoken her name. "Be still. Hold fast."

She stared at him.

"Hold fast to what?"

He did not answer at once and she said, "You won't let me touch you!"

"Not to me —"

"Then to what? There isn't anything!" He thought she was going to cry, but she stood up, took the empty tray, and beat it against the door till it smashed into fragments of wicker and dust. "Come! God damn you! Come, you bastards!" she shouted. "Let us out of here!"

After that she sat down again on the mattress. "Well," she said.

"Listen," he said.

They had heard it before: no city sounds came down to this cellar, wherever it was, but this was something bigger, explosions, they both thought.

The door rattled.

They were both afoot when it opened: not with the usual clash and clang, but slowly. A man waited outside; two men came in. One, armed, they had never seen; the other, the tough-faced young man they called the spokesman, looked as if he had been running or fighting, dusty, worn-out, a little dazed. He closed the door. He had some papers in his hand. The four of them stared at one another in silence for a minute.

"Water," Solly said. "You bastards!"

"Lady," the spokesman said, "I'm sorry." He was not listening to her. His eyes were not on her. He was looking at Teyeo, for the first time. "There is a lot of fighting," he said.

"Who's fighting?" Teyeo asked, hearing himself drop into the even tone of authority, and the young man respond to it as automatically: "Voe Deo. They sent troops. After the funeral, they said they would send troops unless we surrendered. They came yesterday. They go through the city killing. They know all the Old Believer centers. Some of ours." He had a bewildered, accusing note in his voice.

"What funeral?" Solly said.

When he did not answer, Teyeo repeated it: "What funeral?"

"The lady's funeral, yours. Here — I brought net

prints — A state funeral. They said you died in the explosion."

"What Goddamned explosion?" Solly said in her hoarse, parched voice, and this time he answered her: "At the Festival. The Old Believers. The fire, Tual's fire, there were explosives in it. Only it went off too soon. We knew their plan. We rescued you from that, Lady," he said, suddenly turning to her with that same accusatory tone.

"Rescued me, you asshole!" she shouted, and Teyeo's dry lips split in a startled laugh, which he repressed at once.

"Give me those," he said, and the young man handed him the papers.

"Get us water!" Solly said.

"Stay here, please. We need to talk," Teyeo said, instinctively holding on to his ascendancy. He sat down on the mattress with the net prints. Within a few minutes he and Solly had scanned the reports of the shocking disruption of the Festival of Forgiveness, the lamentable death of the Envoy of the Ekumen in a terrorist act executed by the cult of Old Believers, the brief mention of the death of a Voe Dean Embassy guard in the explosion, which had killed over seventy priests and onlookers, the long descriptions of the state funeral, reports of unrest, terrorism, reprisals, then reports of the Palace gratefully accepting offers of assistance from Voe Deo in cleaning out the cancer of terrorism. . . .

"So," he said finally. "You never heard from the Palace. Why did you keep us alive?"

Solly looked as if she thought the question lacked tact, but the spokesman answered with equal bluntness, "We thought your country would ransom you."

"They will," Teyeo said. "Only you have to keep your government from knowing we're alive. If you —"

"Wait," Solly said, touching his hand. "Hold on. I want to think about this stuff. You'd better not leave the Ekumen out of the discussion. But getting in touch with them is the tricky bit."

"If there are Voe Dean troops here, all I need is to get a message to anyone in my command, or the Embassy Guards."

Her hand was still on his, with a warning pressure. She shook the other one at the spokesman, finger outstretched: "You kidnapped an Envoy of the Ekumen, you asshole! Now you have to do the thinking you didn't do ahead of time. And I do too, because I don't want to get blown away by your Goddamned little government for turning up alive and embarrassing them. Where are you hiding, anyhow? Is there any chance of us getting out of this room, at least?"

The man, with that edgy, frantic look, shook his head. "We are all down here now," he said. "Most of the time. You stay here safe."

"Yes, you'd better keep your passports safe!" Solly said. "Bring us some water, damn it! Let us talk a while. Come back in an hour."

The young man leaned towards her suddenly, his face contorted. "What the hell kind of lady you are," he said. "You foreign filthy stinking cunt."

Teyeo was on his feet, but her grip on his hand had tightened: after a moment of silence, the spokesman and the other man turned to the door, rattled the lock, and were let out.

"Ouf," she said, looking dazed.

"Don't," he said, "don't —" He did not know how to say it. "They don't understand," he said. "It's better if I talk."

"Of course. Women don't give orders. Women don't talk. Shitheads! I thought you said they felt so responsible for me!"

"They do," he said. "But they're young men. Fanatics. Very frightened." And you talk to them as if they were assets, he thought, but did not say.

"Well so am I frightened!" she said, with a little spurt of tears. She wiped her eyes and sat down again among the papers. "God," she said. "We've been dead for twenty days. Buried for fifteen. Who do you think they buried?"

Her grip was powerful; his wrist and hand hurt. He massaged the place gently, watching her.

"Thank you," he said. "I would have hit him."

"Oh, I know. Goddamn chivalry. And the one with the gun would have blown your head off. Listen, Teyeo. Are you sure all you have to do is get word to somebody in the Army or the Guard?"

"Yes, of course."

"You're sure your country isn't playing the same game as Gatay?"

He stared at her. As he understood her, slowly the anger he had stifled and denied, all these interminable days of imprisonment with her, rose in him, a fiery flood of resentment, hatred, and contempt.

He was unable to speak, afraid he would speak to her as the young Patriot had done.

He went around to his side of the room and sat on his side of the mattress, somewhat turned from her. He sat cross-legged, one hand lying lightly in the other.

She said some other things. He did not listen or reply.

After a while she said, "We're supposed to be talking, Teyeo. We've only got an hour. I think those kids might do what we tell them, if we tell them something plausible — something that'll work."

He would not answer. He bit his lip and held still.

"Teyeo, what did I say? I said something wrong. I don't know what it was. I'm sorry."

"They would — " He struggled to control his lips and voice. "They would not betray us."

"Who? The Patriots?"

He did not answer.

"Voe Deo, you mean? Wouldn't betray us?"

In the pause that followed her gentle, incredulous question, he knew that she was right; that it was all collusion among the powers of the world; that his loyalty to his country and service was wasted, as futile as the rest of his life. She went on talking, palliating, saying he might very well be right. He put his head into his hands, longing for tears, dry as stone.

She crossed the line. He felt her hand on his shoulder.

"Teyeo, I am very sorry," she said. "I didn't mean to insult you! I honor you. You've been all my hope and help."

"It doesn't matter," he said. "If I — If we had some water."

She leapt up and battered on the door with her fists and a sandal.

"Bastards, bastards," she shouted.

Teyeo got up and walked, three steps and turn, three steps and turn, and halted on his side of the room. "If you're right," he said, speaking slowly and formally, "we and our captors are in danger not only from Gatay but from my own people, who may . . . who have been furthering these anti-Government factions, in order to make an excuse to bring troops here . . . to *pacify* Gatay. That's why they know where to find the factionalists. We are . . . we're lucky our group were . . . were genuine."

She watched him with a tenderness that he found irrelevant.

"What we don't know," he said, "is what side the Ekumen will take. That is . . . There really is only one side."

"No, there's ours, too. The underdogs. If the Embassy sees Voe Deo pulling a takeover of Gatay, they won't interfere, but they won't approve. Especially if it involves as much repression as it seems to."

"The violence is only against the anti-Ekumen factions."

"They still won't approve. And if they find out I'm alive, they're going to be quite pissed at the people who claimed I went up in a bonfire. Our problem is how to get word to them. I was the only person representing the Ekumen in Gatay. Who'd be a safe channel?"

"Any of my men. But . . ."

"They'll have been sent back; why keep Embassy Guards here when the Envoy's dead and buried? I suppose we could try. Ask the boys to try, that is." Presently she said wistfully, "I don't suppose they'd just let us go — in disguise? It would be the safest for them."

"There is an ocean," Teyeo said.

She beat her head. "Oh, why don't they bring some *water*. . . ." Her voice was like paper sliding on paper. He was ashamed of his anger, his grief, himself. He wanted to tell her that she had been a help and hope to him too, that he honored her, that she was brave beyond belief; but none of the words would come. He felt empty, worn-out. He felt old. If only they would bring water!

Water was given them at last; some food, not much and not fresh. Clearly their captors were in hiding and under duress. The spokesman — he gave them his war-name, Kergat, Gatayan for Liberty — told them that whole neighborhoods had been cleared out, set afire, that Voe Dean troops were in control of most of the city including the Palace, and that almost none of this was being reported in the net. "When this is over Voe Deo will own my country," he said with disbelieving fury.

"Not for long," Teyeo said.

"Who can defeat them?" the young man said.

"Yeowe. The idea of Yeowe."

Both Kergat and Solly stared at him.

"Revolution," he said. "How long before Werel becomes New Yeowe?"

"The assets?" Kergat said, as if Teyeo had suggested a revolt of cattle or of flies. "They'll never organise."

"Look out when they do," Teyeo said mildly.

"You don't have any assets in your group?" Solly asked Kergat, amazed. He did not bother to answer. He had classed her as an asset, Teyeo saw. He understood why; he had done so himself, in the other life, when such distinctions made sense.

"Your bondswoman, Rewe," he asked Solly — "was she a friend?"

"Yes," Solly said, then, "No. I wanted her to be."

"The makil?"

After a pause she said, "I think so."

"Is he still here?"

She shook her head. "The troupe was going on with their tour, a few days after the Festival."

"Travel has been restricted since the Festival," Kergat said. "Only government and troops."

"He's Voe Dean. If he's still here, they'll probably send him and his troupe home. Try and contact him, Kergat."

"A makil?" the young man said, with that same distaste and incredulity. "One of your Voe Dean homosexual clowns?"

Teyeo shot a glance at Solly: Patience, patience.

"Bisexual actors," Solly said, disregarding him, but fortunately Kergat was determined to disregard her.

"A clever man," Teyeo said, "with connections. He could help us. You and us. It could be worth it. If he's still here. We must make haste."

"Why would he help us? He is Voe Dean."

"An asset, not a citizen," Teyeo said. "And a member of Hame, the asset underground, which works against the government of Voe Deo. The Ekumen admits the legitimacy of Hame. He'll report to the Embassy that a Patriot group has rescued the Envoy and is holding her safe, in hiding, in extreme danger. The Ekumen, I think, will act promptly and decisively. Correct, Envoy?"

Suddenly reinstated, Solly gave a short, dignified nod. "But discreetly," she said. "They'll avoid violence, if they can use political coercion."

The young man was trying to get it all into his mind and work it through. Sympathetic to his weariness, distrust, and confusion, Teyeo sat quietly waiting. He noticed that Solly was sitting equally quietly, one hand lying in the other. She was thin and dirty and her unwashed, greasy hair was in a lank braid. She was brave, like a brave mare, all nerve. She would break her heart before she quit.

Kergat asked questions; Teyeo answered them, reasoning and reassuring. Occasionally Solly spoke, and Kergat was now listening to her again, uneasily, not wanting to, not after what he had called her. At last he left, not saying what he intended to do; but he had Batikam's name and an identifying message from Teyeo to the Embassy: "Half-pay veots learn to sing old songs quickly."

"What on earth!" Solly said when Kergat was gone.

"Did you know a man named Old Music, in the Embassy?"

"Ah! Is he a friend of yours?"

"He has been kind."

"He's been here on Werel from the start. A First Observer. Rather a powerful man — Yes, and 'quickly,' all right. . . . My mind really isn't working at all. I wish I could lie down beside a little stream, in a meadow, you know, and drink. All day. Every time I wanted to, just stretch my neck out and slup, slup, slup. . . . Running water . . . In the sunshine . . . Oh God, oh God, sunshine. Teyeo, this is very difficult.

This is harder than ever. Thinking that there maybe is really a way out of here. Only not knowing. Trying not to hope and not to not hope. Oh, I am so tired of sitting here!"

"What time is it?"

"Half past twenty. Night. Dark out. Oh God, darkness! Just to be in the darkness . . . Is there any way we could cover up that damned biolume? Partly? To pretend we had night, so we could pretend we had day?"

"If you stood on my shoulders, you could reach it. But how could we fasten a cloth?"

They pondered, staring at the plaque.

"I don't know. Did you notice there's a little patch of it that looks like it's dying? Maybe we don't have to worry about making darkness. If we stay here long enough. Oh, God!"

"Well," he said after a while, curiously self-conscious, "I'm tired." He stood up, stretched, glanced for permission to enter her territory, got a drink of water, returned to his territory, took off his jacket and shoes, by which time her back was turned, took off his trousers, lay down, pulled up the blanket, and said in his mind, "Lord Kamye, let me hold fast to the one noble thing." But he did not sleep.

He heard her slight movements; she pissed, poured a little water, took off her sandals, lay down.

A long time passed.

"Teyeo."

"Yes."

"Do you think . . . that it would be a mistake . . . under the circumstances . . . to make love?"

A pause.

"Not under the circumstances," he said, almost inaudibly. "But — in the other life — "

A pause.

"Short life versus long life," she murmured.

"Yes."

A pause.

"No," he said, and turned to her. "No, that's wrong." They reached out to each other. They clasped each other, cleaved together, in blind haste, greed, need, crying out together the name of God in their different languages and then like animals in the wordless voice. They huddled together, spent, sticky, sweaty, exhausted, reviving, rejoined, reborn in the body's tenderness, in the endless exploration, the ancient discovery, the long flight to the new world.

He woke slowly, in ease and luxury. They were entangled, his face was against her arm and breast; she was stroking his hair, sometimes his neck and shoulder. He lay for a long time aware only of that lazy rhythm and the cool of her skin against his face, under his hand, against his leg.

"Now I know," she said, her half whisper deep in her chest, near his ear, "that I don't know you. Now I need to know you." She bent forward to touch his face with her lips and cheek.

"What do you want to know?"

"Everything. Tell me who Teyeo is. . . ."

"I don't know," he said. "A man who holds you dear."

"Oh, God," she said, hiding her face for a moment in the rough, smelly blanket.

"Who is God?" he asked sleepily. They spoke Voe Dean, but she usually swore in Terran or

Alterran; in this case it had been Alterran, *Seyt,* so he
asked, "Who is Seyt?"

"Oh — Tual — Kamye — what have you. I just
say it. It's just bad language. Do you believe in one
of them? I'm sorry! I feel like such an oaf with you,
Teyeo. Blundering into your soul, invading you —
We *are* invaders, no matter how pacifist and prig-
gish we are —"

"Must I love the whole Ekumen?" he asked,
beginning to stroke her breasts, feeling her tremor of
desire and his own.

"Yes," she said, "yes, yes."

It was curious, Teyeo thought, how little sex
changed anything. Everything was the same, a little easier, less embarrassment and inhibition; and
there was a certain and lovely source of pleasure
for them, when they had enough water and food
to have enough vitality to make love. But the only
thing that was truly different was something he
had no word for. Sex, comfort, tenderness, love,
trust, no word was the right word, the whole
word. It was utterly intimate, hidden in the mutuality of their bodies, and it changed nothing in
their circumstances, nothing in the world, even
the tiny wretched world of their imprisonment.
They were still trapped. They were getting very
tired and were hungry most of the time. They were
increasingly afraid of their increasingly desperate
captors.

"I will be a lady," Solly said. "A good girl. Tell
me how, Teyeo."

"I don't want you to give in," he said, so fiercely, with tears in his eyes, that she went to him and held him in her arms.

"Hold fast," he said.

"I will," she said. But when Kergat or the others came in she was sedate and modest, letting the men talk, keeping her eyes down. He could not bear to see her so, and knew she was right to do so.

The doorlock rattled, the door clashed, bringing him up out of a wretched, thirsty sleep. It was night or very early morning. He and Solly had been sleeping close entangled for the warmth and comfort of it; and seeing Kergat's face now he was deeply afraid. This was what he had feared, to show, to prove her sexual vulnerability. She was still only half-awake, clinging to him.

Another man had come in. Kergat said nothing. It took Teyeo some time to recognise the second man as Batikam.

When he did, his mind remained quite blank. He managed to say the makil's name. Nothing else.

"Batikam?" Solly croaked. "Oh, my God!"

"This is an interesting moment," Batikam said in his warm actor's voice. He was not transvestite, Teyeo saw, but wore Gatayan men's clothing. "I meant to rescue you, not to embarrass you, Envoy, Rega. Shall we get on with it?"

Teyeo had scrambled up and was pulling on his filthy trousers. Solly had slept in the ragged pants their captors had given her. They both had kept on their shirts for warmth.

"Did you contact the Embassy, Batikam?" she was asking, her voice shaking, as she pulled on her sandals.

"Oh, yes. I've been there and come back,

indeed. Sorry it took so long. I don't think I quite realised your situation here."

"Kergat has done his best for us," Teyeo said at once, stiffly.

"I can see that. At considerable risk. I think the risk from now on is low. That is . . ." He looked straight at Teyeo. "Rega, how do you feel about putting yourself in the hands of Hame?" he said. "Any problems with that?"

"Don't, Batikam," Solly said. "Trust him!"

Teyeo tied his shoe, straightened up, and said, "We are all in the hands of the Lord Kamye."

Batikam laughed, the beautiful full laugh they remembered.

"In the Lord's hands, then," he said, and led them out of the room.

In the *Arkamye* it is said, "To live simply is most complicated."

Solly requested to stay on Werel, and after a recuperative leave at the seashore was sent as Observer to South Voe Deo. Teyeo went straight home, being informed that his father was very ill. After his father's death, he asked for indefinite leave from the Embassy Guard, and stayed on the farm with his mother until her death two years later. He and Solly, a continent apart, met only occasionally during those years.

When his mother died, Teyeo freed his family's assets by act of irrevocable manumission, deeded over their farms to them, sold his now almost valueless property at auction, and went to the capital. He knew Solly was temporarily staying at the

Embassy. Old Music told him where to find her. He found her in a small office of the palatial building. She looked older, very elegant. She looked at him with a stricken and yet wary face. She did not come forward to greet or touch him. She said, "Teyeo, I've been asked to be the first Ambassador of the Ekumen to Yeowe."

He stood still.

"Just now — I just came from talking on the ansible with Hain —"

She put her face in her hands. "Oh, my God!" she said.

He said, "My congratulations, truly, Solly."

She suddenly ran at him, threw her arms around him, and cried, "Oh, Teyeo, and your mother died, I never thought, I'm so sorry, I never, I never do — I thought we could — What are you going to do? Are you going to stay there?"

"I sold it," he said. He was enduring rather than returning her embrace. "I thought I might return to the service."

"You sold your *farm*? But I never saw it!"

"I never saw where you were born," he said.

There was a pause. She stood away from him, and they looked at each other.

"You would come?" she said.

"I would," he said.

Several years after Yeowe entered the Ekumen, Mobile Solly Agat Terwa was sent as an Ekumenical liaison to Terra; later she went from there to Hain, where she served with great distinction as a Stabile. In all her travels and posts she was accompanied by her husband, a Werelian army officer, a very handsome man, as reserved as she was outgoing. People who knew them knew their passionate pride and trust in each other. Solly was perhaps the happier person, rewarded and fulfilled in her work; but Teyeo had no regrets. He had lost his world, but he had held fast to the one noble thing.

A Man of the People

Stse

He sat beside his father by the great irrigation tank. Fire-colored wings soared and dipped through the twilight air. Trembling circles enlarged, interlocked, faded on the still surface of the water. "What makes the water go that way?" he asked, softly because it was mysterious, and his father answered softly, "It's where the araha touch it when they drink." So he understood that in the center of each circle was a desire, a thirst. Then it was time to go home, and he ran before his father, pretending he was an araha flying, back through the dusk into the steep, bright-windowed town.

His name was Mattinyehedarheddyuragamuruskets Havzhiva. The word *havzhiva* means "ringed pebble," a small stone with a quartz inclusion running through it that shows as a stripe round it. The people of Stse are particular about stones and names. Boys of the Sky, the Other Sky, and the Static Interference lineages are traditionally given the names of stones or desirable manly qualities such as courage, patience, and grace. The Yehedarhed family were traditionalists, strong on family and lineage. "If you know who your people are, you know who you are," said Havzhiva's father, Granite. A kind, quiet man who took his paternal responsibility seriously, he spoke often in sayings.

Granite was Havzhiva's mother's brother, of course; that is what a father was. The man who had helped his mother conceive Havzhiva lived on a farm; he stopped in sometimes to say hello when he was in town. Havzhiva's mother was the Heir of the Sun. Sometimes Havzhiva envied his cousin Aloe, whose father was only six years older than she was and played with her like a big brother. Sometimes he envied children whose mothers were unimportant. His mother was always fasting or dancing or traveling, had no husband, and rarely slept at home. It was exciting to be with her, but difficult. He had to be important when he was with her. It was always a relief to be home with nobody there but his father and his undemanding grandmother and her sister the Winter Dancekeeper and her husband and whichever Other Sky relatives from farms and other pueblos were visiting at the moment.

There were only two Other Sky households in Stse, and the Yehedarheds were more hospitable than the Doyefarads, so all the relatives came and stayed with them. They would have been hard put to afford it if the visitors hadn't brought all sorts of farm stuff, and if Tovo hadn't been Heir of the Sun.

She got paid richly for teaching and for performing the rituals and handling the protocol at other pueblos. She gave all she earned to her family, who spent it all on their relatives and on ceremonies, festivities, celebrations, and funerals.

"Wealth can't stop," Granite said to Havzhiva. "It has to keep going. Like the blood circulating. You keep it, it gets stopped — that's a heart attack. You die."

"Will Hezhe-old-man die?" the boy asked. Old Hezhe never spent anything on a ritual or a relative; and Havzhiva was an observant child.

"Yes," his father answered. "His araha is already dead."

Araha is enjoyment; honor; the particular quality of one's gender, manhood or womanhood; generosity; the savor of good food or wine.

It is also the name of the plumed, fire-colored, quick-flying mammal that Havzhiva used to see come to drink at the irrigation ponds, tiny flames darting above the darkening water in the evening.

Stse is an almost-island, separated from the mainland of the great south continent by marshes and tidal bogs, where millions of wading birds gather to mate and nest. Ruins of an enormous bridge are visible on the landward side, and another half-sunk fragment of ruin is the basis of the town's boat pier and breakwater. Vast works of other ages encumber all Hain, and are no more and no less venerable or interesting to the Hainish than the rest of the landscape. A child standing on the pier to watch his mother sail off to the mainland might wonder why people had bothered to build a bridge when there were boats and flyers to ride. They must have liked to walk, he thought. I'd rather sail in a boat. Or fly.

But the silver flyers flew over Stse, not landing, going from somewhere else to somewhere else, where historians lived. Plenty of boats came in and out of Stse harbor, but the people of his lineage did not sail them. They lived in the Pueblo of Stse and did the things that their people and their lineage did. They learned what people needed to learn, and lived their knowledge.

"People have to learn to be human," his father said. "Look at Shell's baby. It keeps saying 'Teach me! Teach me!'"

"Teach me," in the language of Stse, is "aowa."

"Sometimes the baby says 'ngaaaaa,'" Havzhiva observed.

Granite nodded. "She can't speak human words very well yet," he said.

Havzhiva hung around the baby that winter, teaching her to say human words. She was one of his Etsahin relatives, his second cousin once removed, visiting with her mother and her father and his wife. The family watched Havzhiva with approval as he patiently said "baba" and "gogo" to the fat, placid, staring baby. Though he had no sister and thus could not be a father, if he went on studying education with such seriousness, he would probably have the honor of being the adopted father of a baby whose mother had no brother.

He also studied at school and in the temple, studied dancing, and studied the local version of soccer. He was a serious student. He was good at soccer but not as good as his best friend, a Buried Cable girl named Iyan Iyan (a traditional name for Buried

Cable girls, a seabird name). Until they were twelve, boys and girls were educated together and alike. Iyan Iyan was the best soccer player on the children's team. They always had to put her on the other side at halftime so that the score would even out and they could go home for dinner without anybody having lost or won badly. Part of her advantage was that she had got her height very early, but most of it was pure skill.

"Are you going to work at the temple?" she asked Havzhiva as they sat on the porch roof of her house watching the first day of the Enactment of the Unusual Gods, which took place every eleven years. No unusual things were happening yet, and the amplifiers weren't working well, so the music in the plaza sounded faint and full of static. The two children kicked their heels and talked quietly. "No, I think I'll learn weaving from my father," the boy said.

"Lucky you. Why do only stupid boys get to use looms?" It was a rhetorical question, and Havzhiva paid it no attention. Women were not weavers. Men did not make bricks. Other Sky people did not operate boats but did repair electronic devices. Buried Cable people did not castrate animals but did maintain generators. There were things one could do and things one could not do; one did those things for people and people did those things for one. Coming up on puberty, Iyan Iyan and Havzhiva were making a first choice of their first profession. Iyan Iyan had already chosen to apprentice in house-building and repair, although the adult soccer team would probably claim a good deal of her time.

A globular silver person with spidery legs came

down the street in long bounds, emitting a shower of sparks each time it landed. Six people in red with tall white masks ran after it, shouting and throwing speckled beans at it. Havzhiva and Iyan Iyan joined in the shouting and craned from the roof to see it go bounding round the corner towards the plaza. They both knew that this Unusual God was Chert, a young man of the Sky lineage, a goalkeeper for the adult soccer team; they both also knew that it was a manifestation of deity. A god called Zarstsa or Ball-Lighting was using Chert to come into town for the ceremony, and had just bounded down the street pursued by shouts of fear and praise and showers of fertility. Amused and entertained by the spectacle, they judged with some acuteness the quality of the god's costume, the jumping, and the fireworks, and were awed by the strangeness and power of the event. They did not say anything for a long time after the god had passed, but sat dreamily in the foggy sunlight on the roof. They were children who lived among the daily gods. Now they had seen one of the unusual gods. They were content. Another one would come along, before long. Time is nothing to the gods.

At fifteen, Havzhiva and Iyan Iyan became gods together.

Stse people between twelve and fifteen were vig-ilantly watched; there would be a great deal of grief and deep, lasting shame if a child of the house, the family, the lineage, the people, should change being prematurely and without ceremony. Virginity was a sacred status, not to be carelessly abandoned; sexual activity was a sacred status, not to be carelessly undertaken. It was assumed that a boy would masturbate and make some homosexual experiments, but not a homosexual pairing; adolescent boys who paired off, and those who incurred suspicion of trying to get alone with a girl, were endlessly lectured and hectored and badgered by older men. A grown man who made sexual advances to a virgin of either sex would forfeit his professional status, his religious offices, and his houseright.

Changing being took a while. Boys and girls had to be taught how to recognise and control their fertility, which in Hainish physiology is a matter of personal decision. Conception does not happen: it is performed. It cannot take place unless both the woman and the man have chosen it. At thirteen, boys began to be taught the technique of deliberately releasing potent sperm. The teachings were full of warnings, threats, and scoldings, though the boys were never actually punished. After a year or two came a series of tests of achieved potency, a threshold ritual, frightening, formal, extremely secret, exclusively male. To have passed the tests was, of course, a matter of intense pride; yet Havzhiva, like most boys, came to his final change-of-being rites very apprehensive, hiding fear under a sullen stoicism.

The girls had been differently taught. The people of Stse believed that a woman's cycle of fertility made it easy for her to learn when and how to conceive, and so the teaching was easy too. Girls' threshold rituals were celebratory, involving praise rather than shame, arousing anticipation rather than fear. Women had been telling them for years, with demonstrations, what a man wants, how to make him stand up tall, how to show him what a woman wants. During this training, most girls asked if they couldn't just go on practicing with each other, and got scolded and lectured. No, they couldn't. Once they had changed status they could do as they pleased, but everybody must go through "the twofold door" once.

The change-of-being rites were held whenever the people in charge of them could get an equal number of fifteen-year-old boys and girls from the pueblo and its farms. Often a boy or girl had to be borrowed from one of the related pueblos to even out the number or to pair the lineages correctly. Magnificently masked and costumed, silent, the participants danced and were honored all day in the plaza and in the house consecrated to the ceremony; in the evening they ate a ritual meal in silence; then they were led off in pairs by masked and silent ritualists. Many of them kept their masks on, hiding their fear and modesty in that sacred anonymity.

Because Other Sky people have sex only with Original and Buried Cable people and they were the only ones of those lineages in the group, Iyan Iyan and Havzhiva had known they must be paired. They had recognised each other as soon as the dancing began. When they were left alone in the consecrated room, they took off their masks at once. Their eyes met. They looked away.

They had been kept apart most of the time for the past couple of years, and completely apart for the last months. Havzhiva had begun to get his growth, and was nearly as tall as she was now. Each saw a stranger. Decorous and serious, they approached each other, each thinking, "Let's get it over with." So they touched, and that god entered them, becoming them; the god for whom they were the doorway; the meaning for which they were the word. It was an awkward god at first, clumsy, but became an increasingly happy one.

When they left the consecrated house the next day, they both went to Iyan Iyan's house. "Havzhiva will live here," Iyan Iyan said, as a woman has a right to say. Everybody in her family made him welcome and none of them seemed surprised.

When he went to get his clothes from his grandmother's house, nobody there seemed surprised, everybody congratulated him, an old woman cousin from Etsahin made some embarrassing jokes, and his father said, "You are a man of this house now; come back for dinner."

So he slept with Iyan Iyan at her house, ate breakfast there, ate dinner at his house, kept his daily clothes at her house, kept his dance clothes at his house, and went on with his education, which now had mostly to do with rug-weaving on the power broadlooms and with the nature of the cosmos. He and Iyan Iyan both played on the adult soccer team.

He began to see more of his mother, because when he was seventeen she asked him if he wanted to learn Sun-stuff with her, the rites and protocols of trade, arranging fair exchange with farmers of Stse and bargaining with other pueblos of the lineages and with foreigners. The rituals were learned by rote, the protocols were learned by practice. Havzhiva went with his mother to the market, to outlying farms, and across the bay to the mainland pueblos. He had been getting restless with weaving, which filled his mind with patterns that left no room outside themselves. The travel was welcome, the work was interesting, and he admired Tovo's authority, wit, and tact. Listening to her and a group of old merchants and Sun people maneuvering around a deal was an education in itself. She did not push him; he played a very minor role in these negotiations. Training in complicated business such as Sun-stuff took years, and there were other, older people in training before him. But she was satisfied with him. "You have a knack for persuading," she told him one afternoon as they were sailing home across the golden water, watching the roofs of Stse solidify out of mist and sunset light. "You could inherit the Sun, if you wanted to."

Do I want to? he thought. There was no response in him but a sense of darkening or softening, which he could not interpret. He knew he liked the work. Its patterns were not closed. It took him out of Stse, among strangers, and he liked that. It gave him something to do which he didn't know how to do, and he liked that.

"The woman who used to live with your father is coming for a visit," Tovo said.

Havzhiva pondered. Granite had never married. The women who had borne the children Granite sired both lived in Stse and always had. He asked nothing, a polite silence being the adult way of signifying that one doesn't understand.

"They were young. No child came," his mother said. "She went away after that. She became a historian."

"Ah," Havzhiva said in pure, blank surprise.

He had never heard of anybody who became a historian. It had never occurred to him that a person could become one, any more than a person could become a Stse. You were born what you were. You were what you were born.

The quality of his polite silence was desperately intense, and Tovo certainly was not unaware of it. Part of her tact as a teacher was knowing when a question needed an answer. She said nothing.

As their sail slackened and the boat slid in toward the pier built on the ancient bridge foundations, he asked, "Is the historian Buried Cable or Original?"

"Buried Cable," his mother said. "Oh, how stiff I am! Boats are such stiff creatures!" The woman who had sailed them across, a ferrywoman of the Grass lineage, rolled her eyes, but said nothing in defense of her sweet, supple little boat.

"A relative of yours is coming?" Havzhiva said to Iyan Iyan that night.

"Oh, yes, she templed in." Iyan Iyan meant a message had been received in the information center of Stse and transmitted to the recorder in her household. "She used to live in your house, my mother said. Who did you see in Etsahin today?"

"Just some Sun people. Your relative is a historian?"

"Crazy people," Iyan Iyan said with indifference, and came to sit naked on naked Havzhiva and massage his back.

The historian arrived, a little short thin woman of fifty or so called Mezha. By the time Havzhiva met her she was wearing Stse clothing and eating breakfast with everybody else. She had bright eyes and was cheerful but not talkative. Nothing about her showed that she had broken the social contract, done things no woman does, ignored her lineage, become another kind of being. For all he knew she was married to the father of her children, and wove at a loom, and castrated animals. But nobody shunned her, and after breakfast the old people of the household took her off for a returning-traveler ceremony, just as if she were still one of them.

He kept wondering about her, wondering what she had done. He asked Iyan Iyan questions about her till Iyan Iyan snapped at him, "I don't know what she does, I don't know what she thinks. Historians are crazy. Ask her yourself!"

When Havzhiva realised that he was afraid to do so, for no reason, he understood that he was in the presence of a god who was requiring something of him. He went up to one of the sitting holes, rock cairns on the heights above the town. Below him the black tile roofs and white walls of Stse nestled under the bluffs, and the irrigation tanks shone silver among fields and orchards. Beyond the tilled land stretched the long sea marshes. He spent a day sitting in silence, looking out to sea and into his soul. He came back down to his own house and slept there. When he turned up for breakfast at Iyan Iyan's house she looked at him and said nothing.

"I was fasting," he said.

She shrugged a little. "So eat," she said, sitting down by him. After breakfast she left for work. He did not, though he was expected at the looms.

"Mother of All Children," he said to the historian, giving her the most respectful title a man of one lineage can give a woman of another, "there are things I do not know, which you know."

"What I know I will teach you with pleasure," she said, as ready with the formula as if she had lived here all her life. She then smiled and forestalled his next oblique question. "What was given me I give," she said, meaning there was no question of payment or obligation. "Come on, let's go to the plaza."

Everybody goes to the plaza in Stse to talk, and sits on the steps or around the fountain or on hot days under the arcades, and watches other people come and go and sit and talk. It was perhaps a little more public than Havzhiva would have liked, but he was obedient to his god and his teacher.

They sat in a niche of the fountain's broad base and conversed, greeting people every sentence or two with a nod or a word.

"Why did —" Havzhiva began, and stuck.

"Why did I leave? Where did I go?" She cocked her head, bright-eyed as an araha, checking that those were the questions he wanted answered. "Yes. Well, I was crazy in love with Granite, but we had no child, and he wanted a child. . . . You look like he did then. I like to look at you. . . . So, I was unhappy. Nothing here was any good to me. And I knew how to do everything here. Or that's what I thought."

Havzhiva nodded once.

"I worked at the temple. I'd read messages that came in or came by and wonder what they were about. I thought, all that's going on in the world! Why should I stay here my whole life? Does my mind have to stay here? So I began to talk with some of them in other places in the temple: who are you, what do you do, what is it like there. . . . Right away they put me in touch with a group of historians who were born in the pueblos, who look out for people like me, to make sure they don't waste time or offend a god."

This language was completely familiar to Havzhiva, and he nodded again, intent.

"I asked them questions. They asked me questions. Historians have to do a lot of that. I found out they have schools, and asked if I could go to one. Some of them came here and talked to me and my family and other people, finding out if there would be trouble if I left. Stse is a conservative pueblo. There hadn't been a historian from here for four hundred years."

She smiled; she had a quick, catching smile, but the young man listened with unchanging, intense seriousness. Her look rested on his face tenderly.

"People here were upset, but nobody was angry. So after they talked about it, I left with those people. We flew to Kathhad. There's a school there. I was twenty-two. I began a new education. I changed being. I learned to be a historian."

"How?" he asked, after a long silence.

She drew a long breath. "By asking hard questions," she said. "Like you're doing now. . . . And by giving up all the knowledge I had — throwing it away."

"How?" he asked again, frowning. "Why?"

"Like this. When I left, I knew I was a Buried Cable woman. When I was there, I had to unknow that knowledge. There, I'm not a Buried Cable woman. I'm a woman. I can have sex with any person I choose. I can take up any profession I choose. Lineage matters, here. It does not matter, there. It has meaning here, and a use. It has no meaning and no use, anywhere else in the universe." She was as intense as he, now. "There are two kinds of knowledge, local and universal. There are two kinds of time, local and historical."

"Are there two kinds of gods?"

"No," she said. "There are no gods there. The gods are here."

She saw his face change.

She said after a while, "There are souls, there. Many, many souls, minds, minds full of knowledge and passion. Living and dead. People who lived on this earth a hundred, a thousand, a hundred thousand years ago. Minds and souls of people from worlds a hundred light-years from this one, all of them with their own knowledge, their own history. The world is sacred, Havzhiva. The cosmos is sacred. That's not a knowledge I ever had to give up. All I learned, here and there, only increased it. There's nothing that is not sacred." She spoke slowly and quietly, the way most people talked in the pueblo. "You can choose the local sacredness or the great one. In the end they're the same. But not in the life one lives. 'To know there is a choice is to have to make the choice: change or stay: river or rock.' The Peoples are the rock. The historians are the river."

After a while he said, "Rocks are the river's bed."

She laughed. Her gaze rested on him again, appraising and affectionate. "So I came home," she said. "For a rest."

"But you're not — you're no longer a woman of your lineage?"

"Yes; here. Still. Always."

"But you've changed being. You'll leave again."

"Yes," she said decisively. "One can be more than one kind of being. I have work to do, there."

He shook his head, slower, but equally decisive. "What good is work without the gods? It makes no sense to me, Mother of All Children. I don't have the mind to understand."

She smiled at the double meaning. "I think you'll understand what you choose to understand, Man of my People," she said, addressing him formally to show that he was free to leave when he wanted.

He hesitated, then took his leave. He went to work, filling his mind and world with the great repeated patterns of the broadloom rugs.

That night he made it up to Iyan Iyan so ardently that she was left spent and a bit amazed. The god had come back to them burning, consuming.

"I want a child," Havzhiva said as they lay melded, sweated together, arms and legs and breasts and breath all mingled in the musky dark.

"Oh," Iyan Iyan sighed, not wanting to talk, decide, resist. "Maybe . . . Later . . . Soon . . ."

"Now," he said, "now."

"No," she said softly. "Hush."

He was silent. She slept.

More than a year later, when they were nineteen, Iyan Iyan said to him before he put out the light, "I want a baby."

"It's too soon."

"Why? My brother's nearly thirty. And his wife

would like a baby around. After it's weaned I'll come sleep with you at your house. You always said you'd like that."

"It's too soon," he repeated. "I don't want it."

She turned to him, laying aside her coaxing, reasonable tone. "What do you want, Havzhiva?"

"I don't know."

"You're going away. You're going to leave the People. You're going crazy. That woman, that damned witch!"

"There are no witches," he said coldly. "That's stupid talk. Superstition."

They stared at each other, the dear friends, the lovers.

"Then what's wrong with you? If you want to move back home, say so. If you want another woman, go to her. But you could give me my child, first! when I ask you for it! Have you lost your araha?" She gazed at him with tearful eyes, fierce, unyielding.

He put his face in his hands. "Nothing is right," he said. "Nothing is right. Everything I do, I have to do because that's how it's done, but it — it doesn't make sense — there are other ways —"

"There's one way to live rightly," Iyan Iyan said, "that I know of. And this is where I live. There's one way to make a baby. If you know another, you can do it with somebody else!" She cried hard after this, convulsively, the fear and anger of months breaking out at last, and he held her to calm and comfort her.

When she could speak, she leaned her head against him and said miserably, in a small, hoarse voice, "To have when you go, Havzhiva."

At that he wept for shame and pity, and whispered, "Yes, yes." But that night they lay holding each other, trying to console each other, till they fell asleep like children.

"I am ashamed," Granite said painfully.

"Did you make this happen?" his sister asked, dry.

"How do I know? Maybe I did. First Mezha, now my son. Was I too stern with him?"

"No, no."

"Too lax, then. I didn't teach him well. Why is he crazy?"

"He isn't crazy, brother. Let me tell you what I think. As a child he always asked why, why, the way children do. I would answer: That's how it is, that's how it's done. He understood. But his mind has no peace. My mind is like that, if I don't remind myself. Learning the Sun-stuff, he always asked, why thus? why this way, not another way? I answered: Because in what we do daily and in the way we do it, we enact the gods. He said: Then the gods are only what we do. I said: In what we do rightly, the gods are: that is the truth. But he wasn't satisfied by the truth. He isn't crazy, brother, but he is lame. He can't walk. He can't walk with us. So, if a man can't walk, what should he do?"

"Sit still and sing," Granite said slowly.

"If he can't sit still? He can fly."

"Fly?"

"They have wings for him, brother."

"I am ashamed," Granite said, and hid his face in his hands.

*   *   *

A Man of the People

Tovo went to the temple and sent a message to Mezha at Kathhad: "Your pupil wishes to join you." There was some malice in the words. Tovo blamed the historian for upsetting her son's balance, offcentering him till, as she said, his soul was lamed. And she was jealous of the woman who in a few days had outdone the teachings of years. She knew she was jealous and did not care. What did her jealousy or her brother's humiliation matter? What they had to do was grieve.

As the boat for Daha sailed away, Havzhiva looked back and saw Stse: a quilt of a thousand shades of green, the sea marshes, the pastures, fields, hedgerows, orchards; the town clambering up the bluffs above, pale granite walls, white stucco walls, black tile roofs, wall above wall and roof above roof. As it diminished it looked like a seabird perched there, white and black, a bird on its nest. Above the town the heights of the island came in view, greyblue moors and high, wild hills fading into the clouds, white skeins of marsh birds flying.

At the port in Daha, though he was farther from Stse than he had ever been and people had a strange accent, he could understand them and read the signs. He had never seen signs before, but their usefulness was evident. Using them, he found his way to the waiting room for the Kathhad flyer. People were sleeping on the cots provided, in their own blankets. He found an empty cot and lay on it, wrapped in the blanket Granite had woven for him years ago. After a short, strange night, people came in with fruit and hot drinks. One of them gave

Havzhiva his ticket. None of the passengers knew anyone else; they were all strangers; they kept their eyes down. Announcements were made, and they all went outside and went into the machine, the flyer.

Havzhiva made himself look at the world as it fell out from under him. He whispered the Staying Chant soundlessly, steadily. The stranger in the seat next to him joined in.

When the world began to tilt and rush up towards him he shut his eyes and tried to keep breathing.

One by one they filed out of the flyer onto a flat, black place where it was raining. Mezha came to him through the rain, saying his name. "Havzhiva, Man of my People, welcome! Come on. There's a place for you at the School."

Kathhad and Ve

By the third year at Kathhad Havzhiva knew a great many things that distressed him. The old knowledge had been difficult but not distressing. It had been all paradox and myth, and it had made sense. The new knowledge was all fact and reason, and it made no sense.

For instance, he knew now that historians did not study history. No human mind could encompass the history of Hain: three million years of it. The events of the first two million years, the Fore-Eras, like layers of metamorphic rock, were so compressed, so distorted by the weight of the succeeding millennia and their infinite events that one could reconstruct only the most sweeping generalities from the tiny surviving details. And if one did chance to find some miraculously preserved document from a thousand millennia ago, what then? A king ruled in Azbahan; the Empire fell to the Infidels; a fusion rocket has landed on Ve. . . . But there had been uncountable kings, empires, inventions, billions of lives lived in millions of countries, monarchies, democracies, oligarchies, anarchies, ages of chaos and ages of order, pantheon upon pantheon of gods, infinite wars and times of peace, incessant discoveries and forgettings, innumerable horrors and triumphs, an endless repetition of unceasing novelty. What is the use trying to describe the flowing of a river at any one moment, and then at the next moment, and then at the next, and the next, and the next? You wear out. You say: There is a great river, and it flows through this land, and we have named it History.

To Havzhiva the knowledge that his life, any life was one flicker of light for one moment on the surface of that river was sometimes distressing, sometimes restful.

What the historians mostly did was explore, in an easy and unhurried fashion, the local reach and moment of the river. Hain itself had been for several thousand years in an unexciting period marked by the coexistence of small, stable, self-contained societies, currently called pueblos, with a high-technology, low-density network of cities and information centers, currently called the temple. Many of the people of the temple, the historians, spent their lives traveling to and gathering knowledge about the other inhabited planets of the nearby Orion Arm, colonised by their ancestors a couple of million years ago during the Fore-Eras. They acknowledged no motive in these contacts and explorations other than curiosity and fellow-feeling. They were getting in touch with their long-lost relatives. They called that greater network of worlds by an alien word, Ekumen, which meant "the household."

By now Havzhiva knew that everything he had learned in Stse, all the knowledge he had had, could be labeled: *typical pueblo culture of northwestern coastal South Continent*. He knew that the beliefs, practices, kinship systems, technologies, and intellectual organising patterns of the different pueblos were entirely different one from another, wildly different, totally bizarre — just as bizarre as the system of Stse — and he knew that such systems were to be met with on every Known World that contained human populations living in small, stable groups with a technology adapted to their environment, a low, constant birth rate, and a political life based on consent.

At first such knowledge had been intensely distressing. It had been painful. It had made him ashamed and angry. First he thought the historians kept their knowledge from the pueblos, then he thought the pueblos kept knowledge from their own people. He accused; his teachers mildly denied. No, they said. You were taught that certain things were true, or necessary; and those things are true and necessary. They are the local knowledge of Stse.

They are childish, irrational beliefs! he said. They looked at him, and he knew he had said something childish and irrational.

Local knowledge is not partial knowledge, they said. There are different ways of knowing. Each has its own qualities, penalties, rewards. Historical knowledge and scientific knowledge are a way of knowing. Like local knowledge, they must be learned. The way they know in the Household isn't taught in the pueblos, but it wasn't hidden from you, by your people or by us. Everybody anywhere on Hain has access to all the information in the temple.

This was true; he knew it to be true. He could have found out for himself, on the screens of the temple of Stse, what he was learning now. Some of his fellow students from other pueblos had indeed taught themselves how to learn from the screens, and had entered history before they ever met a historian.

Books, however, books that were the body of history, the durable reality of it, barely existed in Stse, and his anger sought justification there. You keep the books from us, all the books in the Library of Hain! No, they said mildly. The pueblos choose not to have many books. They prefer the live knowledge, spoken or passing on the screens, passing from the breath to the breath, from living mind to living mind. Would you give up what you learned that way? Is it less than, is it inferior to what you've learned here from books? There's more than one kind of knowledge, said the historians.

By his third year, Havzhiva had decided that there was more than one kind of people. The pueblans, able to accept that existence is fundamentally arbitrary, enriched the world intellectually and spiritually. Those who couldn't be satisfied with mystery were more likely to be of use as historians, enriching the world intellectually and materially.

Meanwhile he had got quite used to people who had no lineage, no relatives, and no religion. Sometimes he said to himself with a glow of pride, "I am a citizen of all history, of the millions of years of Hainish history, and my country is the whole galaxy!" At other times he felt miserably small, and he would leave his screens or his books and go look for company among his fellow students, especially the young women who were so friendly, so companionable.

At the age of twenty-four Havzhiva, or Zhiv as he was now called, had been at the Ekumenical School on Ve for a year.

Ve, the next planet out from Hain, was colonised eons ago, the first step in the vast Hainish expansion of the Fore-Eras. It has gone through many phases as a satellite or partner of Hainish civilizations; at this period it is inhabited entirely by historians and Aliens.

In their current (that is, for at least the past hundred millennia) mood of not tampering, the Hainish have let Ve return to its own norms of coldness, dryness, and bleakness — a climate within human tolerance, but likely to truly delight only people from the Terran Altiplano or the uplands of Chiffewar. Zhiv was out hiking through this stern landscape with his companion, friend, and lover, Tiu.

They had met two years before, in Kathhad. At that point Zhiv had still been reveling in the availability of all women to himself and himself to all women, a freedom that had only gradually dawned on him, and about which Mezha had warned him gently. "You will think there are no rules," she said. "There are always rules." He had been conscious mainly of his own increasingly fearless and careless transgression of what had been the rules. Not all the women wanted to have sex, and not all the women wanted to have sex with men, as he had soon discovered, but that still left an infinite variety. He found that he was considered attractive. And being Hainish was a definite advantage with the Alien women.

The genetic alteration that made the Hainish able to control their fertility was not a simple bit of gene-splicing; involving a profound and radical reconstruction of human physiology, it had probably taken up to twenty-five generations to establish — so say the historians of Hain, who think they know in general terms the steps such a transformation must have followed. However the ancient Hainish did it, they did not do it for any of their colonists. They left the peoples of their colony worlds to work out their own solutions to the First Heterosexual Problem. These have been, of course, various and ingenious; but in all cases so far, to avoid conception you have to do something or have done something or take something or use something — unless you have sex with the Hainish.

Zhiv had been outraged when a girl from Beldene asked him if he was sure he wouldn't get her pregnant. "How do you *know?*" she said. "Maybe I should take a zapper just to be *safe.*" Insulted in the quick of his manhood, he disentangled himself, said, "Maybe it is only safe not to be with me," and stalked out. Nobody else questioned his integrity, fortunately, and he cruised happily on, until he met Tiu.

She was not an Alien. He had sought out women from offworld; sleeping with Aliens added exoticism to transgression, or, as he put it, was an enrichment of knowledge such as every historian should seek. But Tiu was Hainish. She had been born and brought up in Darranda, as had her ancestors before her. She was a child of the Historians as he was a child of the People. He realised very soon that this bond and division was far greater than any mere foreignness: that their unlikeness was true difference and their likeness was true kinship. She was the country he had left his own country to discover. She was what he sought to be. She was what he sought.

What she had — so it seemed to him — was perfect equilibrium. When he was with her he felt that for the first time in his life he was learning to walk. To walk as she did: effortless, unself-conscious as an animal, and yet conscious, careful, keeping in mind all that might unbalance her and using it as tightrope walkers use their long poles. . . . This, he thought, this is a dweller in true freedom of mind, this is a woman free to be fully human, this perfect measure, this perfect grace.

He was utterly happy when he was with her. For a long time he asked nothing beyond that, to be with her. And for a long time she was wary of him, gentle but distant. He thought she had every right to keep her distance. A pueblo boy, a fellow who couldn't tell his uncle from his father — he knew what he was, here, in the eyes of the ill-natured and the insecure. Despite their vast knowledge of human ways of being, historians retained the vast human capacity for bigotry. Tiu had no such prejudices, but what did he have to offer her? She had and was everything. She was complete. Why should she look at him? If she would only let him look at her, be with her, it was all he wanted.

She looked at him, liked him, found him appealing and a little frightening. She saw how he wanted her, how he needed her, how he had made her into the center of his life and did not even know it. That would not do. She tried to be cold, to turn him away. He obeyed. He did not plead. He stayed away.

But after fifteen days he came to her and said, "Tiu, I cannot live without you," and knowing that he was speaking the plain truth she said, "Then live with me a while." For she had missed the passion his presence filled the air with. Everybody else seemed so tame, so balanced.

Their lovemaking was an immediate, immense, and continual delight. Tiu was amazed at herself, at her obsession with Zhiv, at her letting him pull her out of her orbit so far. She had never expected to adore anybody, let alone to be adored. She had led an orderly life, in which the controls were individual and internal, not social and external as they had been in Zhiv's life in Stse. She knew what she wanted to be and do. There was a direction in her, a true north, that she would always follow. Their first year together was a series of continual shifts and changes in their relationship, a kind of exciting love dance, unpredictable and ecstatic. Very gradually, she began to resist the tension, the intensity, the ecstasy. It was lovely but it wasn't right, she thought. She wanted to go on. That constant direction began to pull her away from him again; and then he fought for his life against it.

That was what he was doing, after a long day's hike in the Desert of Asu Asi on Ve, in their miraculously warm Gethenian-made tent. A dry, icy wind moaned among cliffs of crimson stone above them, polished by the endless winds to a shine like lacquer and carved by a lost civilization with lines of some vast geometry.

They might have been brother and sister, as they sat in the glow of the Chabe stove: their red-bronze coloring was the same, their thick, glossy, black hair, their fine, compact body type. The pueblan decorum and quietness of Zhiv's movements and voice met in her an articulate, quicker, more vivid response.

But she spoke now slowly, almost stiffly.

"Don't force me to choose, Zhiv," she said. "Ever since I started in the Schools I've wanted to go to Terra. Since before. When I was a kid. All my life. Now they offer me what I want, what I've worked for. How can you ask me to refuse?"

"I don't."

"But you want me to put it off. If I do, I may lose the chance forever. Probably not. But why risk it — for one year? You can follow me next year!"

He said nothing.

"If you want to," she added stiffly. She was always too ready to forgo her claim on him. Perhaps she had never believed fully in his love for her. She did not think of herself as lovable, as worthy of his passionate loyalty. She was frightened by it, felt inadequate, false. Her self-respect was an intellectual thing. "You make a god of me," she had told him, and did not understand when he replied with happy seriousness, "We make the god together."

"I'm sorry," he said now. "It's a different form of reason. Superstition, if you like. I can't help it, Tiu. Terra is a hundred and forty light-years away. If you go, when you get there, I'll be dead."

"You will not! You'll have lived another year here, you'll be on your way there, you'll arrive a year after I do!"

"I know that. Even in Stse we learned that," he said patiently. "But I'm superstitious. We die to each other if you go. Even in Kathhad you learned that."

"I didn't. It's not true. How can you ask me to give up this chance for what you admit is a superstition? Be fair, Zhiv!"

After a long silence, he nodded.

She sat stricken, understanding that she had won. She had won badly.

She reached across to him, trying to comfort him and herself. She was scared by the darkness in him, his grief, his mute acceptance of betrayal. But it wasn't betrayal — she rejected the word at once. She wouldn't betray him. They were in love. They loved each other. He would follow her in a year, two years at the most. They were adults, they must not cling together like children. Adult relationships are based on mutual freedom, mutual trust. She told herself all these things as she said them to him. He said yes, and held her, and comforted her. In the night, in the utter silence of the desert, the blood singing in his ears, he lay awake and thought, "It has died unborn. It was never conceived."

They stayed together in their little apartment at

the School for the few more weeks before Tiu left. They made love cautiously, gently, talked about history and economics and ethnology, kept busy. Tiu had to prepare herself to work with the team she was going with, studying the Terran concepts of hierarchy; Zhiv had a paper to write on social-energy generation on Werel. They worked hard. Their friends gave Tiu a big farewell party. The next day Zhiv went with her to Ve Port. She kissed and held him, telling him to hurry, hurry and come to Terra. He saw her board the flyer that would take her up to the NAFAL ship waiting in orbit. He went back to the apartment on the South Campus of the School. There a friend found him three days later sitting at his desk in a curious condition, passive, speaking very slowly if at all, unable to eat or drink. Being pueblo-born, the friend recognised this state and called in the medicine man (the Hainish do not call them doctors). Having ascertained that he was from one of the Southern pueblos, the medicine man said, "Havzhiva! The god cannot die in you here!"

After a long silence the young man said softly in a voice which did not sound like his voice, "I need to go home."

"That is not possible now," said the medicine man. "But we can arrange a Staying Chant while I find a person able to address the god." He promptly put out a call for students who were ex–People of the South. Four responded. They sat all night with Havzhiva singing the Staying Chant in two languages and four dialects, until Havzhiva joined them in a fifth dialect, whispering the words hoarsely, till he collapsed and slept for thirty hours.

He woke in his own room. An old woman was

having a conversation with nobody beside him. "You aren't here," she said. "No, you are mistaken. You can't die here. It would not be right, it would be quite wrong. You know that. This is the wrong place. This is the wrong life. You know that! What are you doing here? Are you lost? Do you want to know the way home? Here it is. Listen." She began singing in a thin, high voice, an almost tuneless, almost wordless song that was familiar to Havzhiva, as if he had heard it long ago. He fell asleep again while the old woman went on talking to nobody.

When he woke again she was gone. He never knew who she was or where she came from; he never asked. She had spoken and sung in his own language, in the dialect of Stse.

He was not going to die now, but he was very unwell. The medicine man ordered him to the Hospital at Tes, the most beautiful place on all Ve, an oasis where hot springs and sheltering hills make a mild local climate and flowers and forests can grow. There are paths endlessly winding under great trees, warm lakes where you can swim forever, little misty ponds from which birds rise crying, steam-shrouded hot springs, and a thousand waterfalls whose voices are the only sound all night. There he was sent to stay till he was recovered.

He began to speak into his noter, after he had been at Tes twenty days or so; he would sit in the sunlight on the doorstep of his cottage in a glade of grasses and ferns and talk quietly to himself by way of the little recording machine. "What you select from, in order to tell your story, is nothing less than everything," he said, watching the branches of the old trees dark against the sky. "What you build up your world from, your local, intelligible, rational, coherent world, is nothing less than everything. And so all selection is arbitrary. All knowledge is partial — infinitesimally partial. Reason is a net thrown out into an ocean. What truth it brings in is a fragment, a glimpse, a scintillation of the whole truth. All human knowledge is local. Every life, each human life, is local, is arbitrary, the infinitesimal momentary glitter of a reflection of . . ." His voice ceased; the silence of the glade among the great trees continued.

After forty-five days he returned to the School. He took a new apartment. He changed fields, leaving social science, Tiu's field, for Ekumenical service training, which was intellectually closely related but led to a different kind of work. The change would lengthen his time at the School by at least a year, after which if he did well he could hope for a post with the Ekumen. He did well, and after two years was asked, in the polite fashion of the Ekumenical councils, if he would care to go to Werel. Yes, he said, he would. His friends gave a big farewell party for him.

"I thought you were aiming for Terra," said one of his less-astute classmates. "All that stuff about war and slavery and class and caste and gender — isn't that Terran history?"

"It's current events in Werel," Havzhiva said.

He was no longer Zhiv. He had come back from the Hospital as Havzhiva.

Somebody else was stepping on the unastute classmate's foot, but she paid no attention. "I thought you were going to follow Tiu," she said. " I thought that's why you never slept with anybody.

God, if I'd only known!" The others winced, but Havzhiva smiled and hugged her apologetically.

In his own mind it was quite clear. As he had betrayed and forsaken Iyan Iyan, so Tiu had betrayed and forsaken him. There was no going back and no going forward. So he must turn aside. Though he was one of them, he could no longer live with the People; though he had become one of them, he did not want to live with the historians. So he must go live among Aliens.

He had no hope of joy. He had bungled that, he thought. But he knew that the two long, intense disciplines that had filled his life, that of the gods and that of history, had given him an uncommon knowledge, which might be of use somewhere; and he knew that the right use of knowledge is fulfillment.

The medicine man came to visit him the day before he left, checked him over, and then sat for a while saying nothing. Havzhiva sat with him. He had long been used to silence, and still sometimes forgot that it was not customary among historians.

"What's wrong?" the medicine man said. It seemed to be a rhetorical question, from its meditative tone; at any rate, Havzhiva made no answer.

"Please stand up," the medicine man said, and when Havzhiva had done so, "Now walk a little." He walked a few steps; the medicine man observed him. "You're out of balance," he said. "Did you know it?"

"Yes."

"I could get a Staying Chant together this evening."

"It's all right," Havzhiva said. "I've always been off-balance."

"There's no need to be," the medicine man said. "On the other hand, maybe it's best, since you're going to Werel. So: Good-bye for this life."

They embraced formally, as historians did, especially when as now it was absolutely certain that they would never see one another again. Havzhiva had to give and get a good many formal embraces that day. The next day he boarded the *Terraces of Darranda* and went across the darkness.

Yeowe

During his journey of eighty light-years at NAFAL speed, his mother died, and his father, and Iyan Iyan, everyone he had known in Stse, everyone he knew in Kathhad and on Ve. By the time the ship landed, they had all been dead for years. The child Iyan Iyan had borne had lived and grown old and died.

This was a knowledge he had lived with ever since he saw Tiu board her ship, leaving him to die. Because of the medicine man, the four people who had sung for him, the old woman, and the waterfalls of Tes, he had lived; but he had lived with that knowledge.

Other things had changed as well. At the time he left Ve, Werel's colony planet Yeowe had been a slave world, a huge work camp. By the time he arrived on Werel, the War of Liberation was over, Yeowe had declared its independence, and the institution of slavery on Werel itself was beginning to disintegrate.

Havzhiva longed to observe this terrible and

magnificent process, but the Embassy sent him promptly off to Yeowe. A Hainishman called Sohikelwenyanmurkeres Esdardon Aya counseled him before he left. "If you want danger, it's dangerous," he said, "and if you like hope, it's hopeful. Werel is unmaking itself, while Yeowe's trying to make itself. I don't know if it's going to succeed. I tell you what, Yehedarhed Havzhiva: there are great gods loose on these worlds."

Yeowe had got rid of its Bosses, its Owners, the Four Corporations who had run the vast slave plantations for three hundred years; but though the thirty years of the War of Liberation were over, the fighting had not stopped. Chiefs and warlords among the slaves who had risen to power during the Liberation now fought to keep and extend their power. Factions had battled over the question of whether to kick all foreigners off the planet forever or to admit Aliens and join the Ekumen. The isolationists had finally been voted down, and there was a new Ekumenical Embassy in the old colonial capital. Havzhiva spent a while there learning "the language and the table manners," as they said. Then the Ambassador, a clever young Terran named Solly, sent him south to the region called Yotebber, which was clamoring for recognition.

History is infamy, Havzhiva thought as he rode the train through the ruined landscapes of the world.

The Werelian capitalists who colonised the planet had exploited it and their slaves recklessly, mindlessly, in a long orgy of profit-making. It takes a while to spoil a world, but it can be done. Strip-mining and single-crop agriculture had defaced and sterilised the earth. The rivers were polluted, dead. Huge dust storms darkened the eastern horizon.

The Bosses had run their plantations by force and fear. For over a century they had shipped male slaves only, worked them till they died, imported fresh ones as needed. Work gangs in these all-male compounds developed into tribal hierarchies. At last, as the price of slaves on Werel and the cost of shipping rose, the Corporations began to buy bonds women for Yeowe Colony. So over the next two centuries the slave population grew, and slave-cities were founded, "Assetvilles" and "Dustytowns" spreading out from the old compounds of the plantations. Havzhiva knew that the Liberation movement had arisen first among the women in the tribal compounds, a rebellion against male domination, before it became a war of all slaves against their owners.

The slow train stopped in city after city: miles of shacks and cabins, treeless, whole tracts bombed or burnt out in the war and not yet rebuilt; factories, some of them gutted ruins, some functioning but ancient-looking, rattletrap, smoke-belching. At each station hundreds of people got off the train and onto it, swarming, crowding, shouting out bribes to the porters, clambering up onto the roofs of the cars, brutally shoved off again by uniformed guards and policemen. In the north of the long continent, as on Werel, he had seen many black-skinned people, blue-black; but as the train went farther south there were fewer of these, until in Yotebber the people in the villages and on the desolate sidings were much paler than he was, a bluish, dusty color. These were the "dust people," the descendants of a hundred generations of Werelian slaves.

Yotebber had been an early center of the Liberation. The Bosses had made reprisal with bombs and poison gas; thousands of people had died. Whole towns had been burned to get rid of the unburied dead, human and animal. The mouth of the great river had been dammed with rotting bodies. But all that was past. Yeowe was free, a new member of the Ekumen of the Worlds, and Havzhiva in the capacity of Sub-Envoy was on his way to help the people of Yotebber Region to begin their new history. Or from the point of view of a Hainishman, to rejoin their ancient history.

He was met at the station in Yotebber City by a large crowd surging and cheering and yelling behind barricades manned by policemen and soldiers; in front of the barricades was a delegation of officials wearing splendid robes and sashes of office and variously ornate uniforms: big men, most of them, dignified, very much public figures. There were speeches of welcome, reporters and photographers for the holonet and the neareal news. It wasn't a circus, however. The big men were definitely in control. They wanted their guest to know he was welcome, he was popular, he was — as the Chief said in his brief, impressive speech — the Envoy from the Future.

That night in his luxurious suite in an Owner's city mansion converted to a hotel, Havzhiva thought: If they knew that their man from the future grew up in a pueblo and never saw a neareal till he came here . . .

He hoped he would not disappoint these people. From the moment he had first met them on Werel he had liked them, despite their monstrous society. They were full of vitality and pride, and here on Yeowe they were full of dreams of justice. Havzhiva thought of justice what an ancient Terran said of another god: I believe in it because it is impossible. He slept well, and woke early in the warm, bright morning, full of anticipation. He walked out to begin to get to know the city, his city.

The doorman — it was disconcerting to find that people who had fought so desperately for their freedom had servants — the doorman tried hard to get him to wait for a car, a guide, evidently distressed at the great man's going out so early, afoot, without a retinue. Havzhiva explained that he wanted to walk and was quite able to walk alone. He set off, leaving the unhappy doorman calling after him, "Oh, sir, please, avoid the City Park, sir!"

Havzhiva obeyed, thinking the park must be closed for a ceremony or replanting. He came on a plaza where a market was in full swing, and there found himself likely to become the center of a crowd; people inevitably noticed him. He wore the handsome Yeowan clothes, singlet, breeches, a light narrow robe, but he was the only person with red-brown skin in a city of four hundred thousand people. As soon as they saw his skin, his eyes, they knew him: the Alien. So he slipped away from the market and kept to quiet residential streets, enjoying the soft, warm air and the decrepit, charming colonial architecture of the houses. He stopped to admire an ornate Tualite temple. It looked rather shabby and desolate, but there was, he saw, a fresh offering of flowers at the feet of the image of the Mother at the doorway. Though her nose had been knocked off during the war, she smiled serenely, a little cross-eyed. People called out behind him. Somebody said close to him, "Foreign shit, get off our world," and his arm was seized as his legs were kicked out from under him. Contorted faces, screaming, closed in around him. An enormous, sickening cramp seized his body, doubling him into a red darkness of struggle and voices and pain, then a dizzy shrinking and dwindling away of light and sound.

An old woman was sitting by him, whispering an almost tuneless song that seemed dimly familiar.

She was knitting. For a long time she did not look at him; when she did she said, "Ah." He had trouble making his eyes focus, but he made out that her face was bluish, a pale bluish tan, and there were no whites to her dark eyes.

She rearranged some kind of apparatus that was attached to him somewhere, and said, "I'm the medicine woman — the nurse. You have a concussion, a slight skull fracture, a bruised kidney, a broken shoulder, and a knife wound in your gut; but you'll be all right; don't worry." All this was in a foreign language, which he seemed to understand. At least he understood "don't worry," and obeyed.

He thought he was on the *Terraces of Darranda* in NAFAL mode. A hundred years passed in a bad dream but did not pass. People and clocks had no faces. He tried to whisper the Staying Chant and it had no words. The words were gone. The old woman took his hand. She held his hand and slowly, slowly brought him back into time, into local time, into the dim, quiet room where she sat knitting.

It was morning, hot, bright sunlight in the window. The Chief of Yotebber Region stood by his bedside, a tower of a man in white-and-crimson robes.

"I'm very sorry," Havzhiva said, slowly and thickly because his mouth was damaged. "It was stupid of me to go out alone. The fault was entirely mine."

"The villains have been caught and will be tried in a court of justice," said the Chief.

"They were young men," Havzhiva said. "My ignorance and folly caused the incident —"

"They will be punished," the Chief said.

The day nurses always had the holoscreen up and watched the news and the dramas as they sat with him. They kept the sound down, and Havzhiva could ignore it. It was a hot afternoon; he was watching faint clouds move slowly across the sky, when the nurse said, using the formal address to a person of high status, "Oh, quick — if the gentleman will look, he can see the punishment of the bad men who attacked him!"

Havzhiva obeyed. He saw a thin human body suspended by the feet, the arms and hands twitching, the intestines hanging down over the chest and face. He cried out aloud and hid his face in his arm. "Turn it off," he said, "turn it off!" He retched and gasped for air. "You are not people!" he cried in his own language, the dialect of Stse. There was some coming and going in the room. The noise of a yelling crowd ceased abruptly. He got control of his breath and lay with his eyes shut, repeating one phrase of the Staying Chant over and over until his mind and body began to steady and find a little balance somewhere, not much.

They came with food; he asked them to take it away.

The room was dim, lit only by a night-light somewhere low on the wall and the lights of the city outside the window. The old woman, the night nurse, was there, knitting in the half dark.

"I'm sorry," Havzhiva said at random, knowing he didn't know what he had said to them.

"Oh, Mr. Envoy," the old woman said with a long sigh. "I read about your people. The Hainish people. You don't do things like we do. You don't torture and kill each other. You live in peace. I wonder, I wonder what we seem to you. Like witches, like devils, maybe."

"No," he said, but he swallowed down another wave of nausea.

"When you feel better, when you're stronger, Mr. Envoy, I have a thing I want to speak to you about." Her voice was quiet and full of an absolute, easy authority, which probably could become formal and formidable. He had known people who talked that way all his life.

"I can listen now," he said, but she said, "Not now. Later. You are tired. Would you like me to sing?"

"Yes," he said, and she sat and knitted and sang voicelessly, tunelessly, in a whisper. The names of her gods were in the song: Tual, Kamye. They are not my gods, he thought, but he closed his eyes and slept, safe in the rocking balance.

Her name was Yeron, and she was not old. She was forty-seven. She had been through a thirty-year war and several famines. She had artificial teeth, something Havzhiva had never heard of, and wore eyeglasses with wire frames; body mending was not unknown on Werel, but on Yeowe most people couldn't afford it, she said. She was very thin, and her hair was thin. She had a proud bearing, but moved stiffly from an old wound in the left hip. "Everybody, everybody in this world has a bullet in them, or whipping scars, or a leg blown off, or a dead baby in their heart," she said. "Now you're one of us, Mr. Envoy. You've been through the fire."

He was recovering well. There were five or six medical specialists on his case. The Regional Chief visited every few days and sent officials daily. The Chief was, Havzhiva realised, grateful. The outrageous attack on a representative of the Ekumen had given him the excuse and strong popular support for a strike against the diehard isolationist World Party led by his rival, another warlord hero of the Liberation. He sent glowing reports of his victories to the Sub-Envoy's hospital room. The holonews was all of men in uniforms running, shooting, flyers buzzing over desert hills. As he walked the halls, gaining strength, Havzhiva saw patients lying in bed in the wards wired in to the neareal net, "experiencing" the fighting, from the point of view, of course, of the ones with guns, the ones with cameras, the ones who shot.

At night the screens were dark, the nets were down, and Yeron came and sat by him in the dim light from the window.

"You said there was something you had to tell me," he said. The city night was restless, full of noises, music, voices down in the street below the window she had opened wide to let in the warm, many-scented air.

"Yes, I did." She put her knitting down. "I am your nurse, Mr. Envoy, but also a messenger. When I heard you'd been hurt, forgive me, but I said, 'Praise the Lord Kamye and the Lady of Mercy!' Because I had not known how to bring my message to you, and now I knew how." Her quiet voice paused a minute. "I ran this hospital for fifteen years. During the war. I can still pull a few strings here." Again she paused. Like her voice, her silences were familiar to him. "I'm a messenger to the Ekumen," she said, "from the women. Women here. Women all over Yeowe. We want to make an alliance with you. . . . I know, the government already did that. Yeowe is a member of the Ekumen of the Worlds. We know that. But what does it mean? To us? It means nothing. Do you know what women are, here, in this world? They are nothing. They are not part of the government. Women made the Liberation. They worked and they died for it just like the men. But they weren't generals, they aren't chiefs. They are nobody. In the villages they are less than nobody, they are work animals, breeding stock. Here it's some better. But not good. I was trained in the Medical School at Besso. I am a doctor, not a nurse. Under the Bosses, I ran this hospital. Now a man runs it. Our men are the owners now. And we're what we always were. Property. I don't think that's what we fought the long war for. Do you, Mr. Envoy? I think what we have is a new liberation to make. We have to finish the job."

After a long silence, Havzhiva asked softly, "Are you organised?"

"Oh, yes. Oh, yes! Just like the old days. We can organise in the dark!" She laughed a little. "But I don't think we can win freedom for ourselves alone by ourselves alone. There has to be a change. The men think they have to be bosses. They have to stop thinking that. Well, one thing we have learned in my lifetime, you don't change a mind with a gun. You kill the boss and you become the boss. We must change that mind. The old slave mind, boss mind. We have got to change it, Mr. Envoy. With your help. The Ekumen's help."

"I'm here to be a link between your people and the Ekumen. But I'll need time," he said. "I need to learn."

"All the time in the world. We know we can't turn the boss mind around in a day or a year. This is a matter of education." She said the word as a sacred word. "It will take a long time. You take your time. If we just know that you will *listen.*"

"I will listen," he said.

She drew a long breath, took up her knitting again. Presently she said, "It won't be easy to hear us."

He was tired. The intensity of her talk was more than he could yet handle. He did not know what she meant. A polite silence is the adult way of signifying that one doesn't understand. He said nothing.

She looked at him. "How are we to come to you? You see, that's a problem. I tell you, we are nothing. We can come to you only as your nurse. Your house-maid. The woman who washes your clothes. We don't mix with the chiefs. We aren't on the councils. We wait on table. We don't eat the banquet."

"Tell me —" he hesitated. "Tell me how to start.

Ask to see me if you can. Come as you can, as it . . . if it's safe?" He had always been quick to learn his lessons. "I'll listen. I'll do what I can." He would never learn much distrust.

She leaned over and kissed him very gently on the mouth. Her lips were light, dry, soft.

"There," she said, "no chief will give you that."

She took up her knitting again. He was half-asleep when she asked, "Your mother is living, Mr. Havzhiva?"

"All my people are dead."

She made a little soft sound. "Bereft," she said. "And no wife?"

"No."

"We will be your mothers, your sisters, your daughters. Your people. I kissed you for that love that will be between us. You will see."

"The list of the persons invited to the reception, Mr. Yehedarhed," said Doranden, the Chief's chief liaison to the Sub-Envoy.

Havzhiva looked through the list on the hand-screen carefully, ran it past the end, and said, "Where is the rest?"

"I'm so sorry, Mr. Envoy — are there omissions? This is the entire list."

"But these are all men."

In the infinitesimal silence before Doranden replied, Havzhiva felt the balance of his life poised.

"You wish the guests to bring their wives? Of course! If this is the Ekumenical custom, we shall be delighted to invite the ladies!"

There was something lip-smacking in the way

Yeowan men said "the ladies," a word which Havzhiva had thought was applied only to women of the owner class on Werel. The balance dipped. "What ladies?" he asked, frowning. "I'm talking about women. Do they have no part in this society?"

He became very nervous as he spoke, for he now knew his ignorance of what constituted danger here. If a walk on a quiet street could be nearly fatal, embarrassing the Chief's liaison might be completely so. Doranden was certainly embarrassed — floored. He opened his mouth and shut it.

"I'm sorry, Mr. Doranden," Havzhiva said, "please pardon my poor efforts at jocosity. Of course I know that women have all kinds of responsible positions in your society. I was merely saying, in a stupidly unfortunate manner, that I should be very glad to have such women and their husbands, as well as the wives of these guests, attend the reception. Unless I am truly making an enormous blunder concerning your customs? I thought you did not segregate the sexes socially, as they do on Werel. Please, if I was wrong, be so kind as to excuse the ignorant foreigner once again."

Loquacity is half of diplomacy, Havzhiva had already decided. The other half is silence.

Doranden availed himself of the latter option, and with a few earnest reassurances got himself away. Havzhiva remained nervous until the following morning, when Doranden reappeared with a revised list containing eleven new names, all female. There was a school principal and a couple of teachers; the rest were marked "retired."

"Splendid, splendid!" said Havzhiva. "May I add

one more name?" — Of course, of course, anyone Your Excellency desires — "Dr. Yeron," he said.

Again the infinitesimal silence, the grain of dust dropping on the scales. Doranden knew that name. "Yes," he said.

"Dr. Yeron nursed me, you know, at your excellent hospital. We became friends. An ordinary nurse might not be an appropriate guest among such very distinguished people; but I see there are several other doctors on our list."

"Quite," said Doranden. He seemed bemused. The Chief and his people had become used to patronising the Sub-Envoy, ever so slightly and politely. An invalid, though now well recovered; a victim; a man of peace, ignorant of attack and even of self-defense; a scholar, a foreigner, unworldly in every sense: they saw him as something like that, he knew. Much as they valued him as a symbol and as a means to their ends, they thought him an insignificant man. He agreed with them as to the fact, but not as to the quality, of his insignificance. He knew that what he did might signify. He had just seen it.

"Surely *you* understand the reason for having a bodyguard, Envoy," the General said with some impatience.

"This is a dangerous city, General Denkam, yes, I understand that. Dangerous for everyone. I see on the net that gangs of young men, such as those who attacked me, roam the streets quite beyond the control of the police. Every child, every woman needs a bodyguard. I should be distressed to know that the safety which is every citizen's right was my special privilege."

The General blinked but stuck to his guns. "We can't let you get assassinated," he said.

Havzhiva loved the bluntness of Yeowan honesty. "I don't want to be assassinated," he said. "I have a suggestion, sir. There are policewomen, female members of the city police force, are there not? Find me bodyguards among them. After all, an armed woman is as dangerous as an armed man, isn't she? And I should like to honor the great part women played in winning Yeowe's freedom, as the Chief said so eloquently in his talk yesterday."

The General departed with a face of cast iron.

Havzhiva did not particularly like his bodyguards. They were hard, tough women, unfriendly, speaking a dialect he could hardly understand. Several of them had children at home, but they refused to talk about their children. They were fiercely efficient. He was well protected. He saw when he went about with these cold-eyed escorts that he began to be looked at differently by the city crowds: with amusement and a kind of fellow-feeling. He heard an old man in the market say, "That fellow has some sense."

Everybody called the Chief the Chief except to his face. "Mr. President," Havzhiva said, "the question really isn't one of Ekumenical principles or Hainish customs at all. None of that is or should be of the least weight, the least importance, here on Yeowe. This is your world."

The Chief nodded once, massively.

"Into which," said Havzhiva, by now insuperably

loquacious, "immigrants are beginning to come from Werel now, and many, many more will come, as the Werelian ruling class tries to lessen revolutionary pressure by allowing increasing numbers of the underclass to emigrate. You, sir, know far better than I the opportunities and the problems that this great influx of population will cause here in Yotebber. Now of course at least half the immigrants will be female, and I think it worth considering that there is a very considerable difference between Werel and Yeowe in what is called the construction of gender — the roles, the expectations, the behavior, the relationships of men and women. Among the Werelian immigrants most of the decision-makers, the people of authority, will be female. The Council of the Hame is about nine-tenths women, I believe. Their speakers and negotiators are mostly women. These people are coming into a society governed and represented entirely by men. I think there is the possibility of misunderstandings and conflict, unless the situation is carefully considered beforehand. Perhaps the use of some women as representatives — "

"Among slaves on the Old World," the Chief said, "women were chiefs. Among our people, men are chiefs. That is how it is. The slaves of the Old World will be the free men of the New World."

"And the women, Mr. President?"

"A free man's women are free," said the Chief.

"Well, then," Yeron said, and sighed her deep sigh. "I guess we have to kick up some dust."

"What dust people are good at," said Dobibe.

"Then we better kick up a whole lot," said

Tualyan. "Because no matter what we do, they'll get hysterical. They'll yell and scream about castrating dykes who kill boy babies. If there's five of us singing some damn song, it'll get into the neareals as five hundred of us with machine guns and the end of civilisation on Yeowe. So I say let's go for it. Let's have five thousand women out singing. Let's stop the trains. Lie down on the tracks. Fifty thousand women lying on the tracks all over Yotebber. You think?"

The meeting (of the Yotebber City and Regional Educational Aid Association) was in a schoolroom of one of the city schools. Two of Havzhiva's bodyguards, in plain clothes, waited unobtrusively in the hall. Forty women and Havzhiva were jammed into small chairs attached to blank netscreens.

"Asking for?" Havzhiva said.

"The secret ballot!"

"No job discrimination!"

"Pay for our work!"

"The secret ballot!"

"Child care!"

"The secret ballot!"

"Respect!"

Havzhiva's noter scribbled away madly. The women went on shouting for a while and then settled down to talk again.

One of the bodyguards spoke to Havzhiva as she drove him home. "Sir," she said. "Was those all teachers?"

"Yes," he said. "In a way."

"Be damn," she said. "Different from they used to be."

* * *

"Yehedarhed! What the hell are you doing down there?"

"Ma'am?"

"You were on the news. Along with about a million women lying across railroad tracks and all over flyer pads and draped around the President's Residence. You were talking to women and smiling."

"It was hard not to."

"When the Regional Government begins shooting, will you stop smiling?"

"Yes. Will you back us?"

"How?"

"Words of encouragement to the women of Yotebber from the Ambassador of the Ekumen. Yeowe a model of true freedom for immigrants from the Slave World. Words of praise to the Government of Yotebber — Yotebber a model for all Yeowe of restraint, enlightenment, et cetera."

"Sure. I hope it helps. Is this a revolution, Havzhiva?"

"It is education, ma'am."

The gate stood open in its massive frame; there were no walls.

"In the time of the Colony," the Elder said, "this gate was opened twice in the day: to let the people out to work in the morning, to let the people in from work in the evening. At all other times it was locked and barred." He displayed the great broken lock that hung on the outer face of the gate, the massive bolts rusted in their hasps. His gesture was solemn, measured, like his words, and again Havzhiva admired the dignity these people had kept in degradation, the stateliness they had maintained in, or against, their enslavement. He had begun to appreciate the immense influence of their sacred text, the *Arkamye*, preserved in oral tradition. "This was what we had. This was our belonging," an old man in the city had told him, touching the book which, at sixty-five or seventy, he was learning to read.

Havzhiva himself had begun to read the book in its original language. He read it slowly, trying to understand how this tale of fierce courage and abnegation had for three millennia informed and nourished the minds of people in bondage. Often he heard in its cadences the voices he had heard speak that day.

He was staying for a month in Hayawa Tribal Village, which had been the first slave compound of the Agricultural Plantation Corporation of Yeowe in Yotebber, three hundred fifty years ago. In this immense, remote region of the eastern coast, much of the society and culture of plantation slavery had been preserved. Yeron and other women of the Liberation Movement had told him that to know who the Yeowans were he must know the plantations and the tribes.

He knew that the compounds had for the first century been a domain of men without women and without children. They had developed an internal government, a strict hierarchy of force and favoritism. Power was won by tests and ordeals and kept by a nimble balancing of independence and collusion. When women slaves were brought in at last, they entered this rigid system as the slaves of slaves. By bondsmen as by Bosses, they were used as servants and sexual outlets. Sexual loyalty and partnership continued to be recognized only between men, a nexus of passion, negotiation, status, and tribal politics. During the next centuries the presence of children in the compounds had altered and enriched tribal customs, but the system of male dominance, so entirely advantageous to the slave-owners, had not essentially changed.

"We hope to have your presence at the initiation tomorrow," the Elder said in his grave way, and Havzhiva assured him that nothing could please or honor him more than attendance at a ceremony of such importance. The Elder was sedately but visibly gratified. He was a man over fifty, which meant he had been born a slave and had lived as a boy and man through the years of the Liberation. Havzhiva looked for scars, remembering what Yeron had said, and found them: the Elder was thin, meager, lame, and had no upper teeth; he was marked all through by famine and war. Also he was ritually scarred, four parallel ridges running from neck to elbow over the point of the shoulder like long epaulets, and a dark blue open eye tattooed on his forehead, the sign, in this tribe, of assigned, unalterable chiefdom. A slave chief, a chattel master of chattels, till the walls went down.

The Elder walked on a certain path from the gate to the longhouse, and Havzhiva following him observed that no one else used this path: men, women, children trotted along a wider, parallel road that diverged off to a different entrance to the longhouse. This was the chiefs' way, the narrow way.

That night, while the children to be initiated next day fasted and kept vigil over on the women's side, all the chiefs and elders gathered for a feast. There were inordinate amounts of the heavy food Yeowans were accustomed to, spiced and ornately served, the marsh rice that was the basis of everything fancied up with colorings and herbs; above all there was meat. Women slipped in and out serving ever more elaborate platters, each one with more meat on it — cattle flesh, Boss food, the sure and certain sign of freedom.

Havzhiva had not grown up eating meat, and could count on it giving him diarrhea, but he chewed his way manfully through the stews and steaks, knowing the significance of the food and the meaning of plenty to those who had never had enough.

After huge baskets of fruit finally replaced the platters, the women disappeared and the music began. The tribal chief nodded to his leos, a word meaning "sexual favorite/adopted brother/not heir/not son." The young man, a self-assured, good-natured beauty, smiled; he clapped his long hands very softly once, then began to brush the grey-blue palms in a subtle rhythm. As the table fell silent he sang, but in a whisper.

Instruments of music had been forbidden on most plantations; most Bosses had allowed no singing except the ritual hymns to Tual at the tenthday service. A slave caught wasting Corporation time in singing might have acid poured down his throat. So long as he could work there was no need for him to make noise.

On such plantations the slaves had developed this almost silent music, the touch and brush of palm against palm, a barely voiced, barely varied, long line of melody. The words sung were deliberately broken, distorted, fragmented, so that they seemed meaningless. *Shesh*, the owners had called it, rubbish, and slaves were permitted to "pat hands and sing rubbish" so long as they did it so softly it could not be heard outside the compound walls. Having sung so for three hundred years, they sang so now.

To Havzhiva it was unnerving, almost frightening, as voice after voice joined, always at a whisper, increasing the complexity of the rhythms till the cross-beats nearly, but never quite, joined into a single texture of hushing sibilant sound, threaded by the long-held, quarter-tonal melody sung on syllables that seemed always about to make a word but never did. Caught in it, soon almost lost in it, he kept thinking now — now one of them will raise his voice — now the leos will give a shout, a shout of triumph, letting his voice free! — But he did not. None did. The soft, rushing, waterlike music with its infinitely delicate shifting rhythm went on and on. Bottles of the orange Yote wine passed up and down the table. They drank. They drank freely, at least. They got drunk. Laughter and shouts began to interrupt the music. But they never once sang above a whisper.

They all reeled back to the longhouse on the chiefs' path, embracing, peeing companionably, one or two pausing to vomit here and there. A kind, dark man who had been seated next to Havzhiva now joined him in his bed in his alcove of the longhouse.

Earlier in the evening this man had told him that during the night and day of the initiation heterosexual intercourse was forbidden, as it would change the energies. The initiation would go crooked, and the boys might not become good members of the tribe. Only a witch, of course, would deliberately break the taboo, but many women were witches and would try to seduce a man out of malice. Regular, that is, homosexual, intercourse would encourage the energies, keep the initiation straight, and give the boys strength for their ordeal. Hence every man leaving the banquet would have a partner for the night. Havzhiva was glad he had been assigned to this man, not to one of the chiefs, whom he found daunting, and who might have expected a properly energetic performance. As it was, as well as he could remember in the morning, he and his companion had been too drunk to do much but fall asleep amidst well-intended caresses.

Too much Yote wine left a ringing headache, he knew that already, and his whole skull reconfirmed the knowledge when he woke.

At noon his friend brought him to a place of honor in the plaza, which was filling up with men. Behind them were the men's longhouses, in front of them the ditch that separated the women's side, the inside, from the men's or gate side — still so-called, though the compound walls were gone and the gate alone stood, a monument, towering above the huts and longhouses of the compound and the flat grainfields that stretched away in all directions, shimmering in the windless, shadowless heat.

From the women's huts, six boys came at a run to the ditch. It was wider than a thirteen-year-old could jump, Havzhiva thought; but two of the boys made it. The other four leapt valiantly, fell short, clambered out, one of them hobbling, having hurt a leg or foot in his fall. Even the two who had made the jump successfully looked exhausted and frightened, and all six were bluish grey from fasting and staying awake. Elders surrounded them and got them standing in line in the plaza, naked and shivering, facing the crowd of all the men of the tribe.

No women at all were visible, over on the women's side.

A catechism began, chiefs and elders barking questions which must evidently be answered without delay, sometimes by one boy, sometimes by all together, depending on the questioner's pointing or sweeping gesture. They were questions of ritual, protocol, and ethics. The boys had been well drilled, delivering their answers in prompt yelps. The one who had lamed himself in the jump suddenly vomited and then fainted, slipping quietly down in a little heap. Nothing was done, and some questions were still pointed to him, followed by a moment of painful silence. After a while the boy moved, sat up, sat a while shuddering, then struggled to his feet and stood with the others. His bluish lips moved in answer to all the questions, though no voice reached the audience.

Havzhiva kept his apparent attention fixed on the ritual, though his mind wandered back a long time, a long way. We teach what we know, he thought, and all our knowledge is local.

After the inquisition came the marking: a single deep cut from the base of the neck over the point of the shoulder and down the outer arm to the elbow, made with a hard, sharp stake of wood dragged gouging through skin and flesh to leave, when it healed, the furrowed scar that proved the man. Slaves would not have been allowed any metal tools inside the gate, Havzhiva reflected, watching steadily as behooved a visitor and guest. After each arm and each boy, the officiating elders stopped to resharpen the stake, rubbing it on a big grooved stone that sat in the plaza. The boys' pale blue lips drew back, baring their white teeth; they writhed, half-fainting, and one of them screamed aloud, silencing himself by clapping his free hand over his mouth. One bit on his thumb till blood flowed from it as well as from his lacerated arms. As each boy's marking was finished the Tribal Chief washed the wounds and smeared some ointment on them. Dazed and wobbling, the boys stood again in line; and now the old men were tender with them, smiling, calling them "tribesman," "hero." Havzhiva drew a long breath of relief.

But now six more children were being brought into the plaza, led across the ditch-bridge by old women. These were girls, decked with anklets and bracelets, otherwise naked. At the sight of them a great cheer went up from the audience of men. Havzhiva was surprised. Women were to be made members of the tribe too? That at least was a good thing, he thought.

Two of the girls were barely adolescent, the others were younger, one of them surely not more than six. They were lined up, their backs to the audience, facing the boys. Behind each of them stood the veiled woman who had led her across the bridge; behind each boy stood one of the naked elders. As Havzhiva watched, unable to turn his eyes or mind from what he saw, the little girls lay down face up on the bare, greyish ground of the plaza. One of them, slow to lie down, was tugged and forced down by the woman behind her. The old men came around the boys, and each one lay down on one of the girls, to a great noise of cheering, jeering, and laughter and a chant of "ha-ah-ha-ah!" from the spectators. The veiled women crouched at the girls' heads. One of them reached out and held down a thin, flailing arm. The elders' bare buttocks pumped, whether in actual coitus or an imitation Havzhiva could not tell. "That's how you do it, watch, watch!" the spectators shouted to the boys, amid jokes and comments and roars of laughter. The elders one by one stood up, each shielding his penis with curious modesty.

When the last had stood up, the boys stepped forward. Each lay down on a girl and pumped his buttocks up and down, though not one of them, Havzhiva saw, had had an erection. The men around him grasped their own penises, shouting, "Here, try mine!" and cheering and chanting until the last boy scrambled to his feet. The girls lay flat, their legs parted, like little dead lizards. There was a slight, terrible movement towards them in the crowd of men. But the old women were hauling the girls to their feet, yanking them up, hurrying them back across the bridge, followed by a wave of howls and jeers from the audience.

"They're drugged, you know," said the kind, dark man who had shared Havzhiva's bed, looking into his face. "The girls. It doesn't hurt them."

"Yes, I see," said Havzhiva, standing still in his place of honor.

"These ones are lucky, privileged to assist initiation. It's important that girls cease to be virgin as soon as possible, you know. Always more than one man must have them, you know. So that they can't make claims — 'this is your son,' 'this baby is the chief's son,' you know. That's all witchcraft. A son is chosen. Being a son has nothing to do with bondswomen's cunts. Bondswomen have to be taught that early. But the girls are given drugs now. It's not like the old days, under the Corporations."

"I understand," Havzhiva said. He looked into his friend's face, thinking that his dark skin meant he must have a good deal of owner blood, perhaps indeed was the son of an owner or a Boss. Nobody's son, begotten on a slave woman. A son is chosen. All knowledge is local, all knowledge is partial. In Stse, in the Schools of the Ekumen, in the compounds of Yeowe.

"You still call them bondswomen," he said. His tact, all his feelings were frozen, and he spoke in mere stupid intellectual curiosity.

"No," the dark man said, "no, I'm sorry, the language I learned as a boy — I apologize —"

"Not to me."

Again Havzhiva spoke only and coldly what was in his head. The man winced and was silent, his head bowed.

"Please, my friend, take me to my room now," Havzhiva said, and the dark man gratefully obeyed him.

He talked softly into his noter in Hainish in the dark. "You can't change anything from outside it.

Standing apart, looking down, taking the overview, you see the pattern. What's wrong, what's missing. You want to fix it. But you can't patch it. You have to be in it, weaving it. You have to be part of the weaving." This last phrase was in the dialect of Stse.

Four women squatted on a patch of ground on the women's side, which had roused his curiosity by its untrodden smoothness: some kind of sacred space, he had thought. He walked towards them. They squatted gracelessly, hunched forward between their knees, with the indifference to their appearance, the carelessness of men's gaze, that he had noticed before on the women's side. Their heads were shaved, their skin chalky and pale. Dust people, dusties, was the old epithet, but to Havzhiva their color was more like clay or ashes. The azure tinge of palms and soles and wherever the skin was fine was almost hidden by the soil they were handling. They had been talking fast and quietly, but went silent as he came near. Two were old, withered up, with knobby, wrinkled knees and feet. Two were young women. They all glanced sidelong from time to time as he squatted down near the edge of the smooth patch of ground.

On it, he saw, they had been spreading dust, colored earth, making some kind of pattern or picture. Following the boundaries between colors he made out a long pale figure a little like a hand or a branch, and a deep curve of earthen red.

Having greeted them, he said nothing more, but simply squatted there. Presently they went back to what they were doing, talking in whispers to one another now and then.

When they stopped working, he said, "Is it sacred?"

The old women looked at him, scowled, and said nothing.

"You can't see it," said the darker of the young women, with a flashing, teasing smile that took Havzhiva by surprise.

"I shouldn't be here, you mean."

"No. You can be here. But you can't see it."

He rose and looked over the earth painting they had made with grey and tan and red and umber dust. The lines and forms were in a definite relationship, rhythmical but puzzling.

"It's not all there," he said.

"This is only a little, little bit of it," said the teasing woman, her dark eyes bright with mockery in her dark face.

"Never all of it at once?"

"No," she said, and the others said, "No," and even the old women smiled.

"Can you tell me what the picture is?"

She did not know the word "picture." She glanced at the others; she pondered, and looked up at him shrewdly.

"We make what we know, here," she said, with a soft gesture over the softly colored design. A warm evening breeze was already blurring the boundaries between the colors.

"They don't know it," said the other young woman, ashen-skinned, in a whisper.

"The men? — They never see it whole?"

"Nobody does. Only us. We have it here." The

dark woman did not touch her head but her heart, covering her breasts with her long, work-hardened hands. She smiled again.

The old women stood up; they muttered together, one said something sharply to the young women, a phrase Havzhiva did not understand; and they stumped off.

"They don't approve of your talking of this work to a man," he said.

"A city man," said the dark woman, and laughed. "They think we'll run away."

"Do you want to run away?"

She shrugged. "Where to?"

She rose to her feet in one graceful movement and looked over the earth painting, a seemingly random, abstract pattern of lines and colors, curves and areas.

"Can you see it?" she asked Havzhiva, with that liquid teasing flash of the eyes.

"Maybe someday I can learn to," he said, meeting her gaze.

"You'll have to find a woman to teach you," said the woman the color of ashes.

"We are a free people now," said the Young Chief, the Son and Heir, the Chosen.

"I haven't yet known a free people," Havzhiva said, polite, ambiguous.

"We won our freedom. We made ourselves free. By courage, by sacrifice, by holding fast to the one noble thing. We are a free people." The Chosen was a strong-faced, handsome, intelligent man of forty. Six gouged lines of scarring ran down his upper arms like a rough mantle, and an open blue eye stared between his eyes, unwinking.

"You are free men," Havzhiva said.

There was a silence.

"Men of the cities do not understand our women," the Chosen said. "Our women do not want a man's freedom. It is not for them. A woman holds fast to her baby. That is the noble thing for her. That is how the Lord Kamye made woman, and the Merciful Tual is her example. In other places it may be different. There may be another kind of woman, who does not care for her children. That may be. Here it is as I have said."

Havzhiva nodded, the deep, single nod he had learned from the Yeowans, almost a bow. "That is so," he said.

The Chosen looked gratified.

"I have seen a picture," Havzhiva went on.

The Chosen was impassive; he might or might not know the word. "Lines and colors made with earth on earth may hold knowledge in them. All knowledge is local, all truth is partial," Havzhiva said with an easy, colloquial dignity that he knew was an imitation of his mother, the Heir of the Sun, talking to foreign merchants. "No truth can make another truth untrue. All knowledge is a part of the whole knowledge. A true line, a true color. Once you have seen the larger pattern, you cannot go back to seeing the part as the whole."

The Chosen stood like a grey stone. After a while he said, "If we come to live as they live in the cities, all we know will be lost." Under his dogmatic tone was fear and grief.

"Chosen One," Havzhiva said, "you speak the truth. Much will be lost. I know it. The lesser knowledge must be given to gain the greater. And not once only."

"The men of this tribe will not deny our truth," the Chosen said. His unseeing, unwinking central eye was fixed on the sun that hung in a yellow dust-haze above the endless fields, though his own dark eyes gazed downward at the earth.

His guest looked from that alien face to the fierce, white, small sun that still blazed low above the alien land. "I am sure of that," he said.

When he was fifty-five, Stabile Yehedarhed Havzhiva went back to Yotebber for a visit. He had not been there for a long time. His work as Ekumenical Advisor to the Yeowan Ministry of Social Justice had kept him in the north, with frequent trips to the other hemisphere. He had lived for years in the Old Capital with his partner, but often visited the New Capital at the request of a new Ambassador who wanted to draw on his expertise. His partner — they had lived together for eighteen years, but there was no marriage on Yeowe — had a book she was trying to finish, and admitted that she would like to have the apartment to herself for a couple of weeks while she wrote. "Take that trip south you keep mooning about," she said. "I'll fly down as soon as I'm done. I won't tell any damned politicians where you are. Escape! Go, go, go!"

He went. He had never liked flying, though he had had to do a great deal of it, and so he made the

long journey by train. They were good, fast trains,
terribly crowded, people at every station swarming
and rushing and shouting bribes to the conductors,
though not trying to ride the roofs of the cars, not
at 130 kmh. He had a private room in a through car
to Yotebber City. He spent the long hours in silence
watching the landscape whirl by, the reclamation
projects, the old wastelands, the young forests, the
swarming cities, miles of shacks and cabins and cot-
tages and houses and apartment buildings, sprawling Werel-style compounds with connected houses
and kitchen gardens and worksheds, factories, huge
new plants; and then suddenly the country again,
canals and irrigation tanks reflecting the colors of
the evening sky, a bare-legged child walking with a
great white ox past a field of shadowy grain. The
nights were short, a dark, rocking sweetness of
sleep.

On the third afternoon he got off the train in
Yotebber City Station. No crowds. No chiefs. No
bodyguards. He walked through the hot, familiar
streets, past the market, through the City Park. A little bravado, there. Gangs, muggers were still about,
and he kept his eye alert and his feet on the main
pathways. On past the old Tualite temple. He had
picked up a white flower that had dropped from a
shrub in the park. He set it at the Mother's feet. She
smiled, looking cross-eyed at her missing nose. He
walked on to the big, rambling new compound
where Yeron lived.

She was seventy-four and had retired recently
from the hospital where she had taught, practiced,
and been an administrator for the last fifteen
years. She was little changed from the woman

he had first seen sitting by his bedside, only she seemed smaller all over. Her hair was quite gone, and she wore a glittering kerchief tied round her head. They embraced hard and kissed, and she stroked him and patted him, smiling irrepressibly. They had never made love, but there had always been a desire between them, a yearning to the other, a great comfort in touch. "Look at that, look at that grey!" she cried, petting his hair, "how beautiful! Come in and have a glass of wine with me! How is your Araha? When is she coming? You walked right across the city carrying that bag? You're still crazy!"

He gave her the gift he had brought her, a treatise on *Certain Diseases of Werel-Yeowe* by a team of Ekumenical medical researchers, and she seized it greedily. For some while she conversed only between plunges into the table of contents and the chapter on berlot. She poured out the pale orange wine. They had a second glass. "You look fine, Havzhiva," she said, putting the book down and looking at him steadily. Her eyes had faded to an opaque bluish darkness. "Being a saint agrees with you."

"It's not that bad, Yeron."

"A hero, then. You can't deny that you're a hero."

"No," he said with a laugh. "Knowing what a hero is, I won't deny it."

"Where would we be without you?"

"Just where we are now. . . . " He sighed. "Sometimes I think we're losing what little we've ever won. This Tualbeda, in Detake Province, don't underestimate him, Yeron. His speeches are pure misogyny and anti-immigrant prejudice, and people are eating it up —"

She made a gesture that utterly dismissed the demagogue. "There is no end to that," she said. "But I knew what you were going to be to us. Right away. When I heard your name, even. I knew."

"You didn't give me much choice, you know."

"Bah. You chose, man."

"Yes," he said. He savored the wine. "I did." After a while he said, "Not many people have the choices I had. How to live, whom to live with, what work to do. Sometimes I think I was able to choose because I grew up where all choices had been made for me."

"So you rebelled, made your own way," she said, nodding.

He smiled. "I'm no rebel."

"Bah!" she said again. "No rebel? You, in the thick of it, in the heart of our movement all the way?"

"Oh yes," he said. "But not in a rebellious spirit. That had to be your spirit. My job was acceptance. To keep an acceptant spirit. That's what I learned growing up. To accept. Not to change the world. Only to change the soul. So that it can be in the world. Be rightly in the world."

She listened but looked unconvinced. "Sounds like a woman's way of being," she said. "Men generally want to change things to suit."

"Not the men of my people," he said.

She poured them a third glass of wine. "Tell me about your people. I was always afraid to ask. The Hainish are so old! So learned! They know so much history, so many worlds! Us here with our three hundred years of misery and murder and ignorance — you don't know how small you make us feel."

"I think I do," Havzhiva said. After a while he said, "I was born in a town called Stse."

He told her about the pueblo, about the Other Sky people, his father who was his uncle, his mother the Heir of the Sun, the rites, the festivals, the daily gods, the unusual gods; he told her about changing being; he told her about the historian's visit, and how he had changed being again, going to Kathhad.

"All those rules!" Yeron said. "So complicated and unnecessary. Like our tribes. No wonder you ran away."

"All I did was go learn in Kathhad what I wouldn't learn in Stse," he said, smiling. "What the rules are. Ways of needing one another. Human ecology. What have we been doing here, all these years, but trying to find a good set of rules — a pattern that makes sense?" He stood up, stretched his shoulders, and said, "I'm drunk. Come for a walk with me."

They went out into the sunny gardens of the compound and walked slowly along the paths between vegetable plots and flower beds. Yeron nodded to people weeding and hoeing, who looked up and greeted her by name. She held Havzhiva's arm firmly, with pride. He matched his steps to hers.

"When you have to sit still, you want to fly," he said, looking down at her pale, gnarled, delicate hand on his arm. "If you have to fly, you want to sit still. I learned sitting, at home. I learned flying, with the historians. But I still couldn't keep my balance."

"Then you came here," she said.

"Then I came here."

"And learned?"

"How to walk," he said. "How to walk with my people."

A Woman's Liberation

1. *Shomeke*

My dear friend has asked me to write the story of my life, thinking it might be of interest to people of other worlds and times. I am an ordinary woman, but I have lived in years of mighty changes and have been advantaged to know with my very flesh the nature of servitude and the nature of freedom.

I did not learn to read or write until I was a grown woman, which is all the excuse I will make for the faults of my narrative.

I was born a slave on the planet Werel. As a child I was called Shomekes' Radosse Rakam. That is, Property of the Shomeke Family, Granddaughter of Dosse, Granddaughter of Kamye. The Shomeke family owned an estate on the eastern coast of Voe Deo. Dosse was my grandmother. Kamye is the Lord God.

The Shomekes possessed over four hundred

assets, mostly used to cultivate the fields of gede, to herd the saltgrass cattle, to work in the mills, and as domestics in the House. The Shomeke family had been great in history. Our Owner was an important man politically, often away in the capital.

Assets took their name from their grandmother because it was the grandmother that raised the child. The mother worked all day, and there was no father. Women were always bred to more than one man. Even if a man knew his child he could not care for it. He might be sold or traded away at any time. Young men were seldom kept long on the estates. If they were valuable, they were traded to other estates or sold to the factories. If they were worthless, they were worked to death.

Women were not often sold. The young ones were kept for work and breeding, the old ones to raise the young and keep the compound in order. On some estates women bore a baby a year till they died, but on ours most had only two or three children. The Shomekes valued women as workers. They did not want the men always getting at the women. The grandmothers agreed with them and guarded the young women closely.

I say men, women, children, but you are to understand that we were not called men, women, children. Only our owners were called so. We assets or slaves were called bondsmen, bondswomen, and pups or young. I will use those words, though I have not heard or spoken them for many years, and never before on this blessed world.

The bondsmen's part of the compound, the gateside, was ruled by the Bosses, who were men, some relations of the Shomeke family, others hired by them. On the inside the young and the bondswomen lived. There two cutfrees, castrated bondsmen, were the Bosses in name, but the grandmothers ruled. Indeed nothing in the compound happened without the grandmothers' knowledge.

If the grandmothers said an asset was too sick to work, the Bosses would let that one stay home. Sometimes the grandmothers could save a bondsman from being sold away, sometimes they could protect a girl from being bred by more than one man, or could give a delicate girl a contraceptive. Everybody in the compound obeyed the council of the grandmothers. But if one of them went too far, the Bosses would have her flogged or blinded or her hands cut off. When I was a young child, there lived in our compound a woman we called Great-Grandmother, who had holes for eyes and no tongue. I thought that she was thus because she was so old. I feared that my grandmother Dosse's tongue would wither in her mouth. I told her that. She said, "No. It won't get any shorter, because I don't let it get too long."

I lived in the compound. My mother birthed me there, and was allowed to stay three months to nurse me; then I was weaned to cow's milk, and my mother returned to the House. Her name was Shomekes' Rayowa Yowa. She was light-skinned like most of the assets, but very beautiful, with slender wrists and ankles and delicate features. My grandmother, too, was light, but I was dark, darker than anybody else in the compound.

My mother came to visit, the cutfrees letting her in by their ladder-door. She found me rubbing grey dust on my body. When she scolded me, I told her that I wanted to look like the others.

"Listen, Rakam," she said to me, "they are dust people. They'll never get out of the dust. You're something better. And you will be beautiful. Why do you think you're so black?" I had no idea what she meant. "Someday I'll tell you who your father is," she said, as if she were promising me a gift. I knew that the Shomekes' stallion, a prized and valuable animal, serviced mares from other estates. I did not know a father could be human.

That evening I boasted to my grandmother: "I'm beautiful because the black stallion is my father!" Dosse struck me across the head so that I fell down and wept. She said, "Never speak of your father."

I knew there was anger between my mother and my grandmother, but it was a long time before I understood why. Even now I am not sure I understand all that lay between them.

We little pups ran around in the compound. We knew nothing outside the walls. All our world was the bondswomen's huts and the bondsmen's longhouses, the kitchens and kitchen gardens, the bare plaza beaten hard by bare feet. To me, the stockade wall seemed a long way off.

When the field and mill hands went out the gate in the early morning I didn't know where they went. They were just gone. All day long the whole compound belonged to us pups, naked in the summer, mostly naked in the winter too, running around playing with sticks and stones and mud, keeping away from the grandmothers, until we begged them for something to eat or they put us to work weeding the gardens for a while.

In the evening or the early night the workers

would come back, trooping in the gate guarded by the Bosses. Some were worn out and grim, others would be cheerful and talking and calling back and forth. The great gate was slammed behind the last of them. Smoke went up from all the cooking stoves. The burning cowdung smelled sweet. People gathered on the porches of the huts and longhouses. Bondsmen and bondswomen lingered at the ditch that divided the gateside from the inside, talking across the ditch. After the meal the freedmen led prayers to Tual's statue, and we lifted our own prayers to Kamye, and then people went to their beds, except for those who lingered to "jump the ditch." Some nights, in the summer, there would be singing, or a dance was allowed. In the winter one of the grandfathers — poor old broken men, not strong people like the grandmothers — would "sing the word." That is what we called reciting the *Arkamye*. Every night, always, some of the people were teaching and others were learning the sacred verses. On winter nights one of these old worthless bondsmen kept alive by the grandmothers' charity would begin to sing the word. Then even the pups would be still to listen to that story.

The friend of my heart was Walsu. She was bigger than I, and was my defender when there were fights and quarrels among the young or when older pups called me "Blackie" and "Bossie." I was small but had a fierce temper. Together, Walsu and I did not get bothered much. Then Walsu was sent out the gate. Her mother had been bred and was now stuffed big, so that she needed help in the fields to make her quota. Gede must be hand-harvested. Every day as a new section of the bearing stalk comes ripe it has to be picked, and so gede pickers go through the same field over and over for twenty or thirty days, and then move on to a later planting. Walsu went with her mother to help her pick her rows. When her mother fell ill, Walsu took her place, and with help from other hands she kept up her mother's quota. She was then six years old by owner's count, which gave all assets the same birthday, new year's day at the beginning of spring. She might have truly been seven. Her mother remained ill both before birthing and after, and Walsu took her place in the gede field all that time. She never afterward came back to play, only in the evenings to eat and sleep. I saw her then and we could talk. She was proud of her work. I envied her and longed to go through the gate. I followed her to it and looked through it at the world. Now the walls of the compound seemed very close.

I told my grandmother Dosse that I wanted to go to work in the fields.

"You're too young."

"I'll be seven at the new year."

"Your mother made me promise not to let you go out."

Next time my mother visited the compound, I said, "Grandmother won't let me go out. I want to go work with Walsu."

"Never," my mother said. "You were born for better than that."

"What for?"

"You'll see."

She smiled at me. I knew she meant the House, where she worked. She had told me often of the wonderful things in the House, things that shone and were colored brightly, things that were thin and delicate, clean things. It was quiet in the House, she said. My mother herself wore a beautiful red scarf, her voice was soft, and her clothing and body were always clean and fresh.

"When will I see?"

I teased her until she said, "All right! I'll ask my lady."

"Ask her what?"

All I knew of my-lady was that she too was delicate and clean, and that my mother belonged to her in some particular way, of which she was proud. I knew my-lady had given my mother the red scarf.

"I'll ask her if you can come begin training at the House."

My mother said "the House" in a way that made me see it as a great sacred place like the place in our prayer: *May I enter in the clear house, in the rooms of peace.*

I was so excited I began to dance and sing, "I'm going to the House, to the House!" My mother slapped me to make me stop and scolded me for being wild. She said, "You are too young! You can't behave! If you get sent away from the House, you can never come back."

I promised to be old enough.

"You must do everything right," Yowa told me. "You must do everything I say when I say it. Never question. Never delay. If my lady sees that you're wild, she'll send you back here. And that will be the end of you forever."

I promised to be tame. I promised to obey at once in everything, and not to speak. The more frightening she made it, the more I desired to see the wonderful, shining House.

When my mother left I did not believe she would speak to my-lady. I was not used to promises being kept. But after some days she returned, and I heard her speaking to my grandmother. Dosse was angry at first, speaking loudly. I crept under the window of the hut to listen. I heard my grandmother weep. I was frightened and amazed. My grandmother was patient with me, always looked after me, and fed me well. It had never entered my mind that there was anything more to it than that, until I heard her crying. Her crying made me cry, as if I were part of her.

"You could let me keep her one more year," she said. "She's just a baby. I would never let her out the gate." She was pleading, as if she were powerless, not a grandmother. "She is my joy, Yowa!"

"Don't you want her to do well, then?"

"Just a year more. She's too wild for the House."

"She's run wild too long. She'll get sent out to the fields if she stays. A year of that and they won't have her at the House. She'll be dust. Anyhow, there's no use crying about it. I asked my lady, and she's expected. I can't go back without her."

"Yowa, don't let her come to harm," Dosse said very low, as if ashamed to say this to her daughter, and yet with strength in her voice.

"I'm taking her to keep her out of harm," my mother said. Then she called me, and I wiped my tears and came.

It is queer, but I do not remember my first walk through the world outside the compound or my first sight of the House. I suppose I was frightened and kept my eyes down, and everything was so strange to me that I did not understand what I saw. I know it was a number of days before my mother took me to show me to Lady Tazeu. She had to scrub me and train me and make sure I would not disgrace her. I was terrified when at last she took my hand, scolding me in a whisper all the time, and brought me out of the bondswomen's quarters, through halls and doorways of painted wood, into a bright, sunny room with no roof, full of flowers growing in pots.

I had hardly ever seen a flower, only the weeds in the kitchen gardens, and I stared and stared at them. My mother had to jerk my hand to make me look at the woman lying in a chair among the flowers, in clothes soft and brightly colored like the flowers. I could hardly tell them apart. The woman's hair was long and shining, and her skin was shining and black. My mother pushed me, and I did what she had made me practice over and over: I went and knelt down beside the chair and waited, and when the woman put out her long, narrow, soft hand, black above and azure on the palm, I touched my forehead to it. I was supposed to say "I am your slave Rakam, ma'am," but my voice would not come out.

"What a pretty little thing," she said. "So dark." Her voice changed a little on the last words.

"The Bosses came in . . . that night," Yowa said in a timid, smiling way, looking down as if embarrassed.

"No doubt about that," the woman said. I was able to glance up at her again. She was beautiful. I did not know a person could be so beautiful. I think she saw my wonder. She put out her long, soft hand again and caressed my cheek and neck. "Very, very pretty, Yowa," she said. "You did quite right to bring her here. Has she been bathed?"

She would not have asked that if she had seen me when I first came, filthy and smelling of the cowdung we made our fires with. She knew nothing of the compound at all. She knew nothing beyond the beza, the women's side of the House. She was kept there just as I had been kept in the compound, ignorant of anything outside. She had never smelled cowdung, as I had never seen flowers.

My mother assured her I was clean, and she said, "Then she can come to bed with me tonight. I'd like that. Will you like to come sleep with me, pretty little — " She glanced at my mother, who murmured, "Rakam." Ma'am pursed her lips at the name. "I don't like that," she murmured. "So ugly. Toti. Yes. You can be my new Toti. Bring her this evening, Yowa."

She had had a foxdog called Toti, my mother told me. Her pet had died. I did not know animals ever had names, and so it did not seem odd to me to be given an animal's name, but it did seem strange at first not to be Rakam. I could not think of myself as Toti.

That night my mother bathed me again and oiled my skin with sweet oil and dressed me in a soft gown, softer even than her red scarf. Again she scolded and warned me, but she was excited, too, and pleased with me, as we went to the beza again, through other halls, meeting some other bondswomen on the way, and to the lady's bedroom. It was a wonderful room, hung with mirrors and draperies and paintings. I did not understand what the mirrors were, or the paintings, and was frightened when I saw people in them. Lady Tazeu saw that I was frightened. "Come, little one," she said, making a place for me in her great, wide, soft bed strewn with pillows, "come and cuddle up." I crawled in beside her, and she stroked my hair and skin and held me in her warm, soft arms until I was comfortable and at ease. "There, there, little Toti," she said, and so we slept.

I became the pet of Lady Tazeu Wehoma Shomeke. I slept with her almost every night. Her husband was seldom home and when he was there did not come to her, preferring bondswomen for his pleasure. Sometimes she had my mother or other, younger bondswomen come into her bed, and she sent me away at those times, until I was older, ten or eleven, when she began to keep me and have me join in with them, teaching me how to be pleasured. She was gentle, but she was the mistress in love, and I was her instrument which she played.

I was also trained in household arts and duties. She taught me to sing with her, as I had a true voice. All those years I was never punished and never made to do hard work. I who had been wild in the compound was perfectly obedient in the Great House. I had been rebellious to my grandmother and impatient of her commands, but whatever my lady ordered me to do I gladly did. She held me fast to her by the only kind of love she had to give me. I thought that she was the Merciful Tual come down upon the earth. That is not a way of speaking, that is the truth. I thought she was a higher being, superior to myself.

Perhaps you will say that I could not or should not have had pleasure in being used without my consent by my mistress, and if I did, I should not speak of it, showing even so little good in so great an evil. But I knew nothing of consent or refusal. Those are freedom words.

She had one child, a son, three years older than I. She lived quite alone among us bondswomen. The Wehomas were nobles of the Islands, old-fashioned people whose women did not travel, so she was cut off from her family. The only company she had was when Owner Shomeke brought friends with him from the capital, but those were all men, and she could be with them only at table.

I seldom saw the Owner and only at a distance. I thought he too was a superior being, but a dangerous one.

As for Erod, the Young Owner, we saw him when he came to visit his mother daily or when he went out riding with his tutors. We girls would peep at him and giggle to each other when we were eleven or twelve, because he was a handsome boy, night-black and slender like his mother. I knew that he was afraid of his father, because I had heard him weep when he was with his mother. She would comfort him with candy and caresses, saying, "He'll be gone again soon, my darling." I too felt sorry for Erod, who was like a shadow, soft and harmless. He was sent off to school for a year at fifteen, but his father brought him back before the year was up. Bondsmen told us the Owner had beaten him cruelly and had forbidden him even to ride off the estate.

Bondswomen whom the Owner used told us how brutal he was, showing us where he had bruised and hurt them. They hated him, but my mother would not speak against him. "Who do you think you are?" she said to a girl who was complaining of his use of her. "A lady to be treated like glass?" And when the girl found herself pregnant, stuffed was the word we used, my mother had her sent back to the compound. I did not understand why. I thought Yowa was hard and jealous. Now I think she was also protecting the girl from our lady's jealousy.

I do not know when I understood that I was the Owner's daughter. Because she had kept that secret from our lady, my mother believed it was a secret from all. But the bondswomen all knew it. I do not know what I heard or overheard, but when I saw Erod, I would study him and think that I looked much more like our father than he did, for by then I knew what a father was. And I wondered that Lady Tazeu did not see it. But she chose to live in ignorance.

During these years I seldom went to the compound. After I had been a halfyear or so at the House, I was eager to go back and see Walsu and my grandmother and show them my fine clothes and clean skin and shining hair; but when I went, the pups I used to play with threw dirt and stones at me and tore my clothes. Walsu was in the fields. I had to hide in my grandmother's hut all day. I never wanted to go back. When my grandmother sent for me, I would go only with my mother and always stayed close by her. The people in the compound, even my grandmother, came to look coarse and foul to me. They were dirty and smelled strongly. They had sores, scars from punishment, lopped fingers, ears, or noses. Their hands and feet were coarse, with deformed nails. I was no longer used to people who looked so. We domestics of the Great House were entirely different from them, I thought. Serving the higher beings, we became like them.

When I was thirteen and fourteen Lady Tazeu still kept me in her bed, making love to me often. But also she had a new pet, the daughter of one of the cooks, a pretty little girl though white as clay. One night she made love to me for a long time in ways that she knew gave me great ecstasy of the body. When I lay exhausted in her arms she whispered "good-bye, good-bye," kissing me all over my face and breasts. I was too spent to wonder at this.

The next morning my lady called in my mother and myself to tell us that she intended to give me to her son for his seventeenth birthday. "I shall miss you terribly, Toti darling," she said, with tears in her eyes. "You have been my joy. But there isn't another girl on the place that I could let Erod have. You are the cleanest, dearest, sweetest of them all. I know you are a virgin," she meant a virgin to men, "and I know my boy will enjoy you. And he'll be kind to her, Yowa," she said earnestly to my mother. My mother bowed and said nothing. There was nothing she could say. And she said nothing to me. It was too late to speak of the secret she had been so proud of.

Lady Tazeu gave me medicine to prevent conception, but my mother, not trusting the medicine, went to my grandmother and brought me contraceptive herbs. I took both faithfully that week.

If a man in the House visited his wife he came to the beza, but if he wanted a bondswoman she was "sent across." So on the night of the Young Owner's birthday I was dressed all in red and led over, for the first time in my life, to the men's side of the House.

A Woman's Liberation

My reverence for my lady extended to her son, and I had been taught that owners were superior by nature to us. But he was a boy whom I had known since childhood, and I knew that his blood and mine were half the same. It gave me a strange feeling towards him.

I thought he was shy, afraid of his manhood. Other girls had tried to tempt him and failed. The women had told me what I was to do, how to offer myself and encourage him, and I was ready to do that. I was brought to him in his great bedroom, all of stone carved like lace, with high, thin windows of violet glass. I stood timidly near the door for a while, and he stood near a table covered with papers and screens. He came forward at last, took my hand, and led me to a chair. He made me sit down, and spoke to me standing, which was all improper, and confused my mind.

"Rakam," he said — "that's your name, isn't it?" — I nodded — "Rakam, my mother means only kindness, and you must not think me ungrateful to her, or blind to your beauty. But I will not take a woman who cannot freely offer herself. Intercourse between owner and slave is rape." And he talked on, talking beautifully, as when my lady read aloud from one of her books. I did not understand much, except that I was to come whenever he sent for me and sleep in his bed, but he would never touch me. And I was not to speak of this to anyone. "I am sorry, I am very sorry to ask you to lie," he said, so earnestly that I wondered if it hurt him to lie. That made him seem more like a god than a human being. If it hurt to lie, how could you stay alive?

"I will do just as you say, Lord Erod," I said.

So, most nights, his bondsmen came to bring me across. I would sleep in his great bed, while he worked at the papers on his table. He slept on a couch beneath the windows. Often he wanted to talk to me, sometimes for a long time, telling me his ideas. When he was in school in the capital he had become a member of a group of owners who wished to abolish slavery, called The Community. Getting wind of this, his father had ordered him out of school, sent him home, and forbidden him to leave the estate. So he too was a prisoner. But he corresponded constantly with others in The Community through the net, which he knew how to operate without his father's knowledge, or the government's.

His head was so full of ideas he had to speak them. Often Geu and Ahas, the young bondsmen who had grown up with him, who always came to fetch me across, stayed with us while he talked to all of us about slavery and freedom and many other things. Often I was sleepy, but I did listen, and heard much I did not know how to understand or even believe. He told us there was an organization among assets, called the Hame, that worked to steal slaves from the plantations. These slaves would be brought to members of The Community, who would make out false papers of ownership and treat them well, renting them to decent work in the cities. He told us about the cities, and I loved to hear all that. He told us about Yeowe Colony, saying that there was a revolution there among the slaves.

Of Yeowe I knew nothing. It was a great blue-green star that set after the sun or rose before it, brighter than the smallest of the moons. It was a name in an old song they sang in the compound:

A Woman's Liberation

O, O, Ye-o-we,
Nobody never comes back.

I had no idea what a revolution was. When Erod told me that it meant that assets on plantations in this place called Yeowe were fighting their owners, I did not understand how assets could do that. From the beginning it was ordained that there should be higher and lower beings, the Lord and the human, the man and the woman, the owner and the owned. All my world was Shomeke Estate and it stood on that one foundation. Who would want to overturn it? Everyone would be crushed in the ruins.

I did not like Erod to call assets slaves, an ugly word that took away our value. I decided in my mind that here on Werel we were assets, and in that other place, Yeowe Colony, there were slaves, worthless bondspeople, intractables. That was why they had been sent there. It made good sense.

By this you know how ignorant I was. Sometimes Lady Tazeu had let us watch shows on the holonet with her, but she watched only dramas, not the reports of events. Of the world beyond the estate I knew nothing but what I learned from Erod, and that I could not understand.

Erod liked us to argue with him. He thought it meant our minds were growing free. Geu was good at it. He would ask questions like, "But if there's no assets, who'll do the work?" Then Erod could answer at length. His eyes shone, his voice was eloquent. I loved him very much when he talked to us. He was beautiful and what he said was beautiful. It was like hearing the old men "singing the word," reciting the *Arkamye,* when I was a little pup in the compound.

I gave the contraceptives my lady gave me every month to girls who needed them. Lady Tazeu had aroused my sexuality and accustomed me to being used sexually. I missed her caresses. But I did not know how to approach any of the bondswomen, and they were afraid to approach me, since I belonged to the Young Owner. Being with Erod often, while he talked I yearned to him in my body. I lay in his bed and dreamed that he came and stooped over me and did with me as my lady used to do. But he never touched me.

Geu also was a handsome young man, clean and well mannered, rather dark-skinned, attractive to me. His eyes were always on me. But he would not approach me, until I told him that Erod did not touch me.

Thus I broke my promise to Erod not to tell anyone; but I did not think myself bound to keep promises, as I did not think myself bound to speak the truth. Honor of that kind was for owners, not for us.

After that, Geu used to tell me when to meet him in the attics of the House. He gave me little pleasure. He would not penetrate me, believing that he must save my virginity for our master. He had me take his penis in my mouth instead. He would turn away in his climax, for the slave's sperm must not defile the master's woman. That is the honor of a slave.

Now you may say in disgust that my story is all of such things, and there is far more to life, even a slave's life, than sex. That is very true. I can say only that it may be in our sexuality that we are most easily enslaved, both men and women. It may be there, even as free men and women, that we find freedom hardest to keep. The politics of the flesh are the roots of power.

I was young, full of health and desire for joy. And even now, even here, when I look back across the years from this world to that, to the compound and the House of Shomeke, I see images like those in a bright dream. I see my grandmother's big, hard hands. I see my mother smiling, the red scarf about her neck. I see my lady's black, silky body among the cushions. I smell the smoke of the cowdung fires, and the perfumes of the beza. I feel the soft, fine clothing on my young body, and my lady's hands and lips. I hear the old men singing the word, and my voice twining with my lady's voice in a love song, and Erod telling us of freedom. His face is illuminated with his vision. Behind him the windows of stone lace and violet glass keep out the night. I do not say I would go back. I would die before I would go back to Shomeke. I would die before I left this free world, my world, to go back to the place of slavery. But whatever I knew in my youth of beauty, of love, and of hope, was there.

And there it was betrayed. All that is built upon that foundation in the end betrays itself.

I was sixteen years old in the year the world changed.

The first change I heard about was of no interest to me except that my lord was excited about it, and so were Geu and Ahas and some of the other young bondsmen. Even my grandmother wanted to hear about it when I visited her. "That Yeowe, that slave world," she said, "they made freedom? They sent away their owners? They opened the gates? My lord, my sweet Lord Kamye, how can that be? Praise his name, praise his marvels!" She rocked back and forth as she squatted in the dust, her arms about her knees. She was an old, shrunken woman now. "Tell me!" she said.

I knew little else to tell her. "All the soldiers came back here," I said. "And those other people, those alemens, they're there on Yeowe. Maybe they're the new owners. That's all somewhere way out there," I said, flipping my hand at the sky.

"What's alemens?" my grandmother asked, but I did not know.

It was all mere words to me.

But when our Owner, Lord Shomeke, came home sick, that I understood. He came on a flyer to our little port. I saw him carried by on a stretcher, the whites showing in his eyes, his black skin mottled grey. He was dying of a sickness that was ravaging the cities. My mother, sitting with Lady Tazeu, saw a politician on the net who said that the alemens had brought the sickness to Werel. He talked so fearsomely that we thought everybody was going to die. When I told Geu about it he snorted. "Aliens, not alemens," he said, "and they've got nothing to do with it. My lord talked with the doctors. It's just a new kind of pusworm."

That dreadful disease was bad enough. We knew that any asset found to be infected with it was slaughtered at once like an animal and the corpse burned on the spot.

They did not slaughter the Owner. The House filled with doctors, and Lady Tazeu spent day and night by her husband's bed. It was a cruel death. It went on and on. Lord Shomeke in his suffering made terrible sounds, screams, howls. One would not believe a man could cry out hour after hour as he did. His flesh ulcerated and fell away, he went mad, but he did not die.

As Lady Tazeu became like a shadow, worn and silent, Erod filled with strength and excitement. Sometimes when we heard his father howling his eyes would shine. He would whisper, "Lady Tual have mercy on him," but he fed on those cries. I knew from Geu and Ahas, who had been brought up with him, how the father had tormented and despised him, and how Erod had vowed to be everything his father was not and to undo all he did.

But it was Lady Tazeu who ended it. One night she sent away the other attendants, as she often did, and sat alone with the dying man. When he began his moaning howl, she took her little sewing knife and cut his throat. Then she cut the veins in her arms across and across, and lay down by him, and so died. My mother was in the next room all night. She said she wondered a little at the silence, but was so weary that she fell asleep; and in the morning she went in and found them lying in their cold blood.

All I wanted to do was weep for my lady, but everything was in confusion. Everything in the sickroom must be burned, the doctors said, and the bodies must be burned without delay. The House was under quarantine, so only the priests of the House could hold the funeral. No one was to leave the estate for twenty days. But several of the doctors themselves left when Erod, who was now Lord Shomeke, told them what he intended to do. I heard some confused word of it from Ahas, but in my grief I paid little heed.

That evening, all the House assets stood outside the Lady's Chapel during the funeral service to hear the songs and prayers within. The Bosses and cut-frees had brought the people from the compound, and they stood behind us. We saw the procession come out, the white biers carried by, the pyres lighted, and the black smoke go up. Long before the smoke ceased rising, the new Lord Shomeke came to us all where we stood.

Erod stood up on the little rise of ground behind the chapel and spoke in a strong voice such as I had never heard from him. Always in the House it had been whispering in the dark. Now it was broad day and a strong voice. He stood there black and straight in his white mourning clothes. He was not yet twenty years old. He said, "Listen, you peo-ple: you have been slaves, you will be free. You have been my property, you will own your own lives now. This morning I sent to the Government the Order of Manumission for every asset on the estate, four hundred and eleven men, women, and chil-dren. If you will come to my office in the Counting House in the morning, I will give you your papers. Each of you is named in those papers as a free per-son. You can never be enslaved again. You are free to do as you please from tomorrow on. There will be money for each one of you to begin your new life with. Not what you deserve, not what you have earned in all your work for us, but what I have to give you. I am leaving Shomeke. I will go to the cap-ital, where I will work for the freedom of every slave on Werel. The Freedom Day that came to Yeowe is coming to us, and soon. Any of you who wish to come with me, come! There's work for us all to do!"

I remember all he said. Those are his words as he spoke them. When one does not read and has not had one's mind filled up by the images on the nets, words spoken strike down deep in the mind.

There was such a silence when he stopped speaking as I had never heard.

One of the doctors began talking, protesting to Erod that he must not break the quarantine.

"The evil has been burned away," Erod said, with a great gesture to the black smoke rising. "This has been an evil place, but no more harm will go forth from Shomeke!"

At that a slow sound began among the compound people standing behind us, and it swelled into a great noise of jubilation mixed with wailing, crying, shouting, singing. "Lord Kamye! Lord Kamye!" the men shouted. An old woman came forward: my grandmother. She strode through us House assets as if we were a field of grain. She stopped a good way from Erod. People fell silent to listen to the grandmother. She said, "Lord Master, are you turning us out of our homes?"

"No," he said. "They are yours. The land is yours to use. The profit of the fields is yours. This is your home, and you are free!"

At that the shouts rose up again so loud I cowered down and covered my ears, but I was crying and shouting too, praising Lord Erod and Lord Kamye in one voice with the rest of them.

We danced and sang there in sight of the burning pyres until the sun went down. At last the grandmothers and the cutfrees got the people to go back to the compound, saying they did not have their papers yet. We domestics went straggling back to the House, talking about tomorrow, when we would get our freedom and our money and our land.

All that next day Erod sat in the Counting House and made out the papers for each slave and counted out the same amount of money for each: a hundred kue in cash, and a draft for five hundred kue on the district bank, which could not be drawn for forty days. This was, he explained to each one, to save them from exploitation by the unscrupulous before they knew how best to use their money. He advised them to form a cooperative, to pool their funds, to run the estate democratically. "Money in the bank, Lord!" an old crippled man came out crying, jigging on his twisted legs. "Money in the bank, Lord!"

If they wanted, Erod said over and over, they could save their money and contact the Hame, who would help them buy passage to Yeowe with it.

"*O, O, Ye-o-we,*" somebody began singing, and they changed the words:

> "*Everybody's going to go.*
> *O, O, Ye-o-we,*
> *Everybody's going to go!*"

They sang it all day long. Nothing could change the sadness of it. I want to weep now, remembering that song, that day.

The next morning Erod left. He could not wait to get away from the place of his misery and begin his life in the capital working for freedom. He did not say good-bye to me. He took Geu and Ahas with him. The doctors and their aides and assets had all left the day before. We watched his flyer go up into the air.

We went back to the House. It was like something dead. There were no owners in it, no masters, no one to tell us what to do.

My mother and I went in to pack up our clothing. We had said little to each other, but felt we could not stay there. We heard other women running through the beza, rummaging in Lady Tazeu's rooms, going through her closets, laughing and screaming with excitement, finding jewelry and valuables. We heard men's voices in the hall: Bosses' voices. Without a word my mother and I took what we had in our hands and went out by a back door, slipped through the hedges of the garden, and ran all the way to the compound.

The great gate of the compound stood wide open.

How can I tell you what that was to us, to see that, to see that gate stand open? How can I tell you?

2. *Zeskra*

Erod knew nothing about how the estate was run, because the Bosses ran it. He was a prisoner too. He had lived in his screens, his dreams, his visions.

The grandmothers and others in the compound had spent all that night trying to make plans, to draw our people together so they could defend themselves. That morning when my mother and I came, there were bondsmen guarding the compound with weapons made of farm tools. The grandmothers and cutfrees had made an election of a headman, a strong, well-liked field hand. In that way they hoped to keep the young men with them.

By the afternoon that hope was broken. The young men ran wild. They went up to the House to loot it. The Bosses shot them from the windows, killing many; the others fled away. The Bosses stayed holed up in the House, drinking the wine of the Shomekes. Owners of other plantations were flying reinforcements to them. We heard the flyers land, one after another. The bondswomen who had stayed in the House were at their mercy now.

As for us in the compound, the gates were closed again. We had moved the great bars from the outside to the inside, so we thought ourselves safe for the night at least. But in the midnight they came with heavy tractors and pushed down the wall, and a hundred men or more, our Bosses and owners from all the plantations of the region, came swarming in. They were armed with guns. We fought them with farm tools and pieces of wood. One or two of them were hurt or killed. They killed as many of us as they wanted to kill and then began to rape us. It went on all night.

A group of men took all the old women and men and held them and shot them between the eyes, the way they kill cattle. My grandmother was one of them. I do not know what happened to my mother. I did not see any bondsmen living when they took me away in the morning. I saw white papers lying in the blood on the ground. Freedom papers.

Several of us girls and young women still alive were herded into a truck and taken to the port field. There they made us enter a flyer, shoving and using sticks, and we were carried off in the air. I was not then in my right mind. All I know of this is what the others told me later.

We found ourselves in a compound, like our compound in every way. I thought they had brought us back home. They shoved us in by the cutfrees' ladder. It was still morning and the hands were out at work, only the grandmothers and pups and old men in the compound. The grandmothers came to us fierce and scowling. I could not understand at first why they were all strangers. I looked for my grandmother.

They were frightened of us, thinking we must be runaways. Plantation slaves had been running away, the last years, trying to get to the cities. They thought we were intractables and would bring trouble with us. But they helped us clean ourselves, and gave us a place near the cutfrees' tower. There were no huts empty, they said. They told us this was Zeskra Estate. They did not want to hear about what had happened at Shomeke. They did not want us to be there. They did not need our trouble.

We slept there on the ground without shelter. Some of the bondsmen came across the ditch in the night and raped us because there was nothing to prevent them from it, no one to whom we were of any value. We were too weak and sick to fight them. One of us, a girl named Abye, tried to fight. The men beat her insensible. In the morning she could not talk or walk. She was left there when the Bosses came and took us away. Another girl was left behind too, a big farmhand with white scars on her head like parts in her hair. As we were going I looked at her and saw that it was Walsu, who had been my friend. We had not recognised each other. She sat in the dirt, her head bowed down.

Five of us were taken from the compound to the Great House of Zeskra, to the bondswomen's quarters. There for a while I had a little hope, since I knew how to be a good domestic asset. I did not know then how different Zeskra was from Shomeke. The House at Zeskra was full of people, full of owners and bosses. It was a big family, not a single Lord as at Shomeke but a dozen of them with their retainers and relations and visitors, so there might be thirty or forty men staying on the men's side and as many women in the beza, and a House staff of fifty or more. We were not brought as domestics, but as use-women.

After we were bathed we were left in the use-women's quarters, a big room without any private places. There were ten or more use-women already there. Those of them who liked their work were not glad to see us, thinking of us as rivals; others welcomed us, hoping we might take their places and they might be let to join the domestic staff. But none were very unkind, and some were kind, giving us clothes, for we had been naked all this time, and comforting the youngest of us, Mio, a little compound girl of ten or eleven whose white body was mottled all over with brown-and-blue bruises.

One of them was a tall woman called Sezi-Tual. She looked at me with an ironic face. Something in her made my soul awaken.

"You're not a dusty," she said. "You're as black as old Lord Devil Zeskra himself. You're a Bossbaby, aren't you?"

"No ma'am," I said. "A lord's child. And the Lord's child. My name is Rakam."

A Woman's Liberation

"Your Grandfather hasn't treated you too well lately," she said. "Maybe you should pray to the Merciful Lady Tual."

"I don't look for mercy," I said. From then on Sezi-Tual liked me, and I had her protection, which I needed.

We were sent across to the men's side most nights. When there were dinner parties, after the ladies left the dinner room we were brought in to sit on the owners' knees and drink wine with them. Then they would use us there on the couches or take us to their rooms. The men of Zeskra were not cruel. Some liked to rape, but most preferred to think that we desired them and wanted whatever they wanted. Such men could be satisfied, the one kind if we showed fear or submission, the other kind if we showed yielding and delight. But some of their visitors were another kind of man.

There was no law or rule against damaging or killing a use-woman. Her owner might not like it, but in his pride he could not say so: he was supposed to have so many assets that the loss of one or another did not matter at all. So some men whose pleasure lay in torture came to hospitable estates like Zeskra for their pleasure. Sezi-Tual, a favorite of the Old Lord, could and did protest to him, and such guests were not invited back. But while I was there, Mio, the little girl who had come with us from Shomeke, was murdered by a guest. He tied her down to the bed. He made the knot across her neck so tight that while he used her she strangled to death.

I will say no more of these things. I have told what I must tell. There are truths that are not useful.

All knowledge is local, my friend has said. Is it true, where is it true, that that child had to die in that way? Is it true, where is it true, that she did not have to die in that way?

I was often used by Lord Yaseo, a middle-aged man, who liked my dark skin, calling me "My Lady." Also he called me "Rebel," because what had happened at Shomeke they called a rebellion of the slaves. Nights when he did not send for me I served as a common-girl.

After I had been at Zeskra two years Sezi-Tual came to me one morning early. I had come back late from Lord Yaseo's bed. Not many others were there, for there had been a drinking party the night before, and all the common-girls had been sent for. Sezi-Tual woke me. She had strange hair, curly, in a bush. I remember her face above me, that hair curling out all about it. "Rakam," she whispered, "one of the visitor's assets spoke to me last night. He gave me this. He said his name is Suhame."

"Suhame," I repeated. I was sleepy. I looked at what she was holding out to me: some dirty crumpled paper. "I can't read!" I said, yawning, impatient.

But I looked at it and knew it. I knew what it said. It was the freedom paper. It was my freedom paper. I had watched Lord Erod write my name on it. Each time he wrote a name he had spoken it aloud so that we would know what he was writing. I remembered the big flourish of the first letter of both my names: Radosse Rakam. I took the paper in my hand, and my hand was shaking. "Where did you get this?" I whispered.

"Better ask this Suhame," she said. Now I heard

what that name meant: "from the Hame." It was a password name. She knew that too. She was watching me, and she bent down suddenly and leaned her forehead against mine, her breath catching in her throat. "If I can, I'll help," she whispered.

I met with "Suhame" in one of the pantries. As soon as I saw him I knew him: Ahas, who had been Lord Erod's favorite along with Geu. A slight, silent young man with dusty skin, he had never been much in my mind. He had watchful eyes, and I had thought when Geu and I spoke that he looked at us with ill will. Now he looked at me with a strange face, still watchful, yet blank.

"Why are you here with that Lord Boeba?" I said. "Aren't you free?"

"I am as free as you are," he said.

I did not understand him, then.

"Didn't Lord Erod protect even you?" I asked.

"Yes. I am a free man." His face began to come alive, losing that dead blankness it had when he first saw me. "Lady Boeba's a member of The Community. I work with the Hame. I've been trying to find people from Shomeke. We heard several of the women were here. Are there others still alive, Rakam?"

His voice was soft, and when he said my name my breath caught and my throat swelled. I said his name and went to him, holding him. "Ratual, Ramayo, Keo are still here," I said. He held me gently. "Walsu is in the compound," I said, "if she's still alive." I wept. I had not wept since Mio's death. He too was in tears.

We talked, then and later. He explained to me that we were indeed, by law, free, but that law meant nothing on the Estates. The government would not interfere between owners and those they claimed as their assets. If we claimed our rights, the Zeskras would probably kill us, since they considered us stolen goods and did not want to be shamed. We must run away or be stolen away, and get to the city, the capital, before we could have any safety at all.

We had to be sure that none of the Zeskra assets would betray us out of jealousy or to gain favor. Sezi-Tual was the only one I trusted entirely.

Ahas arranged our escape with Sezi-Tual's help. I pleaded once with her to join us, but she thought that since she had no papers she would have to live always in hiding, and that would be worse than her life at Zeskra.

"You could go to Yeowe," I said.

She laughed. "All I know about Yeowe is nobody ever came back. Why run from one hell to the next one?"

Ratual chose not to come with us; she was a favorite of one of the young lords and content to remain so. Ramayo, the oldest of us from Shomeke, and Keo, who was now about fifteen, wanted to come. Sezi-Tual went down to the compound and found that Walsu was alive, working as a field hand. Arranging her escape was far more difficult than ours. There was no escape from a compound. She could get away only in daylight, in the fields, under the over-seer's and the Boss's eyes. It was difficult even to talk to her, for the grandmothers were distrustful. But Sezi-Tual managed it, and Walsu told her she would do whatever she must do "to see her paper again."

Lady Boeba's flyer waited for us at the edge of a great gede field that had just been harvested. It was late summer. Ramayo, Keo, and I walked away from the House separately at different times of the morning. Nobody watched over us closely, as there was nowhere for us to go. Zeskra lies among other great estates, where a runaway slave would find no friends for hundreds of miles. One by one, taking different ways, we came through the fields and woods, crouching and hiding all the way to the flyer where Ahas waited for us. My heart beat and beat so I could not breathe. There we waited for Walsu.

"There!" said Keo, perched up on the wing of the flyer. She pointed across the wide field of stubble.

Walsu came running from the strip of trees on the far side of the field. She ran heavily, steadily, not as if she were afraid. But all at once she halted. She turned. We did not know why for a moment. Then we saw two men break from the shadow of the trees in pursuit of her.

She did not run from them, leading them towards us. She ran back at them. She leapt at them like a hunting cat. As she made that leap, one of them fired a gun. She bore one man down with her, falling. The other fired again and again. "In," Ahas said, "now." We scrambled into the flyer and it rose into the air, seemingly all in one instant, the same instant in which Walsu made that great leap, she too rising into the air, into her death, into her freedom.

3. *The City*

I had folded up my freedom paper into a tiny packet. I carried it in my hand all the time we were in the flyer and while we landed and went in a public car through the city streets. When Ahas found what I was clutching, he said I need not worry about it. Our manumission was on record in the Government Office and would be honored, here in the City. We were free people, he said. We were gareots, that is, owners who have no assets. "Just like Lord Erod," he said. That meant nothing to me. There was too much to learn. I kept hold of my freedom paper until I had a place to keep it safe. I have it still.

We walked a little way in the streets and then Ahas led us into one of the huge houses that stood side by side on the pavement. He called it a compound, but we thought it must be an owners' house. There a middle-aged woman welcomed us. She was pale-skinned, but talked and behaved like an owner, so that I did not know what she was. She said she was Ress, a rentswoman and an elderwoman of the house.

Rentspeople were assets rented out by their owners to a company. If they were hired by a big company, they lived in the company compounds, but there were many, many rentspeople in the City who worked for small companies or businesses they managed themselves, and they occupied buildings run for profit, called open compounds. In such places the occupants must keep curfew, the doors being locked at night, but that was all; they were self-governed. This was such an open compound. It was supported by The Community. Some of the occupants were rentspeople, but many were like us, gareots who had been slaves. Over a hundred people lived there in forty apartments. It was supervised by several women, whom I would have called grandmothers, but here they were called elderwomen.

On the estates deep in the country, deep in the past, where the life was protected by miles of land and by the custom of centuries and by determined ignorance, any asset was absolutely at the mercy of any owner. From there we had come into this great crowd of two million people where nothing and nobody was protected from chance or change, where we had to learn as fast as we could how to stay alive, but where our life was in our own hands.

I had never seen a street. I could not read a word. I had much to learn.

Ress made that clear at once. She was a City woman, quick-thinking and quick-talking, impatient, aggressive, sensitive. I could not like or understand her for a long time. She made me feel stupid, slow, a clod. Often I was angry at her.

There was anger in me now. I had not felt anger while I lived at Zeskra. I could not. It would have eaten me. Here there was room for it, but I found no use for it. I lived with it in silence. Keo and Ramayo had a big room together, I had a small one next to theirs. I had never had a room to myself. At first I felt lonely in it and as if ashamed, but soon I came to like it. The first thing I did freely, as a free woman, was to shut my door.

Nights, I would shut my door and study. Days, we had work training in the morning, classes in the afternoon: reading and writing, arithmetic, history. My work training was in a small shop which made boxes of paper and thin wood to hold cosmetics, candies, jewelry, and such things. I was trained in all the different steps and crafts of making and ornamenting the boxes, for that is how most work was done in the City, by artisans who knew all their trade. The shop was owned by a member of The Community. The older workers were rentspeople. When my training was finished I too would be paid wages.

Till then Lord Erod supported me as well as Keo and Ramayo and some men from Shomeke compound, who lived in a different house. Erod never came to the house. I think he did not want to see any of the people he had so disastrously freed. Ahas and Geu said he had sold most of the land at Shomeke and used the money for The Community and to make his way in politics, as there was now a Radical Party which favored emancipation.

Geu came a few times to see me. He had become a City man, dapper and knowing. I felt when he looked at me he was thinking I had been a use-woman at Zeskra, and I did not like to see him.

Ahas, whom I had never thought about in the old days, I now admired, knowing him brave, resolute, and kind. It was he who had looked for us, found us, rescued us. Owners had paid the money but Ahas had done it. He came often to see us. He was the only link that had not broken between me and my childhood.

And he came as a friend, a companion, never driving me back into my slave body. I was angry now at every man who looked at me as men look at women. I was angry at women who looked at me seeing me sexually. To Lady Tazeu all I had been was my body. At Zeskra that was all I had been. Even to Erod who would not touch me that was all I had been. Flesh to touch or not to touch, as they pleased. To use or not to use, as they chose. I hated the sexual parts of myself, my genitals and breasts and the swell of my hips and belly. Ever since I was a child, I had been dressed in soft clothing made to display all that sexuality of a woman's body. When I began to be paid and could buy or make my own clothing, I dressed in hard, heavy cloth. What I liked of myself was my hands, clever at their work, and my head, not clever at learning, but still learning, no matter how long it took.

What I loved to learn was history. I had grown up without any history. There was nothing at Shomeke or Zeskra but the way things were. Nobody knew anything about any time when things had been different. Nobody knew there was any place where things might be different. We were enslaved by the present time.

Erod had talked of change, indeed, but the owners were going to make the change. We were to be changed, we were to be freed, just as we had been owned. In history I saw that any freedom has been made, not given.

The first book I read by myself was a history of Yeowe, written very simply. It told about the days of the Colony, of the Four Corporations, of the terrible first century when the ships carried slave men to Yeowe and precious ores back. Slave men were so cheap then they worked them to death in a few years in the mines, bringing in new shipments continually. *O, O, Yeowe, nobody never comes back.* Then the Corporations began to send women slaves to work and breed, and over the years the assets spilled out of the compounds and made cities — whole great cities like this one I was living in. But not run by the owners or Bosses. Run by the assets, the way this house was run by us. On Yeowe the assets had belonged to the Corporations. They could rent their freedom by paying the Corporation a part of what they earned, the way sharecropper assets paid their owners in parts of Voe Deo. On Yeowe they called those assets freedpeople. Not free people, but freedpeople. And then, this history I was reading said, they began to think, why aren't we free people? So they made the revolution, the Liberation. It began on a plantation called Nadami, and spread from there. Thirty years they fought for their freedom. And just three years ago they had won the war, they had driven the Corporations, the owners, the bosses, off their world. They had danced and sung in the streets, freedom, freedom! This book I was reading (slowly, but reading it) had been printed there — there on Yeowe, the Free World. The Aliens had brought it to Werel. To me it was a sacred book.

I asked Ahas what it was like now on Yeowe, and he said they were making their government, writing a perfect Constitution to make all men equal under the Law.

On the net, on the news, they said they were fighting each other on Yeowe, there was no government at all, people were starving, savage tribesmen in the countryside and youth gangs in the cities running amuck, law and order broken down. Corruption, ignorance, a doomed attempt, a dying world, they said.

Ahas said that the Government of Voe Deo, which had fought and lost the war against Yeowe, now was afraid of a Liberation on Werel. "Don't believe any news," he counseled me. "Especially

don't believe the neareals. Don't ever go into them.
They're just as much lies as the rest, but if you feel
and see a thing, you will believe it. And they know
that. They don't need guns if they own our minds."
The owners had no reporters, no cameras on Yeowe,
he said; they invented their "news," using actors.
Only some of the Aliens of the Ekumen were
allowed on Yeowe, and the Yeowans were debating
whether they should send them away, keeping the
world they had won for themselves alone.

"But then what about us?" I said, for I had
begun dreaming of going there, going to the Free
World, when the Hame could charter ships and send
people.

"Some of them say assets can come. Others say
they can't feed so many, and would be overwhelmed. They're debating it democratically. It will
be decided in the first Yeowan elections, soon." Ahas
was dreaming of going there too. We talked together of our dream the way lovers talk of their love.

But there were no ships going to Yeowe now. The
Hame could not act openly and The Community was
forbidden to act for them. The Ekumen had offered
transportation on their own ships to anyone who
wanted to go, but the government of Voe Deo refused
to let them use any spaceport for that purpose. They
could carry only their own people. No Werelian was to
leave Werel.

It had been only forty years since Werel had at
last allowed the Aliens to land and maintain diplomatic relations. As I went on reading history I began
to understand a little of the nature of the dominant
people of Werel. The black-skinned race that conquered all the other peoples of the Great Continent,

and finally all the world, those who call themselves the owners, have lived in the belief that there is only one way to be. They have believed they are what people should be, do as people should do, and know all the truth that is known. All the other peoples of Werel, even when they resisted them, imitated them, trying to become them, and so became their property. When a people came out of the sky looking differently, doing differently, knowing differently, and would not let themselves be conquered or enslaved, the owner race wanted nothing to do with them. It took them four hundred years to admit that they had equals.

I was in the crowd at a rally of the Radical Party, at which Erod spoke, as beautifully as ever. I noticed a woman beside me in the crowd listening. Her skin was a curious orange-brown, like the rind of a pini, and the whites showed in the corners of her eyes. I thought she was sick — I thought of the pusworm, how Lord Shomeke's skin had changed and his eyes had shown their whites. I shuddered and drew away. She glanced at me, smiling a little, and returned her attention to the speaker. Her hair curled in a bush or cloud, like Sezi-Tual's. Her clothing was of a delicate cloth, a strange fashion. It came upon me very slowly what she was, that she had come here from a world unimaginably far. And the wonder of it was that for all her strange skin and eyes and hair and mind, she was human, as I am human: I had no doubt of that. I felt it. For a moment it disturbed me deeply. Then it ceased to trouble me and I felt a great curiosity, almost a yearning, a drawing to her. I wished to know her, to know what she knew.

In me the owner's soul was struggling with the free soul. So it will do all my life.

Keo and Ramayo stopped going to school after they had learned to read and write and use the calculator, but I kept on. When there were no more classes to take from the school the Hame kept, the teachers helped me find classes in the net. Though the government controlled such courses, there were fine teachers and groups from all over the world, talking about literature and history and the sciences and arts. Always I wanted more history.

Ress, who was a member of the Hame, first took me to the Library of Voe Deo. As it was open only to owners, it was not censored by the government. Freed assets, if they were light-skinned, were kept out by the librarians on one pretext or another. I was dark-skinned, and had learned here in the City to carry myself with an indifferent pride that spared one many insults and offenses. Ress told me to stride in as if I owned the place. I did so, and was given all privileges without question. So I began to read freely, to read any book I wanted in that great library, every book in it if I could. That was my joy, that reading. That was the heart of my freedom.

Beyond my work at the boxmaker's, which was well paid, pleasant, and among pleasant companions, and my learning and reading, there was not much to my life. I did not want more. I was lonely, but felt that loneliness was no high price to pay for what I wanted.

Ress, whom I had disliked, was a friend to me. I went with her to meetings of the Hame, and also to entertainments that I would have known nothing about without her guidance. "Come on, Bumpkin," she would say. "Got to educate the plantation pup." And she would take me to the makil theater, or to asset dance halls where the music was good. She always wanted to dance. I let her teach me, but was not very happy dancing. One night as we were dancing the "slow-go" her hands began pressing me to her, and looking in her face I saw the mask of sexual desire on it, soft and blank. I broke away. "I don't want to dance," I said.

We walked home. She came up to my room with me, and at my door she tried to hold and kiss me. I was sick with anger. "I don't want that!" I said.

"I'm sorry, Rakam," she said, more gently than I had ever heard her speak. "I know how you must feel. But you've got to get over that, you've got to have your own life. I'm not a man, and I do want you."

I broke in — "A woman used me before a man ever did. Did you ask me if I wanted you? I will never be used again!"

That rage and spite came bursting out of me like poison from an infection. If she had tried to touch me again, I would have hurt her. I slammed my door in her face. I went trembling to my desk, sat down, and began to read the book that was open on it.

Next day we were both ashamed and stiff. But Ress had patience under her City quickness and roughness. She did not try to make love to me again, but she got me to trust her and talk to her as I could not talk to anybody else. She listened intently and told me what she thought. She said, "Bumpkin, you have it all wrong. No wonder. How could you have got it right? You think sex is something that gets done to you. It's not. It's something you do. With somebody else. Not to them. You never had any sex. All you ever knew was rape."

"Lord Erod told me all that a long time ago," I said. I was bitter. "I don't care what it's called. I had enough of it. For the rest of my life. And I'm glad to be without it."

Ress made a face. "At twenty-two?" she said. "Maybe for a while. If you're happy, then fine. But think about what I said. It's a big part of life to just cut out."

"If I have to have sex, I can pleasure myself," I said, not caring if I hurt her. "Love has nothing to do with it."

"That's where you're wrong," she said, but I did not listen. I would learn from teachers and books which I chose for myself, but I would not take advice I had not asked for. I refused to be told what to do or what to think. If I was free, I would be free by myself. I was like a baby when it first stands up.

Ahas had been giving me advice too. He said it was foolish to pursue education so far. "There's nothing useful you can do with so much book learning," he said. "It's self-indulgent. We need leaders and members with practical skills."

"We need teachers!"

"Yes," he said, "but you knew enough to teach a year ago. What's the good of ancient history, facts about alien worlds? We have a revolution to make!"

I did not stop my reading, but I felt guilty. I took a class at the Hame school teaching illiterate assets and freedpeople to read and write, as I myself had been taught only three years before. It was hard work. Reading is hard for a grown person to learn, tired, at night, after work all day. It is much easier to let the net take one's mind over.

I kept arguing with Ahas in my mind, and one day I said to him, "Is there a Library on Yeowe?"

"I don't know."

"You know there isn't. The Corporations didn't leave any libraries there. They didn't have any. They were ignorant people who knew nothing but profit. Knowledge is a good in itself. I keep on learning so that I can bring my knowledge to Yeowe. If I could, I'd bring them the whole Library!"

He stared. "What owners thought, what owners did — that's all their books are about. They don't need that on Yeowe."

"Yes they do," I said, certain he was wrong, though again I could not say why.

At the school they soon called on me to teach history, one of the teachers having left. These classes went well. I worked hard preparing them. Presently I was asked to speak to a study group of advanced students, and that, too, went well. People were interested in the ideas I drew from history and the comparisons I had learned to make of our world with other worlds. I had been studying the way various peoples bring up their children, who takes the responsibility for them and how that responsibility is understood, since this seemed to me a place where a people frees or enslaves itself.

To one of these talks a man from the Embassy of the Ekumen came. I was frightened when I saw the alien face in my audience. I was worse frightened when I recognised him. He had taught the first course in Ekumenical History that I had taken in the net. I had listened to it devotedly though I never participated in the discussion. What I learned had had a great influence on me. I thought he would find me presumptuous for talking of things he truly knew. I stammered on through my lecture, trying not to see his white-cornered eyes.

He came up to me afterwards, introduced himself politely, complimented my talk, and asked if I had read such-and-such a book. He engaged me so deftly and kindly in conversation that I had to like and trust him. And he soon earned my trust. I needed his guidance, for much foolishness has been written and spoken, even by wise people, about the balance of power between men and women, on which depend the lives of children and the value of their education. He knew useful books to read, from which I could go on by myself.

His name was Esdardon Aya. He worked in some high position, I was not sure what, at the Embassy. He had been born on Hain, the Old World, humanity's first home, from which all our ancestors came.

Sometimes I thought how strange it was that I knew about such things, such vast and ancient matters, I who had not known anything outside the compound walls till I was six, who had not known the name of the country I lived in till I was eighteen! When I was new to the City someone had spoken of "Voe Deo," and I had asked, "Where is that?" They had all stared at me. A woman, a hard-voiced old City rentswoman, had said, "Here, Dusty. Right here's Voe Deo. Your country and mine!"

I told Esdardon Aya that. He did not laugh. "A country, a people," he said. "Those are strange and very difficult ideas."

"My country was slavery," I said, and he nodded.

By now I seldom saw Ahas. I missed his kind friendship, but it had all turned to scolding. "You're puffed up, publishing, talking to audiences all the time," he said. "You're putting yourself before our cause."

I said, "But I talk to people in the Hame, I write about things we need to know. Everything I do is for freedom."

"The Community is not pleased with that pamphlet of yours," he said, in a serious, counseling way, as if telling me a secret I needed to know. "I've been asked to tell you to submit your writings to the committee before you publish again. That press is run by hotheads. The Hame is causing a good deal of trouble to our candidates."

"Our candidates!" I said in a rage. "No owner is my candidate! Are you still taking orders from the Young Owner?"

That stung him. He said, "If you put yourself first, if you won't cooperate, you bring danger on us all."

"I don't put myself first — politicians and capitalists do that. I put freedom first. Why can't you cooperate with me? It goes two ways, Ahas!"

He left angry, and left me angry.

I think he missed my dependence on him. Perhaps he was jealous, too, of my independence, for he did remain Lord Erod's man. His was a loyal heart. Our disagreement gave us both much bitter pain. I wish I knew what became of him in the troubled times that followed.

There was truth in his accusation. I had found that I had the gift in speaking and writing of moving people's minds and hearts. Nobody told me that such a gift is as dangerous as it is strong. Ahas said I was putting myself first, but I knew I was not doing that. I was wholly in the service of the truth and of liberty. No one told me that the end cannot purify the means, since only the Lord Kamye knows what the end may be. My grandmother could have told me that. The *Arkamye* would have reminded me of it, but I did not often read in it, and in the City there were no old men singing the word, evenings. If there had been, I would not have heard them over the sound of my beautiful voice speaking the beautiful truth.

I believe I did no harm, except as we all did, in bringing it to the attention of the rulers of Voe Deo that the Hame was growing bolder and the Radical Party was growing stronger, and that they must move against us.

The first sign was a divisive one. In the open compounds, as well as the men's side and the women's side there were several apartments for couples. This was a radical thing. Any kind of marriage between assets was illegal. They were allowed to live in pairs only by their owners' indulgence. Assets' only legitimate loyalty was to their owner. The child did not belong to the mother, but to the owner. But since gareots were living in the same place as owned assets, these apartments for couples had been tolerated or ignored. Now suddenly the law was invoked, asset couples were arrested, fined if they were wage earners, separated, and sent to company-run compound houses. Ress and the other elderwomen who ran our house were fined and warned that if "immoral arrangements" were discovered again, they would be held responsible and sent to the labor camps. Two little children of one of the couples were not on the government's list and so were left, abandoned, when their parents were taken off. Keo and Ramayo took them in. They became wards of the women's side, as orphans in the compounds always did.

There were fierce debates about this in meetings of the Hame and The Community. Some said the right of assets to live together and to bring up their children was a cause the Radical Party should support. It was not directly threatening to ownership, and might appeal to the natural instincts of many owners, especially the women, who could not vote but who were valuable allies. Others said that private affections must be overridden by loyalty to the cause of liberty, and that any personal issue must take second place to the great issue of emancipation. Lord Erod spoke thus at a meeting. I rose to answer him. I said that there was no freedom without sexual freedom, and that until women were allowed and men were willing to take responsibility for their children, no woman, whether owner or asset, would be free.

"Men must bear the responsibility for the public side of life, the greater world the child will enter; women, for the domestic side of life, the moral and physical upbringing of the child. This is a division enjoined by God and Nature," Erod answered.

"Then will emancipation for a woman mean she's free to enter the beza, be locked in on the women's side?"

"Of course not," he began, but I broke in again, fearing his golden tongue — "Then what is freedom for a woman? Is it different from freedom for a man? Or is a free person free?"

A Woman's Liberation

The moderator was angrily thumping his staff, but some other asset women took up my question. "When will the Radical Party speak for us?" they said, and one elderwoman cried, "Where are your women, you owners who want to abolish slavery? Why aren't they here? Don't you let them out of the beza?"

The moderator pounded and finally got order restored. I was half-triumphant and half-dismayed. I saw Erod and also some of the people from the Hame now looking at me as an open troublemaker. And indeed my words had divided us. But were we not already divided?

A group of us women went home talking through the streets, talking aloud. These were my streets now, with their traffic and lights and dangers and life. I was a City woman, a free woman. That night I was an owner. I owned the City. I owned the future.

The arguments went on. I was asked to speak at many places. As I was leaving one such meeting, the Hainishman Esdardon Aya came to me and said in a casual way, as if discussing my speech, "Rakam, you're in danger of arrest."

I did not understand. He walked along beside me away from the others and went on: "A rumor has come to my attention at the Embassy. . . . The government of Voe Deo is about to change the status of manumitted assets. You're no longer to be considered gareots. You must have an owner-sponsor."

This was bad news, but after thinking it over I said, "I think I can find an owner to sponsor me. Lord Boeba, maybe."

"The owner-sponsor will have to be approved

by the government. . . . This will tend to weaken The Community both through the asset and the owner members. It's very clever, in its way," said Esdardon Aya.

"What happens to us if we don't find an approved sponsor?"

"You'll be considered runaways."

That meant death, the labor camps, or auction.

"O Lord Kamye," I said, and took Esdardon Aya's arm, because a curtain of dark had fallen across my eyes.

We had walked some way along the street. When I could see again I saw the street, the high houses of the City, the shining lights I had thought were mine.

"I have some friends," said the Hainishman, walking on with me, "who are planning a trip to the Kingdom of Bambur."

After a while I said, "What would I do there?"

"A ship to Yeowe leaves from there."

"To Yeowe," I said.

"So I hear," he said, as if we were talking about a streetcar line. "In a few years, I expect Voe Deo will begin offering rides to Yeowe. Exporting intractables, troublemakers, members of the Hame. But that will involve recognising Yeowe as a nation state, which they haven't brought themselves to do yet. They are, however, permitting some semilegitimate trade arrangements by their client states. . . . A couple of years ago, the King of Bambur bought one of the old Corporation ships, a genuine old Colony Trader. The King thought he'd like to visit the moons of Werel. But he found the moons boring. So he rented the ship to a consortium of scholars from the University of Bambur and businessmen from his capital. Some manufacturers in Bambur carry on a little trade with Yeowe in it, and some scientists at the university make scientific expeditions in it at the same time. Of course each trip is very expensive, so they carry as many scientists as they can whenever they go."

I heard all this not hearing it, yet understanding it.

"So far," he said, "they've gotten away with it."

He always sounded quiet, a little amused, yet not superior.

"Does The Community know about this ship?" I asked.

"Some members do, I believe. And people in the Hame. But it's very dangerous to know about. If Voe Deo were to find out that a client state was exporting valuable property . . . In fact, we believe they may have some suspicions. So this is a decision that can't be made lightly. It is both dangerous and irrevocable. Because of that danger, I hesitated to speak of it to you. I hesitated so long that you must make it very quickly. In fact, tonight, Rakam."

I looked from the lights of the City up to the sky they hid. "I'll go," I said. I thought of Walsu.

"Good," he said. At the next corner he changed the direction we had been walking, away from my house, towards the Embassy of the Ekumen.

I never wondered why he did this for me. He was a secret man, a man of secret power, but he always spoke truth, and I think he followed his own heart when he could.

As we entered the Embassy grounds, a great park softly illuminated in the winter night by groundlights, I stopped. "My books," I said. He looked his question. "I wanted to take my books to Yeowe," I said. Now my voice shook with a rush of tears, as if everything I was leaving came down to that one thing. "They need books on Yeowe, I think," I said.

After a moment he said, "I'll have them sent on our next ship. I wish I could put you on that ship," he added in a lower voice. "But of course the Ekumen can't give free rides to runaway slaves. . . . "

I turned and took his hand and laid my forehead against it for a moment, the only time in my life I ever did that of my own free will.

He was startled. "Come, come," he said, and hurried me along.

The Embassy hired Werelian guards, mostly veots, men of the old warrior caste. One of them, a grave, courteous, very silent man, went with me on the flyer to Bambur, the island kingdom east of the Great Continent. He had all the papers I needed. From the flyer port he took me to the Royal Space Observatory, which the King had built for his spaceship. There without delay I was taken to the ship, which stood in its great scaffolding ready to depart.

I imagine that they had made comfortable apartments up front for the King when he went to see the moons. The body of the ship, which had belonged to the Agricultural Plantation Corporation, still consisted of great compartments for the produce of the Colony. It would be bringing back grain from Yeowe in four of the cargo bays that now held farm machinery made in Bambur. The fifth compartment held assets.

The cargo bay had no seats. They had laid felt pads on the floor, and we lay down and were strapped to stanchions, as cargo would have been.

There were about fifty "scientists." I was the last to come aboard and be strapped in. The crew were hasty and nervous and spoke only the language of Bambur. I could not understand the instructions we were given. I needed very badly to relieve my bladder, but they had shouted "No time, no time!" So I lay in torment while they closed the great doors of the bay, which made me think of the doors of Shomeke compound. Around me people called out to one another in their language. A baby screamed. I knew that language. Then the great noise began, beneath us. Slowly I felt my body pressed down on the floor, as if a huge soft foot were stepping on me, till my shoulder blades felt as if they were cutting into the mat, and my tongue pressed back into my throat as if to choke me, and with a sharp stab of pain and hot relief my bladder released its urine.

Then we began to be weightless — to float in our bonds. Up was down and down was up, either was both or neither. I heard people all around me calling out again, saying one another's names, saying what must be, "Are you all right? Yes, I'm all right." The baby had never ceased its fierce, piercing yells. I began to feel at my restraints, for I saw the woman next to me sitting up and rubbing her arms and chest where the straps had held her. But a great blurry voice came bellowing over the loudspeaker, giving orders in the language of Bambur and then in Voe Dean: "Do not unfasten the straps! Do not attempt to move about! The ship is under attack! The situation is extremely dangerous!"

So I lay floating in my little mist of urine, listening to the strangers around me talk, understanding nothing. I was utterly miserable, and yet fearless as I had never been. I was carefree. It was like dying. It would be foolish to worry about anything while one died.

The ship moved strangely, shuddering, seeming to turn. Several people were sick. The air filled with the smell and tiny droplets of vomit. I freed my hands enough to draw the scarf I was wearing up over my face as a filter, tucking the ends under my head to hold it.

Inside the scarf I could no longer see the huge vault of the cargo bay stretching above or below me, making me feel I was about to fly or fall into it. It smelled of myself, which was comforting. It was the scarf I often wore when I dressed up to give a talk, fine gauze, pale red with a silver thread woven in at intervals. When I bought it at a City market, paying my own earned money for it, I had thought of my mother's red scarf, given her by Lady Tazeu. I thought she would have liked this one, though it was not as bright. Now I lay and looked into the pale red dimness it made of the vault, starred with the lights at the hatches, and thought of my mother, Yowa. She had probably been killed that morning in the compound. Perhaps she had been carried to another estate as a use-woman, but Ahas had never found any trace of her. I thought of the way she had of carrying her head a little to the side, deferent yet alert, gracious. Her eyes had been full and bright, "eyes that hold the seven moons," as the song says. I thought then: But I will never see the moons again.

At that I felt so strange that to comfort myself and distract my mind I began to sing under my breath, there alone in my tent of red gauze warm with my own breath. I sang the freedom songs we sang in the Hame, and then I sang the love songs Lady Tazeu had taught me. Finally I sang "O, O, Yeowe," softly at first, then a little louder. I heard a voice somewhere out in that soft red mist world join in with me, a man's voice, then a woman's. Assets from Voe Deo all know that song. We sang it together. A Bambur man's voice picked it up and put words in his own language to it, and others joined in singing it. Then the singing died away. The baby's crying was weak now. The air was very foul.

We learned many hours later, when at last clean air entered the vents and we were told we could release our bonds, that a ship of the Voe Dean Space Defense Fleet had intercepted the freighter's course just above the atmosphere and ordered it to stop. The captain chose to ignore the signal. The warship had fired, and though nothing hit the freighter the blast had damaged the controls. The freighter had gone on, and had seen and heard nothing more of the warship. We were now about eleven days from Yeowe. The warship, or a group of them, might be in wait for us near Yeowe. The reason they gave for ordering the freighter to halt was "suspected contraband merchandise."

That fleet of warships had been built centuries ago to protect Werel from the attacks they expected from the Alien Empire, which is what they then called the Ekumen. They were so frightened by that imagined threat that they put all their energy into the technology of space flight; and the colonisation of Yeowe was a result. After four hundred years without any threat of attack, Voe Deo had finally let the Ekumen send envoys and ambassadors. They had used the Defense Fleet to transport troops and weapons during the War of Liberation. Now they were using them the way estate owners used hunting dogs and hunting cats, to hunt down runaway slaves.

I found the two other Voe Deans in the cargo bay, and we moved our "bedstraps" together so we could talk. Both of them had been brought to Bambur by the Hame, who had paid their fare. It had not occurred to me that there was a fare to be paid. I knew who had paid mine.

"Can't fly a spaceship on love," the woman said. She was a strange person. She really was a scientist. Highly trained in chemistry by the company that rented her, she had persuaded the Hame to send her to Yeowe because she was sure her skills would be needed and in demand. She had been making higher wages than many gareots did, but she expected to do still better on Yeowe. "I'm going to be rich," she said.

The man, only a boy, a mill hand in a northern city, had simply run away and had the luck to meet people who could save him from death or the labor camps. He was sixteen, ignorant, noisy, rebellious, sweet-natured. He became a general favorite, like a puppy. I was in demand because I knew the history of Yeowe and through a man who knew both our languages I could tell the Bamburs something about where they were going — the centuries of Corporation slavery, Nadami, the War, the Liberation. Some of them were rentspeople from the cities, others were a group of estate slaves bought at auction by the Hame with false money and under a false name and hurried onto this flight, knowing very little of where they were going. It was that trick that had drawn Voe Deo's attention to this flight.

Yoke, the mill boy, speculated endlessly about how the Yeowans would welcome us. He had a story, half a joke, half a dream, about the bands playing and the speeches and the big dinner they would have for us. The dinner grew more and more elaborate as the days went on. They were long, hungry days, floating in the featureless great space of the cargo bay, marked only by the alternation every twelve hours of brighter and dimmer lighting and the issuing of two meals during the "day," food and water in tubes you squeezed into your mouth. I did not think much about what might happen. I was between happenings. If the warships found us, we would probably die. If we got to Yeowe, it would be a new life. Now we were floating.

4. *Yeowe*

The ship came down safe at the Port of Yeowe. They unloaded the crates of machinery first, then the other cargo. We came out staggering and holding on to one another, not able to stand up to the great pull of this new world drawing us down to its center, blinded by the light of the sun that we were closer to than we had ever been.

"Over here! Over here!" a man shouted. I was grateful to hear my language, but the Bamburs looked apprehensive.

Over here — in here — strip — wait — All we heard when we were first on the Free World was orders. We had to be decontaminated, which was painful and exhausting. We had to be examined by doctors. Anything we had brought with us had to be decontaminated and examined and listed. That did not take long for me. I had brought the clothes I wore and had worn for two weeks now. I was glad to get decontaminated. Finally we were told to stand in line in one of the big empty cargo sheds. The sign over the doors still read APCY — Agricultural Plantation Corporation of Yeowe. One by one we were processed for entry. The man who processed me was short, white, middle-aged, with spectacles, like any clerk asset in the City, but I looked at him with reverence. He was the first Yeowan I had spoken to. He asked me questions from a form and wrote down my answers. "Can you read?" — "Yes." — "Skills?" — I stammered a moment and said, "Teaching — I can teach reading and history." He never looked up at me.

I was glad to be patient. After all, the Yeowans had not asked us to come. We were admitted only because they knew if they sent us back, we would die horribly in a public execution. We were a profitable cargo to Bambur, but to Yeowe we were a problem. But many of us had skills they must need, and I was glad they asked us about them.

When we had all been processed, we were separated into two groups: men and women. Yoke hugged me and went off to the men's side laughing and waving. I stood with the women. We watched all the men led off to the shuttle that went to the Old Capital. Now my patience failed and my hope darkened. I prayed, "Lord Kamye, not here, not here too!" Fear made me angry. When a man came giving us orders again, come on, this way, I went up to him and said, "Who are you? Where are we going? We are free women!"

He was a big fellow with a round, white face and bluish eyes. He looked down at me, huffy at first, then smiling. "Yes, Little Sister, you're free," he said. "But we've all got to work, don't we? You ladies are going south. They need people on the rice plantations. You do a little work, make a little money, look around a little, all right? If you don't like it down there, come on back. We can always use more pretty little ladies round here."

I had never heard the Yeowan country accent, a singing, blurry softening, with long, clear vowels. I had never heard asset women called ladies. No one had ever called me Little Sister. He did not mean the word "use" as I took it, surely. He meant well. I was bewildered and said no more. But the chemist, Tualtak, said, "Listen, I'm no field hand, I'm a trained scientist —"

"Oh, you're all scientists," the Yeowan said with his big smile. "Come on now, ladies!" He strode ahead, and we followed. Tualtak kept talking. He smiled and paid no heed.

We were taken to a train car waiting on a siding. The huge, bright sun was setting. All the sky was orange and pink, full of light. Long shadows ran black along the ground. The warm air was dusty and sweet-smelling. While we stood waiting to climb up into the car I stooped and picked up a little reddish stone from the ground. It was round, with a tiny stripe of white clear through it. It was a piece of Yeowe. I held Yeowe in my hand. That little stone, too, I still have.

Our car was shunted along to the main yards

and hooked onto a train. When the train started we were served dinner, soup from great kettles wheeled through the car, bowls of sweet, heavy marsh rice, pini fruit — a luxury on Werel, here a commonplace. We ate and ate. I watched the last light die away from the long, rolling hills that the train was passing through. The stars came out. No moons. Never again. But I saw Werel rising in the east. It was a great blue-green star, looking as Yeowe looks from Werel. But you would never see Yeowe rising after sunset. Yeowe followed the sun.

I'm alive and I'm here, I thought. I'm following the sun. I let the rest go, and fell asleep to the swaying of the train.

We were taken off the train on the second day at a town on the great river Yot. Our group of twenty-three was separated there, and ten of us were taken by oxcart to a village, Hagayot. It had been an APCY compound, growing marsh rice to feed the Colony slaves. Now it was a cooperative village, growing marsh rice to feed the Free People. We were enrolled as members of the cooperative. We lived share and share alike with the villagers until payout, when we could pay them back what we owed the cooperative.

It was a reasonable way to handle immigrants without money who did not know the language or who had no skills. But I did not understand why they had ignored our skills. Why had they sent the men from Bambur plantations, field hands, into the city, not here? Why only women?

I did not understand why, in a village of free people, there was a men's side and a women's side, with a ditch between them.

I did not understand why, as I soon discovered, the men made all the decisions and gave all the orders. But, it being so, I did understand that they were afraid of us Werelian women, who were not used to taking orders from our equals. And I understood that I must take orders and not even look as if I thought of questioning them. The men of Hagayot Village watched us with fierce suspicion and a whip as ready as any Boss's. "Maybe you told men what to do back over there," the foreman told us the first morning in the fields. "Well, that's back over there. That's not here. Here we free people work together. You think you're Bosswomen. There aren't any Bosswomen here."

There were grandmothers on the women's side, but they were not the powers our grandmothers had been. Here, where for the first century there had been no slave women at all, the men had had to make their own life, set up their own powers. When women slaves at last were sent into those slave-kingdoms of men, there was no power for them at all. They had no voice. Not till they got away to the cities did they ever have a voice on Yeowe.

I learned silence.

But it was not as bad for me and Tualtak as for our eight Bambur companions. We were the first immigrants any of these villagers had ever seen. They knew only one language. They thought the Bambur women were witches because they did not talk "like human beings." They whipped them for talking to each other in their own language.

I will confess that in my first year on the Free World my heart was as low as it had been at Zeskra. I hated standing all day in the shallow water of the rice paddies. Our feet were always sodden and swollen and full of tiny burrowing worms we had to pick out every night. But it was needed work and not too hard for a healthy woman. It was not the work that bore me down.

Hagayot was not a tribal village, not as conservative as some of the old villages I learned about later. Girls here were not ritually raped, and a woman was safe on the women's side. She "jumped the ditch" only with a man she chose. But if a woman went anywhere alone, or even got separated from the other women working in the paddies, she was supposed to be "asking for it," and any man thought it his right to force himself on her.

I made good friends among the village women and the Bamburs. They were no more ignorant than I had been a few years before and some were wiser than I would ever be. There was no possibility of having a friend among men who thought themselves our owners. I could not see how life here would ever change. My heart was very low, nights, when I lay among the sleeping women and children in our hut and thought, Is this what Walsu died for?

In my second year there, I resolved to do what I could to keep above the misery that threatened me. One of the Bambur women, meek and slow of understanding, whipped and beaten by both women and men for speaking her language, had drowned in one of the great rice paddies. She had lain down there in the warm shallow water not much deeper than her ankles, and had drowned. I feared that yielding, that water of despair. I made up my mind to use my skill, to teach the village women and children to read.

I wrote out some little primers on rice cloth and made a game of it for the little children, first. Some of the older girls and women were curious. Some of them knew that people in the towns and cities could read. They saw it as a mystery, a witchcraft that gave the city people their great power. I did not deny this.

For the women, I first wrote down verses and passages of the *Arkamye,* all I could remember, so that they could have it and not have to wait for one of the men who called themselves "priests" to recite it. They were proud of learning to read these verses. Then I had my friend Seugi tell me a story, her own recollection of meeting a wild hunting cat in the marshes as a child. I wrote it down, entitling it "The Marsh Lion, by Aro Seugi," and read it aloud to the author and a circle of girls and women. They marveled and laughed. Seugi wept, touching the writing that held her voice.

The chief of the village and his headmen and foremen and honorary sons, all the hierarchy and government of the village, were suspicious and not pleased by my teaching, yet did not want to forbid me. The government of Yotebber Region had sent word that they were establishing country schools where village children were to be sent for half the year. The village men knew that their sons would be advantaged if they could already read and write when they went there.

The Chosen Son, a big, mild, pale man, blind in one eye from a war wound, came to me at last. He wore his coat of office, a tight, long coat such as Werelian owners had worn three hundred years ago. He told me that I should not teach girls to read, only boys.

I told him I would teach all the children who wanted to learn or none of them.

"Girls do not want to learn this," he said.

"They do. Fourteen girls have asked to be in my class. Eight boys. Do you say girls do not need religious training, Chosen Son?"

This gave him pause. "They should learn the life of the Merciful Lady," he said.

"I will write the Life of Tual for them," I said at once. He walked away, saving his dignity.

I had little pleasure in my victory, such as it was. At least I went on teaching.

Tualtak was always at me to run away, run away to the city downriver. She had grown very thin, for she could not digest the heavy food. She hated the work and the people. "It's all right for you, you were a plantation pup, a dusty, but I never was, my mother was a rentswoman, we lived in fine rooms on Haba Street, I was the brightest trainee they ever had in the laboratory," and on and on, over and over, living in the world she had lost.

Sometimes I listened to her talk about running away. I tried to remember the maps of Yeowe in my lost books. I remembered the great river, the Yot, running from far inland three thousand kilos to the South Sea. But where were we on its vast length, how far from Yotebber City on its delta? Between Hagayot and the city might be a hundred villages like this one. "Have you been raped?" I asked Tualtak.

She took offense. "I'm a rentswoman, not a use-woman," she snapped.

I said, "I was a use-woman for two years. If I was raped again, I would kill the man or kill myself. I think two Werelian women walking alone here would be raped. I can't do it, Tualtak."

"It can't all be like this place!" she cried, so desperate that I felt my own throat close up with tears.

"Maybe when they open the schools — there will be people from the cities then —" It was all I had to offer her, or myself, as hope. "Maybe if the harvest's good this year, if we can get our money, we can get on the train. . . ."

That indeed was our best hope. The problem was to get our money from the chief and his cohorts. They kept the cooperative's income in a stone hut which they called the Bank of Hagayot, and only they ever saw the money. Each individual had an account, and they kept tally faithfully, the old Banker Headman scratching your account out in the dirt if you asked for it. But women and children could not withdraw money from their account. All we could get was a kind of scrip, clay pieces marked by the Banker Headman, good to buy things from one another, things people in the village made, clothes, sandals, tools, bead necklaces, rice beer. Our real money was safe, we were told, in the bank. I thought of that old lame bondsman at Shomeke, jigging and singing, "Money in the bank, Lord! Money in the bank!"

Before we ever came, the women had resented this system. Now there were nine more women resenting it.

One night I asked my friend Seugi, whose hair was as white as her skin, "Seugi, do you know what happened at a place called Nadami?"

"Yes," she said. "The women opened the door. All the women rose up and then the men rose up against the Bosses. But they needed weapons. And a woman ran in the night and stole the key from the owner's box and opened the door of the strong place where the Bosses kept their guns and bullets, and she held it open with the strength of her body, so that the slaves could arm themselves. And they killed the Corporations and made that place, Nadami, free."

"Even on Werel they tell that story," I said. "Even there women tell about Nadami, where the women began the Liberation. Men tell it too. Do men here tell it? Do they know it?"

Seugi and the other women nodded.

"If a woman freed the men of Nadami," I said, "maybe the women of Hagayot can free their money."

Seugi laughed. She called out to a group of grandmothers, "Listen to Rakam! Listen to this!"

After plenty of talk for days and weeks, it ended in a delegation of women, thirty of us. We crossed the ditch bridge onto the men's side and ceremoniously asked to see the chief. Our principal bargaining counter was shame. Seugi and other village women did the speaking, for they knew how far they could shame the men without goading them into anger and retaliation. Listening to them, I heard dignity speak to dignity, pride speak to pride. For the first time since I came to Yeowe I felt I was one of these people, that this pride and dignity were mine.

Nothing happens fast in a village. But by the next harvest, the women of Hagayot could draw their own earned share out of the bank in cash.

"Now for the vote," I said to Seugi, for there was

no secret ballot in the village. When there was a regional election, even in the worldwide Ratification of the Constitution, the chiefs polled the men and filled out the ballots. They did not even poll the women. They wrote in the votes they wanted cast.

But I did not stay to help bring about that change at Hagayot. Tualtak was really ill and half-crazy with her longing to get out of the marshes, to the city. And I too longed for that. So we took our wages, and Seugi and other women drove us in an oxcart on the causeway across the marshes to the freight station. There we raised the flag that signaled the next train to stop for passengers.

It came along in a few hours, a long train of boxcars loaded with marsh rice, heading for the mills of Yotebber City. We rode in the crew car with the train crew and a few other passengers, village men. I had a big knife in my belt, but none of the men showed us any disrespect. Away from their compounds they were timid and shy. I sat up in my bunk in that car watching the great, wild, plumy marshes whirl by, and the villages on the banks of the wide river, and wished the train would go on forever.

But Tualtak lay in the bunk below me, coughing and fretful. When we got to Yotebber City she was so weak I knew I had to get her to a doctor. A man from the train crew was kind, telling us how to get to the hospital on the public cars. As we rattled through the hot, crowded city streets in the crowded car, I was still happy. I could not help it.

At the hospital they demanded our citizen's registration papers.

I had never heard of such papers. Later I found

that ours had been given to the chiefs at Hagayot, who had kept them, as they kept all "their" women's papers. At the time, all I could do was stare and say, "I don't know anything about registration papers."

I heard one of the women at the desk say to the other, "Lord, how dusty can you get?"

I knew what we looked like. I knew we looked dirty and low. I knew I seemed ignorant and stupid. But when I heard that word "dusty" my pride and dignity woke up again. I put my hand into my pack and brought out my freedom paper, that old paper with Erod's writing on it, all crumpled and folded, all dusty.

"This is my Citizen's Registration paper," I said in a loud voice, making those women jump and turn. "My mother's blood and my grandmother's blood is on it. My friend here is sick. She needs a doctor. Now bring us to a doctor!"

A thin little woman came forward from the corridor. "Come on this way," she said. One of the deskwomen started to protest. This little woman give her a look.

We followed her to an examination room.

"I'm Dr. Yeron," she said, then corrected herself. "I'm serving as a nurse," she said. "But I am a doctor. And you — you come from the Old World? from Werel? Sit down there, now, child, take off your shirt. How long have you been here?"

Within a quarter of an hour she had diagnosed Tualtak and got her a bed in a ward for rest and observation, found out our histories, and sent me off with a note to a friend of hers who would help me find a place to live and a job.

"Teaching!" Dr. Yeron said. "A teacher! Oh, woman, you are rain to the dry land!"

Indeed the first school I talked to wanted to hire me at once, to teach anything I wanted. Because I come of a capitalist people, I went to other schools to see if I could make more money at them. But I came back to the first one. I liked the people there.

Before the War of Liberation, the cities of Yeowe, which were cities of Corporation-owned assets who rented their own freedom, had had their own schools and hospitals and many kinds of training programs. There was even a University for assets in the Old Capital. The Corporations, of course, had controlled all the information that came to such institutions, and watched and censored all teaching and writing, keeping everything aimed towards the maximization of their profits. But within that narrow frame the assets had been free to use the information they had as they pleased, and city Yeowans had valued education deeply. During the long war, thirty years, all that system of gathering and teaching knowledge had broken down. A whole generation grew up learning nothing but fighting and hiding, famine and disease. The head of my school said to me, "Our children grew up illiterate, ignorant. Is it any wonder the plantation chiefs just took over where the Corporation Bosses left off? Who was to stop them?"

These men and women believed with a fierce passion that only education would lead to freedom. They were still fighting the War of Liberation.

Yotebber City was a big, poor, sunny, sprawling city with wide streets, low buildings, and huge old shady trees. The traffic was mostly afoot, with cycles tinging and public cars clanging along among the slow crowds. There were miles of shacks and shanties down in the old floodplain of the river behind the levees, where the soil was rich for gardening. The center of the city was on a low rise, the mills and train yards spreading out from it. Downtown it looked like the City of Voe Deo, only older and poorer and gentler. Instead of big stores for owners, people bought and sold everything from stalls in open markets. The air was soft here in the south, a warm, soft sea air full of mist and sunlight. I stayed happy. I have by the grace of the Lord a mind that can leave misfortune behind, and I was happy in Yotebber City.

Tualtak recovered her health and found a good job as a chemist in a factory. I saw her seldom, as our friendship had been a matter of necessity, not choice. Whenever I saw her she talked about Haba Street and her laboratory on Werel and complained about her work and the people here.

Dr. Yeron did not forget me. She wrote a note and told me to come visit her, which I did. Presently, when I was settled, she asked me to come with her to a meeting of an educational society. This, I found, was a group of democrats, mostly teachers, who sought to work against the autocratic power of the tribal and regional chiefs under the new Constitution, and to counteract what they called the slave mind, the rigid, misogynistic hierarchy that I had encountered in Hagayot. My experience was useful to them, for they were all city people who had met the slave mind only when they found themselves governed by it. The women of the group were the angriest. They had lost the most at

Liberation and now had less to lose. In general the men were gradualists, the women ready for revolution. As a Werelian, ignorant of politics on Yeowe, I listened and did not talk. It was hard for me not to talk. I am a talker, and sometimes I had plenty to say. But I held my tongue and heard them. They were people worth hearing.

Ignorance defends itself savagely, and illiteracy, as I well knew, can be shrewd. Though the Chief, the President of Yotebber Region, elected by a manipulated ballot, might not understand our counter-manipulations of the school curriculum, he did not waste much energy trying to control the schools, merely sending his inspectors to meddle with our classes and censor our books. But what he saw as important was the fact that, just as the Corporations had, he controlled the net. The news, the information programs, the puppets of the neareals, all danced to his strings. Against that, what harm could a lot of teachers do? Parents who had no schooling had children who entered the net to hear and see and feel what the Chief wanted them to know: that freedom is obedience to leaders, that virtue is violence, that manhood is domination. Against the enactment of such truths in daily life and in the heightened sensational experience of the neareals, what good were words?

"Literacy is irrelevant," one of our group said sorrowfully. "The chiefs have jumped right over our heads into the postliterate information technology."

I brooded over that, hating her fancy words, *irrelevant*, *postliterate*, because I was afraid she was right.

To the next meeting of our group, to my surprise; an Alien came: the Sub-Envoy of the Ekumen. He was supposed to be a great feather in our Chief's cap, sent down from the Old Capital apparently to support the Chief's stand against the World Party, which was still strong down here and still clamoring that Yeowe should keep out all foreigners. I had heard vaguely that such a person was here, but I had not expected to meet him at a gathering of subversive schoolteachers.

He was a short man, red-brown, with white corners to his eyes, but handsome if one could ignore that. He sat in the seat in front of me. He sat perfectly still, as if accustomed to sitting still, and listened without speaking, as if accustomed to listening. At the end of the meeting he turned around and his queer eyes looked straight at me.

"Radosse Rakam?" he said.

I nodded, dumb.

"I'm Yehedarhed Havzhiva," he said. "I have some books for you from old music."

I stared. I said, "Books?"

"From old music," he said again. "Esdardon Aya, on Werel."

"My books?" I said.

He smiled. He had a broad, quick smile.

"Oh, where?" I cried.

"They're at my house. We can get them tonight, if you like. I have a car." There was something ironic and light in how he said that, as if he was a man who did not expect to have a car, though he might enjoy it.

Dr. Yeron came over. "So you found her," she said to the Sub-Envoy. He looked at her with such a bright face that I thought, these two are lovers.

Though she was much older than he, there was nothing unlikely in the thought. Dr. Yeron was a magnetic woman. It was odd to me to think it, though, for my mind was not given to speculating about people's sexual affairs. That was no interest of mine.

He put his hand on her arm as they talked, and I saw with peculiar intensity how gentle his touch was, almost hesitant, yet trustful. That is love, I thought. Yet they parted, I saw, without that look of private understanding that lovers often give each other.

He and I rode in his government electric car, his two silent bodyguards, policewomen, sitting in the front seat. We spoke of Esdardon Aya, whose name, he explained to me, meant Old Music. I told him how Esdardon Aya had saved my life by sending me here. He listened in a way that made it easy to talk to him. I said, "I was sick to leave my books, and I've thought about them, missing them, as if they were my family. But I think maybe I'm a fool to feel that way."

"Why a fool?" he asked. He had a foreign accent, but he had the Yeowan lilt already, and his voice was beautiful, low and warm.

I tried to explain everything at once: "Well, they mean so much to me because I was illiterate when I came to the City, and it was the books that gave me freedom, gave me the world — the worlds — But now, here, I see how the net, the holos, the neareals mean so much more to people, giving them the present time. Maybe it's just clinging to the past to cling to books. Yeowans have to go towards the future. And we'll never change people's minds just with words."

He listened intently, as he had done at the meeting, and then answered slowly, "But words are an essential way of thinking. And books keep the words true. . . . I didn't read till I was an adult, either."

"You didn't?"

"I knew how, but I didn't. I lived in a village. It's cities that have to have books," he said, quite decisively, as if he had thought about this matter. "If they don't, we keep on starting over every generation. It's a waste. You have to save the words."

When we got to his house, up at the top end of the old part of town, there were four crates of books in the entrance hall.

"These aren't all mine!" I said.

"Old Music said they were yours," Mr. Yehedarhed said, with his quick smile and a quick glance at me. You can tell where an Alien is looking much better than you can tell with us. With us, except for the few people with bluish eyes, you have to be close enough to see the dark pupil move in the dark eye.

"I haven't got anywhere to put so many," I said, amazed, realising how that strange man, Old Music, had helped me to freedom yet again.

"At your school, maybe? The school library?"

It was a good idea, but I thought at once of the Chief's inspectors pawing through them, perhaps confiscating them. When I spoke of that, the Sub-Envoy said, "What if I present them as a gift from the Embassy? I think that might embarrass the inspectors."

"Oh," I said, and burst out, "Why are you so kind? You, and he — Are you Hainish too?"

"Yes," he said, not answering my other question. "I was. I hope to be Yeowan."

He asked me to sit down and drink a little glass of wine with him before his guard drove me home. He was easy and friendly, but a quiet man. I saw he had been hurt. There were scars on his face and a gap in his hair where he had had a head injury. He asked me what my books were, and I said, "History."

At that he smiled, slowly this time. He said nothing, but he raised his glass to me. I raised mine, imitating him, and we drank.

Next day he had the books delivered to our school. When we opened and shelved them, we realised we had a great treasure. "There's nothing like this at the University," said one of the teachers, who had studied there for a year.

There were histories and anthropologies of Werel and of the worlds of the Ekumen, works of philosophy and politics by Werelians and by people of other worlds, there were compendiums of literature, poetry and stories, encyclopedias, books of science, atlases, dictionaries. In a corner of one of the crates were my own few books, my own treasure, even that first little crude *History of Yeowe, Printed at Yeowe University in the Year One of Liberty.* Most of my books I left in the school library, but I took that one and a few others home for love, for comfort.

I had found another love and comfort not long since. A child at school had brought me a present, a spotted-cat kitten, just weaned. The boy gave it to me with such loving pride that I could not refuse it. When I tried to pass it on to another teacher they all laughed at me. "You're elected, Rakam!" they said. So unwillingly I took the little being home, afraid of its frailty and delicacy and near to feeling a disgust for it. Women in the beza at Zeskra had had pets, spotted cats and foxdogs, spoiled little animals fed better than we were. I had been called by the name of a pet animal once.

I alarmed the kitten taking it out of its basket, and it bit my thumb to the bone. It was tiny and frail but it had teeth. I began to have some respect for it.

That night I put it to sleep in its basket, but it climbed up on my bed and sat on my face until I let it under the covers. There it slept perfectly still all night. In the morning it woke me by dancing on me, chasing dust motes in a sunbeam. It made me laugh, waking, which is a pleasant thing. I felt that I had never laughed very much, and wanted to.

The kitten was all black, its spots showing only in certain lights, black on black. I called it Owner. I found it pleasant to come home evenings to be greeted by my little Owner.

Now for the next half year we were planning the great demonstration of women. There were many meetings, at some of which I met the Sub-Envoy again, so that I began to look for him. I liked to watch him listen to our arguments. There were those who argued that the demonstration must not be limited to the wrongs and rights of women, for equality must be for all. Others argued that it should not depend in any way on the support of foreigners, but should be a purely Yeowan movement. Mr. Yehedarhed listened to them, but I got angry. "I'm a foreigner," I said. "Does that make me no use to you? That's owner talk — as if you were better than other people!" And Dr. Yeron said, "I will believe equality is for all when I see it written in the Constitution of Yeowe." For our Constitution, ratified by a world vote during the time I was at

Hagayot, spoke of citizens only as men. That is finally what the demonstration became, a demand that the Constitution be amended to include women as citizens, provide for the secret ballot, and guarantee the right to free speech, freedom of the press and of assembly, and free education for all children.

I lay down on the train tracks along with seventy thousand women, that hot day. I sang with them. I heard what that sounds like, so many women singing together, what a big, deep sound it makes.

I had begun to speak in public again when we were gathering women for the great demonstration. It was a gift I had, and we made use of it. Sometimes gang boys or ignorant men would come to heckle and threaten me, shouting, "Bosswoman, Owner-woman, black cunt, go back where you came from!" Once when they were yelling that, go back, go back, I leaned into the microphone and said, "I can't go back. We used to sing a song on the plantation where I was a slave," and I sang it,

> *O, O, Ye-o-we,*
> *Nobody never comes back.*

The singing made them be still for a moment. They heard it, that awful grief, that yearning.

After the great demonstration the unrest never died down, but there were times that the energy flagged, the Movement didn't move, as Dr. Yeron said. During one of those times I went to her and proposed that we set up a printing house and publish books. This had been a dream of mine, growing from that day in Hagayot when Seugi had touched her words and wept.

"Talk goes by," I said, "and all the words and images in the net go by, and anybody can change them. But books are there. They last. They are the body of history, Mr. Yehedarhed says."

"Inspectors," said Dr. Yeron. "Until we get the free press amendment, the chiefs aren't going to let anybody print anything they didn't dictate themselves."

I did not want to give up the idea. I knew that in Yotebber Region we could not publish anything political, but I argued that we might print stories and poems by women of the region. Others thought it a waste of time. We discussed it back and forth for a long time. Mr. Yehedarhed came back from a trip to the Embassy, up north in the Old Capital. He listened to our discussions, but said nothing, which disappointed me. I had thought that he might support my project.

One day I was walking home from school to my apartment, which was in a big, old, noisy house not far from the levee. I liked the place because my windows opened into the branches of trees, and through the trees I saw the river, four miles wide here, easing along among sandbars and reedbeds and willow isles in the dry season, brimming up the levees in the wet season when the rainstorms scudded across it. That day as I came near the house, Mr. Yehedarhed appeared, with two sour-faced policewomen close behind him as usual. He greeted me and asked if we might talk. I was confused and did not know what to do but to invite him up to my room.

His guards waited in the lobby. I had just the one big room on the third floor. I sat on the bed and the Sub-Envoy sat in the chair. Owner went round and round his legs, saying roo? roo?

I had observed that the Sub-Envoy took pleasure in disappointing the expectations of the Chief and his cohorts, who were all for pomp and fleets of cars and elaborate badges and uniforms. He and his policewomen went all over the city, all over Yotebber, in his government car or on foot. People liked him for it. They knew, as I knew now, that he had been assaulted and beaten and left for dead by a World Party gang his first day here, when he went out afoot alone. The city people liked his courage and the way he talked with everybody, anywhere. They had adopted him. We in the Liberation Movement thought of him as "our Envoy," but he was theirs, and the Chief's too. The Chief may have hated his popularity, but he profited from it.

"You want to start a publishing house," he said, stroking Owner, who fell over with his paws in the air.

"Dr. Yeron says there's no use until we get the Amendments."

"There's one press on Yeowe not directly controlled by the government," Mr. Yehedarhed said, stroking Owner's belly.

"Look out, he'll bite," I said. "Where is that?"

"At the University. I see," Mr. Yehedarhed said, looking at his thumb. I apologized. He asked me if I was certain that Owner was male. I said I had been told so, but never had thought to look. "My impression is that your Owner is a lady," Mr. Yehedarhed said, in such a way that I began to laugh helplessly.

He laughed along with me, sucked the blood off his thumb, and went on. "The University never amounted to much. It was a Corporation ploy — let the assets pretend they're going to college. During the last years of the War it was closed down. Since Liberation Day it's reopened and crawled along with no one taking much notice of it. The faculty are mostly old. They came back to it after the War. The National Government gives it a subsidy because it sounds well to have a University of Yeowe, but they don't pay it any attention, because it has no prestige. And because many of them are unenlightened men." He said this without scorn, descriptively. "It does have a printing house."

"I know," I said. I reached out for my old book and showed it to him.

He looked through it for a few minutes. His face was curiously tender as he did so. I could not help watching him. It was like watching a woman with a baby, a constant, changing play of attention and response.

"Full of propaganda and errors and hope," he said at last, and his voice too was tender. "Well, I think this could be improved upon. Don't you? All that's needed is an editor. And some authors."

"Inspectors," I warned, imitating Dr. Yeron.

"Academic freedom is an easy issue for the Ekumen to have some influence upon," he said, "because we invite people to attend the Ekumenical Schools on Hain and Ve. We certainly want to invite graduates of the University of Yeowe. But of course, if their education is severely defective because of the lack of books, of information . . ."

I said, "Mr. Yehedarhed, are you *supposed* to subvert government policies?" The question broke out of me unawares.

He did not laugh. He paused for quite a long time before he answered. "I don't know," he said. "So far the Ambassador has backed me. We may both get reprimanded. Or fired. What I'd like to do . . ." His strange eyes were right on me again. He looked down at the book he still held. "What I'd like is to become a Yeowan citizen," he said. "But my usefulness to Yeowe, and to the Liberation Movement, is my position with the Ekumen. So I'll go on using that, or misusing it, till they tell me to stop."

When he left I had to think about what he had asked me to do. That was to go to the University as a teacher of history, and once there to volunteer for the editorship of the press. That all seemed so preposterous, for a woman of my background and my little learning, that I thought I must be misunderstanding him. When he convinced me that I had understood him, I thought he must have very badly misunderstood who I was and what I was capable of. After we had talked about that for a little while, he left, evidently feeling that he was making me uncomfortable, and perhaps feeling uncomfortable himself, though in fact we laughed a good deal and I did not feel uncomfortable, only a little as if I were crazy.

I tried to think about what he had asked me to do, to step so far beyond myself. I found it difficult to think about. It was as if it hung over me, this huge choice I must make, this future I could not imagine. But what I thought about was him, Yehedarhed Havzhiva. I kept seeing him sitting there in my old chair, stooping down to stroke Owner. Sucking blood off his thumb. Laughing.

Looking at me with his white-cornered eyes. I saw his red-brown face and red-brown hands, the color of pottery. His quiet voice was in my mind.

I picked up the kitten, half-grown now, and looked at its hinder end. There was no sign of any male parts. The little black silky body squirmed in my hands. I thought of him saying, "Your Owner is a lady," and I wanted to laugh again, and to cry. I stroked the kitten and set her down, and she sat sedately beside me, washing her shoulder. "Oh poor little lady," I said. I don't know who I meant. The kitten, or Lady Tazeu, or myself.

He had said to take my time thinking about his proposal, all the time I wanted. But I had not really thought about it at all when, the next day but one, there he was, on foot, waiting for me as I came out of the school. "Would you like to walk on the levee?" he said.

I looked around.

"There they are," he said, indicating his cold-eyed bodyguards. "Everywhere I am, they are, three to five meters away. Walking with me is dull, but safe. My virtue is guaranteed."

We walked down through the streets to the levee and up onto it in the long early evening light, warm and pink-gold, smelling of river and mud and reeds. The two women with guns walked along just about four meters behind us.

"If you do go to the University," he said after a long silence, "I'll be there constantly."

"I haven't yet —" I stammered.

"If you stay here, I'll be here constantly," he said. "That is, if it's all right with you."

I said nothing. He looked at me without turning

his head. I said without intending to, "I like it that I can see where you're looking."

"I like it that I can't see where you're looking," he said, looking directly at me.

We walked on. A heron rose up out of a reed islet and its great wings beat over the water, away. We were walking south, downriver. All the western sky was full of light as the sun went down behind the city in smoke and haze.

"Rakam, I would like to know where you came from, what your life on Werel was," he said very softly.

I drew a long breath. "It's all gone," I said. "Past."

"We are our past. Though not only that. I want to know you. Forgive me. I want very much to know you."

After a while I said, "I want to tell you. But it's so bad. It's so ugly. Here, now, it's beautiful. I don't want to lose it."

"Whatever you tell me I will hold valuable," he said, in his quiet voice that went to my heart. So I told him what I could about Shomeke compound, and then hurried on through the rest of my story. Sometimes he asked a question. Mostly he listened. At some time in my telling he had taken my arm, I scarcely noticing at the time. When he let me go, thinking some movement I made meant I wanted to be released, I missed that light touch. His hand was cool. I could feel it on my forearm after it was gone.

"Mr. Yehedarhed," said a voice behind us: one of the bodyguards. The sun was down, the sky flushed with gold and red. "Better head back?"

"Yes," he said, "thanks." As we turned I took his arm. I felt him catch his breath.

I had not desired a man or a woman — this is the truth — since Shomeke. I had loved people, and I had touched them with love, but never with desire. My gate was locked.

Now it was open. Now I was so weak that at the touch of his hand I could scarcely walk on.

I said, "It's a good thing walking with you is so safe."

I hardly knew what I meant. I was thirty years old but I was like a young girl. I had never been that girl.

He said nothing. We walked along in silence between the river and the city in a glory of failing light.

"Will you come home with me, Rakam?" he said.

Now I said nothing.

"They don't come in with us," he said, very low, in my ear, so that I felt his breath.

"Don't make me laugh!" I said, and began crying. I wept all the way back along the levee. I sobbed and thought the sobs were ceasing and then sobbed again. I cried for all my sorrows, all my shames. I cried because they were with me now and always would be. I cried because the gate was open and I could go through at last, go into the country on the other side, but I was afraid to.

When we got into the car, up near my school, he took me in his arms and simply held me, silent. The two women in the front seat never looked round.

We went into his house, which I had seen once

before, an old mansion of some owner of the Corporation days. He thanked the guards and shut the door. "Dinner," he said. "The cook's out. I meant to take you to a restaurant. I forgot." He led me to the kitchen, where we found cold rice and salad and wine. After we ate he looked at me across the kitchen table and looked down again. His hesitance made me hold still and say nothing. After a long time he said, "Oh, Rakam! will you let me make love to you?"

"I want to make love to you," I said. "I never did. I never made love to anyone."

He got up smiling and took my hand. We went upstairs together, passing what had been the entrance to the men's side of the house. "I live in the beza," he said, "in the harem. I live on the woman's side. I like the view."

We came to his room. There he stood still, looking at me, then looked away. I was so frightened, so bewildered, I thought I could not go to him or touch him. I made myself go to him. I raised my hand and touched his face, the scars by his eye and on his mouth, and put my arms around him. Then I could hold him to me, closer and closer.

Some time in that night as we lay drowsing entangled I said, "Did you sleep with Dr. Yeron?"

I felt Havzhiva laugh, a slow, soft laugh in his belly, which was against my belly. "No," he said. "No one on Yeowe but you. And you, no one on Yeowe but me. We were virgins, Yeowan virgins. . . . Rakam, *araha*. . . ." He rested his head in the hollow of my shoulder and said something else in a foreign language and fell asleep. He slept deeply, silently.

Later that year I came up north to the University,

where I was taken on the faculty as a teacher of history. By their standards at that time, I was competent. I have worked there ever since, teaching and as editor of the press.

As he had said he would be, Havzhiva was there constantly, or almost.

The Amendments to the Constitution were voted, by secret ballot, mostly, in the Yeowan Year of Liberty 18. Of the events that led to this, and what has followed, you may read in the new three-volume *History of Yeowe* from the University Press. I have told the story I was asked to tell. I have closed it, as so many stories close, with a joining of two people. What is one man's and one woman's love and desire, against the history of two worlds, the great revolutions of our lifetimes, the hope, the unending cruelty of our species? A little thing. But a key is a little thing, next to the door it opens. If you lose the key, the door may never be unlocked. It is in our bodies that we lose or begin our freedom, in our bodies that we accept or end our slavery. So I wrote this book for my friend, with whom I have lived and will die free.

Notes on Werel and Yeowe

1. *Pronunciation of Names and Words*

In VOE DEAN (which is also the language of Yeowe) and GATAYAN, vowels have the usual "European values":

  a as in father (ah)
  e as in hey (ay) or let (eh)
  i as in machine (ee) or it (ih)
  o as in go (o) or off (oh)
  u as in ruby (oo)

In Voe Dean the accent is normally on the next-to-last syllable. Thus:

  Arkamye — ar-KAHM-yeh
  Bambur — BAHM-boor
  Boeba — bo-AY-bah
  Dosse — DOHS-seh
  Erod — EH-rod

gareot — gah-RAY-ot
Gatay — gah-TAH-ee
gede — GHEH-deh
Geu — GAY-oo
Hame — HAH-meh
Hagayot — hah-GAH-yot
Hayawa — hah-YAH-wah
Kamye — KAHM-yeh
Keo — KAY-o
makil — MAH-kihl
Nadami — nah-DAH-mee
Noeha — no-AY-hah
Ramayo — rah-MAH-yo
rega — RAY-gah
Rewe — REH-weh
San Ubattat — sahn-oo-BAHT-taht
Seugi — say-OO-ghee
Shomeke — sho-MEH-keh
Suhame — soo-HAH-meh
Tazeu — tah-ZAY-oo
Teyeo — teh-YAY-o
Tikuli — tee-KOO-lee
Toebawe — to-eh-BAH-weh
Tual — too-AHL or TWAHL
veot — VAY-ot
Voe Deo — vo-eh-DAY-o
Walsu — WAHL-soo
Werel — WEH-rehl
Yeowe — yay-O-way
Yeron — YEH-rohn
Yoke — YO-keh
Yotebber — yo-TEHB-ber
Yowa — YO-wah

* * *

Notes on Werel and Yeowe

Names formed with the name of the deities Kamye (Kam) and Tual tend to keep a stress on that element, thus:

Abberkam — AHB-ber-KAHM
Batikam — BAH-tih-KAHM
Rakam — RAH-KAHM
Sezi-Tual — SAY-zih-TWAHL
Tualtak — TWAHL-tahk

HAINISH

(The extremely long lineage-names common among the Hainish are cut down for daily use; thus Mattin-yehedarhed-dyura-ga-muruskets becomes Yehedarhed.)

araha — ah-RAH-ha
Ekumen *(from an Ancient Terran word)* — EK-yoo-men
Esdardon Aya — ez-DAR-don-AH-ya
Havzhiva — HAHV-zhi-vah
Iyan Iyan — ee-YAHN-ee-YAHN
Kathhad — KAHTH-hahd
Mezhe — MEH-zheh
Stse — STSEH *(like the capitalized letters in English "beST SEt")*
Tiu — TYOO
Ve — VEH
Yehedarhed — yeh-heh-DAR-hed

2. The Planets Werel and Yeowe

From <u>A Handbook of the Known Worlds</u>, printed in Darranda, Hain, Hainish Cycle 93, Local Year 5467.

Ekumenical Year 2102 is counted as Present when historical dates are given as years Before Present (BP).

The Werel-Yeowe solar system consists of 16 planets orbiting a yellow-white star (RK-tamo-5544-34). Life developed on the third, fourth, and fifth planets. The fifth, called Rakuli in Voe Dean, has only invertebrate life-forms tolerant of arid cold, and has not been exploited or colonised. The third and fourth planets, Yeowe and Werel, are well within the Hainish Norm of atmosphere, gravity, climate, etc. Werel was colonised by Hain late in the Expansion, within the last million years. It appears that there was no native fauna to displace, as all animal life-forms found on Werel, as well as some flora, are of Hainish derivation. Yeowe had no animal life until Werel colonised it 365 years BP.

Werel

Natural History

The fourth planet out from its sun, Werel has seven small moons. Its current climate is cool temperate, severely cold at the poles. Its flora is largely indigenous, its fauna entirely of Hainish origin, modified deliberately to obtain cobiosis with the native plants, and further modified through genetic drift and adaptation. Human adaptations include a cyanotic skin coloration (from black to pale, with a bluish cast) and eyes without visible whites, both evidently adjustments to elements in the solar radiation spectrum.

Voe Deo: *Recent History:* 4000–3500 years BP, aggressive, progressive black-skinned people from south of the equator on the single great continent (the region that is now the nation of Voe Deo) invaded and dominated the lighter-skinned peoples of the north. These conquerors instituted a master-slave society based on skin color.

Voe Deo is the largest, most numerous, wealthiest nation on the planet; all other nations in both hemispheres are dependencies, client states, or economically dependent on Voe Deo. Voe Dean economics have been based on capitalism and slavery for at least 3000 years. Voe Dean hegemony permits the general description of Werel as if it were all one society. As the society is in rapid change, however, this account will be put in the past tense.

Social Classes under Slavery

Class: master (**owner** or **gareot**) and slave (**asset**). Your class was your mother's class, without exception.

Skin color ranges from blue-black through bluish or greyish beige to an almost depigmented white. (Only albinism affects hair and eyes, which are dark). Ideally and in the abstract, class was skin color: owners black, assets white. Actually, many owners were black, most were dark; some assets were black, most beige, some white.

OWNERS were called men, women, children.

The unqualified word *owner* meant either the

class as a whole or an individual/family owning two or more slaves.

The owner of one slave or no slaves was a staff-less owner or *gareot*.

The *veot* was a member of an hereditary warrior caste of owners; the ranks were *rega, zadyo, oga*. Veot men almost invariably joined the Army; most veot families were landed proprietors; most were owners, some gareots.

Owner women formed a subclass or inferior caste. An owner woman was legally the property of a man (father, uncle, brother, husband, son, or guardian). Most observers hold that the gender division of Werelian society was as profound and essential as the master/slave division, but less visible, as it cut across it, owner women being considered socially superior to assets of both sexes. Since women were property, they could not own property, including human property. They could, however, manage property.

ASSETS were called bondsmen, bondswomen, pups or young. Pejorative terms: slaves, dusties, chalks, whites.

Luls were work-slaves, owned by a person or a family. All slaves on Werel were luls, except makils and asset-soldiers.

Makils were sold to and owned by the Entertainment Corporation.

Asset-soldiers were sold to and owned by the Army.

"Cutfrees" or eunuchs were male slaves castrated (more or less voluntarily, depending on age, etc.) to gain status and privilege. Werelian histories describe a number of cutfrees who rose to great power in var-

ious governments; many held posts of influence throughout the bureaucracy. The Bosses of the bondswomen's side of the compound were invariably cutfrees.

Manumission was extremely rare up until the last century, restricted to a few famous historical/legendary cases of slaves whose supernal loyalty and virtue induced their masters to give them freedom. About the time the War of Liberation began on Yeowe, the practice of manumission became more frequent on Werel, led by the owner group **The Community**, which advocated the abolition of slavery. A manumitted asset ranked legally, though seldom socially, as a gareot.

In Voe Deo at the time of the Liberation the proportion of assets to owners was 7:1. (About half these owners were gareots, owners of one or no assets.) In poorer countries the proportion dropped lower or reversed; in the Equatorial States the proportion of assets to owners was 1:5. In Werel as a whole, the proportion was estimated to be about three assets to one owner.

The House and the Compound

Historically and in the country, on the estates, farms, and plantations, the assets lived in a fenced or walled compound with a single gate. The compound was divided in halves by a ditch running parallel to the gate wall. The *gateside* was the men's quarters, the *inside* was the women's. Children lived on the inside, until boys reaching working age (8 to 10) were sent over to the longhouse. Women lived in huts, mothers and daughters, sisters or friends usually sharing a hut, two to four women with their children. The men and boys lived in gateside barracks called long-houses. Kitchen gardens were maintained by the old people and small children who did not go out to work; the old people generally cooked for the working people. The grandmothers ruled the compound.

Cutfrees (eunuchs) lived in separate houses built against the outside wall, with a surveillance station on the wall; they served as Compound Bosses, intermediaries between the grandmothers and the Work Bosses (members of the owner family, or hired gareots, in charge of the working assets). Work Bosses lived in houses outside the compound.

The owning family and their owner-class dependents occupied the House. The term House included any number of outbuildings, the Work Bosses' quarters, and animal barns, but specifically meant the family's large house. In conventional Houses the men's side (azade) and the women's side (beza) were strictly divided. The degree of restriction on the women reflected the wealth, power, and social pretension of the family. Gareot women might have considerable freedom of movement and occupation, but women of wealthy or distinguished family were kept indoors or in the walled gardens, never going out without numerous male escorts.

A number of female assets lived on the women's side as domestics and for use of the male owners. Some Houses kept male domestics, usually boys or old men; some kept cutfrees as servants.

In factories, mills, mines, etc., the compound system was maintained with some modifications. Where there was division of labor, all-male compounds were controlled entirely by hired gareots; in all-female compounds the grandmothers were allowed to keep order as in country compounds. Men rented to the all-male compounds had a life expectancy of about 28 years. During the shortage of assets caused by the slave trade to Yeowe in the early years of the Colony, some owners formed cooperative breeding compounds, where bonds-women were kept and bred annually, doing light work; some of these "breeders" bore a baby annually for twenty or more years.

Rentspeople: On Werel, all assets were individually owned. (The Corporations of Yeowe changed this practice; the Corporations owned the slaves, who had no private masters.)

In Werelian cities, assets traditionally lived in their owners' households as domestics. During the last millennium it became increasingly common for owners of superfluous assets to rent them to businesses and factories as skilled or unskilled labor. The owners or shareholders of a company bought and owned individual assets individually; the company rented the assets, controlled their use, and shared the profits. An owner could live on the rental of two skilled assets. Thus rentsmen and rentswomen became the largest group of assets in all cities and many towns. Rentspeople lived in "union compounds" — apartment houses supervised by hired gareot Bosses. They were required to keep curfew and check in and out.

(Note the difference between Werelian *rentspeople*, rented out by their owner, and the far more autonomous Yeowan *freedpeople*, slaves who paid their owner a tithe or tax on freely chosen work, called "freedom rental." One of the early objectives of the **Hame**, the Voe Dean underground asset liberation group, was to institute "freedom rental" on Werel.)

Most union compounds and all city households were gender-divided into azade and beza, but some private owners and some companies allowed their assets or rentspeople to live as couples, though not to marry. Their owners could separate them for any reason at any time. The mother's owner owned the children of any such asset couple.

In the conventional compound, heterosexual access was controlled by the owners, the Bosses, and the grandmothers. People who "jumped the ditch" did so at their peril. The owner myth-ideal was of total separation of male and female assets, with the Bosses managing selective breeding, chosen stud asset males servicing the females at optimal intervals to produce the desired number of young. Female assets were mainly concerned, on exploitive farms, to avoid undesired breeding and yearly pregnancy. In the hands of benevolent owners, the grandmothers and cutfrees often could protect girls and women from rape, and even allow some affectional pairing. But bonding was discouraged both by the owners and the grandmothers; and no form of slave marriage was admitted by law or custom on Werel.

Religions

The worship of Tual, a Kwan Yin–like maternal deity of peace and forgiveness, was the state religion of Voe Deo. *Philosophically*, Tual is seen as the most important incarnation of Ama the Increate or Creator Spirit. *Historically*, she is an amalgam of many local and nature deities, and locally often refragments into multiplicity. *Nationally*, enforcement of the national religion tended to accompany Voe Dean hegemony in other countries, although the religion is not inherently a proselytising or aggressive one. Tualite priests can and do hold high office in the government. *Class:* Tualite images and worship were maintained by the owners in all slave compounds, both on Werel and Yeowe. Tualism was the owners' religion. The assets' practice of it was enforced, and while including aspects of Tualite myth and worship in their rituals, most assets were Kamyites. By considering Kamye as "the Bondsman" and a lesser aspect of Ama, the Tualite priesthood included and tolerated Kamyite practice (which had no official clergy) among slaves and soldiers (most veots were Kamyites).

The *Arkamye* or Life of Kamye the Swordsman (Kamye is also the Herdsman, a beastmaster deity, and the Bondsman, having been long in service to Lord Nightfall): a warrior epic, adopted about 3,000 years ago by the assets, pretty much worldwide, as the sourcebook of their own religion. It cultivates such warrior/slave virtues as obedience, courage, patience, and selflessness, as well as spiritual independence, a stoical indifference to the things of this world, and a passionate mysticism: reality is to be won only by letting the seeming-real go. Assets and veots include Tual in their worship as an incarnation of Kamye, himself an incarnation of Ama the Increate. The "stages of life" and "going into silence" are among the mystical ideas and practices shared by Kamyites and Tualites.

Relations with the Ekumen

The First Envoy (EY 1724) was met with extreme suspicion. After a closely guarded deputation was allowed to land from the ship *Hugum*, alliance was rejected. Aliens were forbidden to enter the solar system by the Government of Voe Deo and its allies. Werel, led by Voe Deo, then entered on a rapid, competitive development of space technology and intensification of all techno-industrial development. For many decades, Voe Dean government, industry, and military were driven by a paranoid expectation of the armed return of conquering Aliens. It was this development that led within only thirteen years to the colonisation of Yeowe.

During the next three centuries the Ekumen made contact at intervals with Werel. An exchange of information was initiated at the insistence of the University of Bambur, joined by a consortium of universities and research institutions. Finally, after over three hundred years, the Ekumen was permitted to send a few Observers. During the War of Liberation on Yeowe, the Ekumen was invited to send Ambassadors to Voe Deo and Bambur, and later Envoys to Gatay, the Forty States, and other nations. For some time nonobservance of the Arms Convention kept Werel from joining the Ekumen, despite pressure from Voe Deo on the other states, which insisted on retaining their weaponry. After the abrogation of the Arms Convention, Werel joined the Ekumen, 359 years after first contact and 14 years after the end of the War of Liberation.

As a property of the Corporations, having no government of its own, Yeowe Colony was considered by its Werelian owners to be ineligible for Ekumenical membership. The Ekumen continued to question the right of the Four Corporations to ownership of the planet and its people. During the last years of the War of Liberation, the Freedom Party invited Ekumenical observers to Yeowe, and the establishment of a regular Envoy there coincided with the end of the War. The Ekumen helped Yeowe negotiate an end to the economic control of the planet by the Corporations and the Government of Voe Deo. The World Party nearly succeeded in driving the Aliens as well as the Werelians off the planet, but when that movement collapsed, the Ekumen supported the Provisional Government until elections could be held. Yeowe joined the Ekumen in Year of Liberation 11, three years before Werel did.

Yeowe

Natural History

The third planet out from its sun, Yeowe has a warm-moderate climate with little seasonal variation.

Bacterial life is ancient and of normally vast complexity and adaptive variety. A number of microscopic marine Yeowan species are defined as animals; otherwise, the native biota of the planet were plants.

On land there was a great variety of complex species, photosynthetic or saprophytic. Most were sessile, with some "creepers," colonial or individual plants capable of slow movement. Trees were the principal large life-form. South Continent was almost entirely tropical jungle/temperate rain forest from the coastlines up to timberline in the Polar Range and to the taiga of the Antarctic Circle. Great Continent, forested in the extreme north and south, was a steppe and savannah landscape at the higher central altitudes, with immense areas of bog, marsh, and sea marsh on the coastal plains. In the absence of pollinating animals, the plants had many devices to use wind and rain to cross-fertilise and propagate: explosive seeds, winged seeds, seednets that catch the wind and float for hundreds of miles, waterproof spores, "burrowing" seeds, "swimming" seeds, and plants with mobile vanes, cilia, etc.

The seas, which are warm and relatively shallow, and the vast sea marshes nourish a huge variety of sessile and floating plants, on the order of plankton, algaes, seaweeds, coral-type and sponge-type plants forming permanent constructions (mostly of silicon), and unique plants such as the "sailers" and the "mirrorweed." Vast connected "lily mats" were harvested by the Corporations so efficiently as to render the species extinct within thirty years.

Heedless introduction of Werelian plant and animal species killed off or crowded out about 3/5 of the native species, aided by industrial pollution and war. The owners brought in deer, hunting dogs, hunting cats, and greathorses for their hunts. The deer thrived and destroyed a great deal of native habitat. Most introduced animal species failed in the long run. Werelian animal survivors other than humankind on Yeowe include:

   birds (domestic fowl brought in as game or as
      poultry; songbirds were released, and a few
      species adapted and survived)
   foxdogs and spotted cats (pets)
   cattle (domestic; many wild in abandoned dis-
      tricts)
   deer (wild, called fendeer, adapted to the marsh
      regions)
   hunting cats (feral, rare, in marshlands)

The introduction of some fish species in the rivers was disastrous to the native plant life, and what fish survived were destroyed by poison. All attempts to introduce ocean fish failed.

Horses were slaughtered during the War of Liberation, as symbolic possessions of the owners; none remain.

The Colony: The Settlement

Early Werelian rockets reached Yeowe 365 years BP. Exploration, mapping, and prospecting were eagerly pursued. The Yeowe Mines Corporation, owned principally by Voe Dean investors, was given sole right to prospecting. Within twenty-five years, larger and more efficient ships made mining profitable, and the YMC began regular shipments of slaves to Yeowe and ores and minerals to Werel.

The next major company established was the Second Planet Forest Woods Corporation, cutting and shipping Yeowan timber to Werel, where industrial and population expansion had reduced forests drastically.

Exploitation of the oceans became a major industry by the end of the first century, the Yeowan Shippers Corporation harvesting the lily mats with immense profit. Having used up that resource, the YSC turned to the exploitation and processing of other sea species, especially the oil-rich bladder-weed.

During the Colony's first century, the Agricultural Plantation Company of Yeowe began systematic culture of introduced grains and fruits and of native species such as the oe-reed and the pini fruit. The warm, equable climate of most of Yeowe and the absence of insect and animal pests (maintained by scrupulous quarantine regulations) permitted an enormous expansion of agriculture.

The individual enterprises of these four Corporations and the regions where they operated, whether in mining, forestry, mariculture, or agriculture, were called "Plantations."

The four great Corporations maintained absolute control over their respective products, though there were over the decades many battles (legal and physical) over conflicting rights to the exploitation of an area. No rival company was able to break the Corporations' monopoly, which had the full, active support — military, political, and scientific — of the Government of Voe Deo, a major beneficiary of Corporation profits. The principal investment of capital in the Corporations was always from the government and capitalists of Voe Deo. A powerful country at the time of the Settlement, after three centuries of the Colony Voe Deo was by far the richest country on Werel, dominating and controlling all the others. Its control over the Corporations on Yeowe, however, was nominal. It negotiated with them as with sovereign powers.

Population and Slavery

For the first century only male slaves were exported to Yeowe Colony by the Corporations, whose monopoly on slave shipment, via the Interplanet Cartel, was complete. In the first century, a high proportion of these slaves were from the poorer nations of Werel; later, as slave-breeding for the Yeowan market became profitable, more of them were sent from Bambur, the Forty States, and Voe Deo.

During this period, the population grew to about 40,000 of the owner class (80% male) and about 800,000 slaves (all male).

There were several experimental "Emigration Towns," settlements of gareots (owner-class people without slaves), mostly mills and service communities. These settlements were first tolerated, then abolished, by the Corporations, who induced the Werelian governments to limit emigration to Corporation personnel. The gareot settlers were shipped back to Werel and the services they had set up were staffed by slaves. The "middle class" of townsfolk and tradespeople on Yeowe thus came to be composed of semiindependent slaves (freedpeople) rather than gareots and rentspeople as on Werel.

Prices on bondsmen kept going up, as the Mining and Agricultural Corporations in particular squandered slave life (a mine slave during the first century was expected to have a "worklife" of five years). Individual owners increasingly often smuggled in female slaves as sexual and domestic servants. The Corporations, under these pressures, changed their rule and permitted the importation of bondswomen (238 BP).

At first bondswomen, considered as breeding stock, were restricted to the compounds on the plantations. As their usefulness for all kinds of work became evident, these restrictions were eased by the owners on most plantations. Slave women, however, had to fit into the century-old social system of slave men, which they entered as inferiors, slaves' slaves.

On Werel, all assets were personally owned,

except the makils (bought from their owners by the Entertainment Corporation), and asset-soldiers (bought from their owners by the government). On Yeowe, all slaves were Corporation-owned, bought by the Corporation from their Werelian owners. No slave on Yeowe could be privately owned. No slave on Yeowe could be freed. Even those brought in as personal servants, such as maids of plantation owners' wives, had their ownership transferred to the Corporation that owned the plantation.

Though manumission was not allowed, as the slave population increased very rapidly, causing a surplus on many plantations, the status of *freedperson* became increasingly common. Freedpeople found work for hire or independently and "rented freedom," paying one or more Corporations monthly or annually whatever fee (usually about 50%) was levied on them as a tax on their independent work. Most freedpeople worked as sharecroppers, shopkeepers, or mill hands, and in service industries; during the Colony's third century a professional class of freedpeople became well established in the cities.

By the end of the third century, when the population growth had slowed somewhat, the total population of Yeowe was about 450 million; the proportion of owners to slaves was less than one to one hundred. About half the slave population were freedpeople. (The population 20 years after Liberation was again 450 million, all free.)

On the plantations, the original all-male social structure set the pattern of slave society. Work gangs early developed into social groups (called gangs), and gangs into tribes, each with a hierarchy of power:

Tribesmen under a slave Headman or Chief, under the Boss, under the owner, under the Corporation. Bonding, competition, rivalry, homosexual privileges, and adoptive lineages became institutionalised and often elaborately codified. The only safety for a slave was membership in a tribe and strict adherence to its rules. Slaves sold away from their plantation had to serve as slaves' slaves, often for years, before they were accepted into membership of the local tribe.

As women slaves were brought in, most of them became tribal, as well as Corporate, property. The Corporations encouraged this. It was to their advantage to have slave women controlled by the tribes, as the tribes were controlled by the Corporations.

Opposition and insurrection, never able to organise widely, were always crushed with the instant and brutal finality of infinitely superior armaments. Headmen and chiefs colluded with the Bosses, who, working in the interest of owners and Corporations, exploited the rivalries between tribes and the power struggles within them, while maintaining an absolute embargo on "ideology," by which they meant education, information of any kind from outside the local plantation. (On most plantations, well into the second century, literacy was a crime. A slave caught reading was blinded by dropping acid in the eyes or scraping the eyes from the sockets. A slave caught using a radio or network outlet was deafened by white-hot picks thrust through the eardrums. The "Fit Punishment Lists" of the Corporations and plantations were long, detailed, and explicit.)

In the second century, as slave population shot

up to the point of surplus on most plantations, a gradual trickle of both men and women towards the "shop-strips" run by freedpeople grew to a steady stream. Over the decades, the "shop-strips" grew into towns and the towns into cities entirely populated by freedpeople.

Although doomsayers among the owners began to point to the ever-increasing size and independence of the "Assetvilles" and "Whiteytowns" and "Dustyburgs" as a looming threat, the Corporations considered the cities safely under control. No large buildings were allowed, no defensive structures of any kind; possession of a firearm was punished by disembowelment; no slave was allowed to operate any flying vehicle; the Corporations kept tight guard on raw materials and industrial processes that could provide weaponry of any kind to the slaves or freedpeople.

"Ideology," education, did exist in the cities. Late in the second century of the Colony, the Corporations, while censoring, filtering, and altering information, formally gave permission for freedpeople's children and some tribal children to be schooled up to age 14. They allowed slave communities to set up schools, and sold them books and other materials. In the third century the Corporations instituted and maintained an information and entertainment network for the cities. Educated workers were becoming valuable. The limitations of the tribes had become increasingly evident. Rigidly conservative, most tribal chiefs and Bosses were unable or unwilling to change any practices in any way, at a time when the abuse of the planet's resources called for radical changes in methods and objectives. It was clear that profit on Yeowe would increasingly come not from strip-mining, clear-cutting, and monoculture, but from refined industry, modern plants staffed by skilled workers capable of learning new techniques and following unfamiliar orders.

On Werel, a capitalist slave society, work was done by people. Slave labor, whether simple brawn-work or highly skilled, was hand labor, aided by an elegant but ancillary machine technology: "The trained asset is the finest machine, and the cheapest." Production, even of very high-technology items, was essentially traditional craft of very high quality. Neither speed nor great volume was particularly valued.

On Yeowe, late in the third century of the Colony, as raw material exports failed, slave labor was used in a new way. The assembly line was developed, with the conscious purpose not only of speeding and cheapening production, but also of keeping the worker ignorant of the work process as a whole. The Second Planet Corporation, dropping the words Forest Woods from its name, led the new manufacture. The SPC quickly surpassed the old giants, Mines and Agriculture, reaping huge profits from the sale of mass-produced finished goods to the poorer nations of Werel. By the time of the Uprising, more than half the freedworkers of Yeowe were owned by or rented to the Second Planet Corporation.

There was far more social unrest in the mills and mill towns than on the tribal plantations. Corporation executives ascribed it to the increase in the number of "uncontrolled" freedpersons, and many advocated closing the schools, destruction of the cities, and reinstitution of sealed compounds for all slaves. The Corporations' city militia (gareots hired and brought from Werel, plus a police force of unarmed freedmen) increased to a considerable standing army, its gareot members heavily armed. Much of the unrest in the cities and attempts at protest centered on mills that used the assembly line. Workers who, feeling themselves part of an intelligible process, would tolerate very harsh conditions, found meaningless work intolerable, even though working conditions were in some ways improved.

The Liberation began, however, not in the cities, but in the compounds of the plantations.

The Uprising and the Liberation

The Uprising had its origin in organisations of tribal women in plantations of Great Continent, joining together to prevent ritual rape of girl-children and to demand tribal laws against sexual enslavement of bondswomen by bondsmen, gang rape, and the beating and murder of women, for none of which was there any penalty.

They acted first by educating women and children of both sexes, then by demanding proportional voice in the all-male tribal councils. Their organisations, called Woman Clubs, spread across both continents throughout the third century of the Colony. The Clubs spirited so many girls and women off the plantations into the cities that the chiefs' and Bosses' complaints began to be heard by the Corporations. Local tribesman and Bosses were encouraged to "go into the cities and get their women back."

These incursions, often led by plantation police and aided by the Corporation city militia, were often carried out with extreme brutality. City freed-people, unused to the kind of violence normal on the plantations, reacted with outrage. City bonds-men were drawn to defend and fight with the women.

In 61 BP, in Eyu Province, in the town of Soyeso, the slaves' successful resistance to a police raid from Nadami Plantation (APC) escalated into an attack on the plantation itself. The police barracks were stormed and burned. Some of the chiefs of Nadami joined the uprising, opening their compounds to the rebels. Others joined in the defense of their owners in the Plantation House. A slave woman unlocked the doors of the plantation armory to the insurrection — the first time in the history of Yeowe Colony that any large group of slaves had access to powerful weapons. A massacre of owners followed, but it was partially restrained: most of the children of the Plantation House, and twenty women and men, were spared and put on a train to the capital. No adult slave who had fought against the uprising was spared.

From Nadami the Uprising spread, by way of guns and ammunition, to three neighboring plantations. All the tribes joined, defeating Corporation forces in the quick, fierce Battle of Nadami. Slaves and freedpeople from neighboring provinces poured into Eyu. The chiefs, the grandmothers of the compounds, and the leaders of the insurrection met at Nadami and declared Eyu Province a free state.

Within ten days, Corporation bombing raids and land troops had smashed the insurrection.

Captured rebels were tortured and executed. Particular revenge was taken on the town of Soyeso: all the people left there, mostly children and the old, were herded into the town squares and trucks and tread-wheeled ore-carriers ran over and over them. This was called "paving with dust."

The Corporations' victory had been quick and easy, but it was followed by a new insurrection at a different plantation, the murder of an owner's family here, a strike of city freedworkers there, all over the world.

The unrest did not cease. Many attacks on plantation armories and militia barracks were successful; the insurrectionists now had weapons, and learned how to make bombs and mines. Hit-and-run warfare in the jungles and the great marshes gave the guerrillas' advantage to the rebels. It became clear that the Corporations needed more armaments and more manpower. They imported mercenary soldiers from the poorer nations of Werel. Not all of these were loyal or effective troops. The Corporations soon persuaded the government of Voe Deo to safeguard its national interest by investing troops in the defense of the Owners of Yeowe. At first the commitment was reluctant, but 23 years after Nadami, Voe Deo decided to put down the unrest once and for all, sending 45,000 troops, all veots (members of the hereditary warrior caste) or owner-volunteers.

Seven years later, at the end of the war, 300,000 soldiers from Werel had been killed on Yeowe, most of them from Voe Deo, and most of them veots.

The Corporations began to take their people off Yeowe several years before the end of the war, and during the final year of fighting there were almost no civilian owners left on the planet.

Throughout the thirty years of the War of Liberation, some tribes and many individual slaves sided with the Corporations, which promised them safety and rewards and furnished them with weapons. Even during the Liberation there were battles between rival tribes. After the Corporations and the army pulled out, tribal wars smouldered and flared up all over Great Continent. No central government was able to establish itself until Abberkam's World Party, defeating the Freedom Party in many local elections, seemed to be on the point of setting up the first World Council elections. In Year 2 of Liberation the World Party collapsed abruptly under accusation of corruption. The Envoys of the Ekumen (invited to Yeowe by the Freedom Party during the final year of the war) supported the Freedom Party in activating their constitution and setting up elections. The First Election (Year 3 of the Liberation), managed by the Freedom Party, established the new Constitution on rather shaky ground; women were not allowed to vote, many tribal votes were cast by the chiefs alone, and some of the hierarchic tribal structures were retained and legalised. There were several more fierce tribal wars and years of unrest and protest while the society of free Yeowe constructed itself. Yeowe joined the Ekumen in Year 11 of the Liberation, 19 BP, and the First Ambassador was sent in that year. Major amendments to the Yeowan Constitution, assuring all people over 18 the vote by secret ballot and guaranteeing equal rights, were voted by free general election in Year 18 of the Liberation.

O Yeowe

O, O, Ye-o-we, No-bo-dy ne-ver come back.

▄ HarperPrism

A Fisherman of the Inland Sea
by Ursula K. Le Guin

The National Book Award-winning author's new collection has all the majesty and appeal of her major works. Here we have starships that sail, literally, on wings of song . . . musical instruments to be played at funerals only. . . *ansibles*, faster-than-light communication . . . orbiting arks designed to save a doomed humanity.

Also by Ursula K. Le Guin

Searoad: Chronicles of Klatsand
Here is the culmination of Le Guin's lifelong fascination with small island cultures. In a sense, the Klatsand of these stories is a modern world apart from our own, but part of it as well.

The Dispossessed
A brilliant physicist makes an unprecedented journey to the utopian mother planet to challenge the complex structures of life and living, and ignite the fires of change.

The Beginning Place
Two young people meet in a strange and wonderful place across the creek and escape from their dreary daily lives. But when their place of peace becomes a realm of horror, they suddenly face a terrible and chilling choice that could cost them everything, including their lives.

The Eye of the Heron
The People of the Peace are brutalized and dominated by the City criminals. They would have broken vows and shed blood if not for one bold young woman who leaves her City father to lead the People on a perilous quest to discover a world of hope within this world of chaos . . . a place they will call Heron.

The Compass Rose
Twenty astonishing stories that carry us to worlds of wonder and horror, desire and destiny, enchantment and doom.

Orsinian Tales
In this enchanting collection, Ursula K. Le Guin brings to mainstream fiction the same compelling mastery of word and deed, of story and character, of violence and love, that has won the Hugo, the Nebula, and the National Book Awards.